THE PEER'S ROGUISH WORD

The Dukes' Pact Series
Book Five

By Kate Archer

ARE YOU SIGNED UP FOR DRAGONBLADE'S BLOG?

You'll get the latest news and information on exclusive giveaways, exclusive excerpts, coming releases, sales, free books, cover reveals and more.

Check out our complete list of authors, too!

No spam, no junk. That's a promise!

Sign Up Here

www.dragonbladepublishing.com

Dearest Reader;

Thank you for your support of a small press. At Dragonblade Publishing, we strive to bring you the highest quality Historical Romance from the some of the best authors in the business. Without your support, there is no 'us', so we sincerely hope you adore these stories and find some new favorite authors along the way.

Happy Reading!

CEO, Dragonblade Publishing

Additional Dragonblade books by Author Kate Archer

The Dukes' Pact Series
The Viscount's Sinful Bargain (Book 1)
The Marquess' Daring Wager (Book 2)
The Lord's Desperate Pledge (Book 3)
The Baron's Dangerous Contract (Book 4)
The Peer's Roguish Word (Book 5)

PROLOGUE

White's, 1818

THE SIX ELDERLY dukes had once more gathered in their favored room at the club. When the dukes had arrived, they'd found a gaggle of younger gentlemen occupying the room, these presumptuous cubs imagining their card game to be of vital importance. Those youthful and very mistaken fellows had been chased out as if they were of no more account than a group of clerks. Servants had scurried to move the furniture and set up the room as the dukes liked it—six chairs round a cheery fire with plentiful claret and a tray of meats and cheeses piled high on a side table.

The dukes did not engage in idle chatter, that was never their habit on these occasions. The discussion would revolve around the pact between them to ensure their sons found wives so that grandsons might be produced. Before any further actions could be debated, they waited patiently for the Duke of Wentworth to settle his gouty foot and claim his recent victory.

After much rearranging of pillows on a stool, the duke and his foot were finally in place. "Well, gentlemen," he said, "I hardly dared imagine it, but my son has married. You will know by now that it was Mendbridge's daughter, Penelope Darlington. The two of them have ridden off to Dorset, where I suspect they are riding still. Naturally, I hope the lady will dismount her horse at some point and produce an heir."

"We congratulate you, Wentworth," the Duke of Gravesley said. "In the meantime, I never imagined we would actually have to take the thing so far, but the two scoundrels that are left have been entirely cut off from their funds. It appears we have arrived at a far steeper hill to climb."

The dukes nodded at one another, as if this were a fact well-known amongst them.

"There are *two* hills left, though—do you hint that Bainbridge's son or my own is the steeper of them?" the Duke of Glastonburg said.

"It is mine," the Duke of Bainbridge said. "Dalton may be scarred and sullen, but he does not spend half his life dressing himself and is not one of the most unfortunate scoundrels to ever grace London. My eldest spawn is getting a reputation for breaking hearts, although his own is never amongst them."

"Then let us hope," the Duke of Carlisle said, "that a new season brings a new lady who may finally capture our lothario and tie him down."

"I'd tie him down myself and point the girl to his location if I thought it'd help," the Duke of Bainbridge said.

CHAPTER ONE

KATHERINE DELL, OR Kitty as her friends knew her, debated what could be brought with her to London for the season. It was not anywhere near the amount of things she would like to bring, but then there were only so many trunks, and only so many times the carriages would make the trip back and forth from Devon. Most young ladies might be singularly focused on their wardrobe, but those decisions had long been dispensed with. The current question was, how to move the telescope and precisely how many books could she fit into the luggage carriage? While there was a perfectly good library in their house in town, she was just now in the middle of upwards of sixteen books and had her eye on a few dozen more.

"We are not bringing the telescope," a laughing voice said at her doorway.

Kitty turned to find her brother, Frederick, leaning against the doorframe and appearing highly amused. He was tall and handsome and they were only two years apart. They had been great friends and great combatants since their days in the nursery.

"So says Martha, too," Kitty said. "Though she calls it the *contraption.*"

"Then your maid has more sense than you do," Frederick answered. "Nobody takes their telescope to London."

"Oh, I am not so certain," Kitty said, with a mischievous look.

"It is my guess that people may wish to bring all sorts of unusual things to London. I might even imagine that a dear brother would not mind packing a certain Miss Crimpleton in one of his trunks."

Frederick straightened a cuff. "You would be wrong," he said. "Miss Crimpleton has a particular delicacy of feeling and would scream like a stuck pig if I attempted it."

"You will miss her, though?"

"Enough of that, Kitty," her brother said brusquely. "She will have her season next year, not a hundred years from now. I can easily wait."

Kitty shrugged, well knowing when not to take a thing further. Her brother was perfectly amenable to a teasing…up to the point he was not. When it came to Miss Crimpleton, he was generally *not*.

"In any event," Frederick said, "your telescope is emblematic of what I wished to speak to you about."

Kitty crossed her arms and prepared for battle.

Seeing his sister donning her armor and ready for a war, Frederick sighed. In a kinder tone, he said, "Kit-cat, you are going up for your launch season, not to give a speech at the Royal Society. I understand your interests, but there are practicalities to consider."

Kitty turned away at the mention of the Royal Society. Had she been a man, induction into that great institution would have been her primary aim in life. Had she been a man, she'd already be a member. Through rigorous experiments, she had proved that Cornish eyebright was hemi-parasitic on Western Gorse. Men had been inducted for less. In truth, men had been inducted for nothing at all, though the great Caroline Herschel might discover a slew of comets and be excluded.

She bent and looked through her beloved telescope; it stood in its permanent place on the wide window ledge. It was afternoon and so no stars were to be noted and it was an overcast and drizzly sort of day. The most interesting thing she could discover was a herd of cows huddled together against the weather on a far hillside.

"You sound very like mama with your scoldings," Kitty said, "though you are more roundabout than she is. She does not remind me of *practicalities*—she calls it marriage."

"Marriage is very practical," Frederick said. "Dinners and balls and routs are the most established way to achieve that very practical aim. Please put aside your intellectual pursuits for a few months at least. You cannot wish to be an old maid. I *know* you cannot wish it. You shall want children and your own house."

Kitty knew that was perfectly true. And yet, she was not eager to leave her father's house. Her dear papa treated her as his intellectual equal. How was she to transform herself into somebody's wife, only responsible for seeing that the right calls were made and a house ran smooth and dinner parties came off well? She suspected those mundane tasks would be the height of her wifely career—she had not the skill or temperament to be as her mother was. The baroness was the vital root of the family, keeping her various offshoots supplied with sunlight and water.

Kitty understood what was expected of her. She understood that most gentlemen did not wish to have a serious discussion with her about the advancements of the day. She supposed they all had lively debates at their clubs. Lively debates where new questions, or even conclusions, were posited. But nobody seemed to wish to discuss with *her* Herschel's fascinating paper on telescopes, or Carlisle's examination of the peculiarities of the arteries in slow-moving animals, or Henry's experiments on muriatic acid. She had suspected that it would be the case all along, but she'd been thoroughly convinced of it after she'd visited Penny Darlington at Newmarket.

Though she'd not been technically out, she'd been allowed certain entertainments under the watchful eye of Lord Mendbridge and Mrs. Wellburton. Along with the entertainments had come the gentlemen. It appeared, through those conversations at dinner or at dancing, that her sole value was her looks. And, she supposed, her dowry too. She might have arrived with complete emptiness between her ears and it would not signify. None of those gentlemen had shown her the truth more clearly than Lord Grayson.

Oh, she had been so struck by his person when she'd first seen him in the drawing room at Mendbridge Cottage. Tall, the sort of cheekbones a sculptor might dream up, and looking so urbane. His dress was impeccable and he wore it with such ease. She was not so foolish as to deny any reaction she might have had involving a fluttering of the stomach.

It was a pity he'd ruined the sensation by being so patronizing! Each time she'd attempted to discuss anything rational, he'd looked at her as if she were a puppy doing something charming. It was near-enraging—as he condescended to her, he at the same time proved himself to be the most uneducated person she had ever encountered. Even her maid was better read than he. Of course, one who spent as much time as he on his person would have little time for education. His neckcloths were a veritable building of the pyramids and likely took just as long.

She had pretended good humor over his condescension and had appeased her feelings by torturing Lord Grayson with questions he had no hope of answering. She had given him a book on Cardinal Wolsey and quizzed him on it ruthlessly. For all the entertainment of it, she still could not help but be offended at how he viewed her. How they *all* viewed her.

Lord Grayson had taken every opportunity to steer the conversation away from anything approaching the intellectual to land firmly on her person. As she had listened to his ridiculous compliments, she had thought it was a shame he was so handsome. An injustice, really. Those chiseled features had been better suited to a learned man and not wasted on the dandified Lord Grayson.

She *did* wish to marry, to an intelligent man who would be intelligent enough to recognize her own intelligence. A man she could debate things with, as two equals. She could only pray that such a man existed. If he happened to be as handsome as Lord Grayson, so much the better. Though, it was not an absolute requirement.

"You will find somebody you like, Kitty," her brother said. "Mendbridge says Lord Grayson was an admirer at Newmarket. I do not know the fellow and he is part of that ridiculous dukes' pact, but on the other hand, he's a Marquess and will be a duke. You could do worse than duchess, is all I say."

Kitty turned away from her telescope and stared at her brother. "You are quite mistaken, Frederick. I am convinced I could in fact *not* do worse than Lord Grayson."

"Never mind him, then," Frederick said. "The town will be teeming with suitable fellows. If only you would put your thoughts wholly on the matter at hand."

Kitty knew well enough that it would not be possible to put her thoughts wholly on dressing and making calls and going to parties. On the other hand, she was not oblivious to the expense of a season, she would not insult her parents with outright defiance, and she *did* like dancing. Naturally, she was also not opposed to a good dinner. There must be some middle ground they might all comfortably stand on.

"Frederick," she said, "I will be the dutiful young lady just out, *if* you do not attempt to suppress my natural inclinations altogether. You know of what I speak."

"Lackington & Allen," Frederick said.

Kitty nodded. Mr. Lackington ran the largest bookstore in London. No, not just the largest. It was the Temple Muse and carried over eight hundred thousand volumes. Lackington's was the sun and the world revolved around it.

Over the past two years, she had maintained a correspondence with Mr. Lackington. She would write him a letter and give it to her father. Her father would review the letter, enclose a note of his own, and send it off to Mr. Lackington. Then a letter would come back to her father and be passed on to her. In that way, she'd had rousing debates on a variety of subjects and got important recommendations on books she ought to own. Kitty was determined to experience the establishment for herself and be introduced to the great man.

"You shall find me remarkably good humored and compliant if I have my visits to Lackington and Allen," Kitty said, her chin jutting out in rock solid stubbornness.

"Finsbury Square it is, then," Frederick said.

GILES DERMOT, THE Marquess of Grayson and eldest son of the Duke of Bainbridge, hurried down the stairs. As his funds had been entirely eliminated thanks to the devilish pact his father and his old cronies had dreamed up, he was entirely at the mercy of Dalton's hospitality. This should have necessitated being prompt for a drink before going to the theater, but nobody could hurry LaRue. If his valet was not satisfied with the fall of his neckcloth, and he rarely was, then it would require starting over again with a fresh one. The lord did not own above forty-five cloths on a whim, it was a necessity when one employed such a temperamental scoundrel.

He passed Bellamy in the hall and the old butler stared at him as grim as ever. Giles had been in the house long enough to know that Bellamy's annoyance had little to do with if his master would be inconvenienced by his houseguest's tardiness. Bellamy would be irritated that *Bellamy* was inconvenienced. The old fellow had one aim in life—get the lords out of the house so he and his footmen could vandalize the wine cellar and make merry. Should one require anything late at night in Dalton's house, one might do best to get it oneself. Ringing the bell would only bring a swaying and bleary-eyed footman to the door. LaRue called Dalton's retinue *the barbarians* and claimed he would not dignify the horde by using individual names.

Giles entered the library, that being the preferred room in the house for gathering. Dalton had already a glass in hand. "Prompt as ever," his friend said.

"I've told you over and over, LaRue has his own timetable," Giles said. "There's no use trying to hurry him, I did it once and he descended into some sort of French madness. I did not get the whole of it, but crimes against mankind were thrown about."

"Why don't you just give him the wrong time?" Dalton asked. "Tell him you've got to be out the door an hour before you actually do?"

"I do not see how that will work," Giles said. "He'll know, somehow."

"He did not *somehow know* this evening. I said we would depart at eight, but we do not in fact go until nine. Here it is at half past the hour and for once you are arrived in good time. I suspect not all of the blame for your shocking habits can be laid at your valet's door."

Giles shrugged. He supposed Dalton was right, he *could* be undecided about which coat would suit. "Well, in any case, very jolly that I am not late, is it not?"

"It is about the only jolly thing I can think of just now," Dalton said. "We are reduced to attending parties to get a good dinner these days and I do not even have the funds to open my house in Brighton this summer. If we are not invited to a series of country house parties, we will broil alone in London. Or, God forbid, we'd have to fly to our respective family's coups."

"Yes, we are near penniless," Giles said, "but I am sure we will not be forced to return to our father's estates. The fates are not so cruel as that. I think this circumstance cannot go on forever. Once our fathers perceive that we cannot be forced to marry, they will give it up. The old cabal will have to satisfy themselves that they've had their way with Hampton, Lockwood, Ashworth, and Cabot."

"I knew we'd be the last hold outs," Dalton said. "Cabot was hopeless. A horse-mad gentleman develops a preference for a horse-mad lady. I did my best to throw them off, but I suspected all along it was a losing proposition."

"So far, all of your propositions have been losing. You could not even keep Lockwood safely above stairs behind a sturdy locked door. By the by, there is a whispered rumor going about that Miss Darlington rode Cabot's horse for the thousand guinea stakes," Giles said. "Apparently, the ladies are all finding it highly romantic."

Dalton downed his brandy. "Watch that *you* do not find anything highly romantic this season. Miss Dell, in particular. You fancy yourself in love with her, no doubt."

"What matter if I do?" Giles said. "She is a charming lady."

"As you may have noted, had you paid the slightest bit of attention, flirtations have a way of getting out of hand. Right out of hand and to an altar."

"Come now, Dalton," Giles said, laughing. "How many years have you known me to be infatuated with a lady?"

"As many years as I have known you."

"And how many years has it been the same lady?"

"None," Dalton admitted.

"There you have it," Giles said. "Being in love is as air to me, I must have it. However, it is a fickle and fleeting thing."

In truth, though Giles was in the habit of spouting off about love, what he felt for the parade of ladies over the seasons was not love. Not in its finest sense. Not as Shakespeare would have it. Not as Byron or Wordsworth or Blake would have it. His experience of love began with a merry chase—and then when the chase was over, the feeling reliably faded. He was fairly sure that love as poets and playwrights imagined it did not even exist.

He ought to be *more* than fairly sure. His own parents had come to hate each other. It could not have ever been real love. Nobody in the same house with them now could fail to feel the icicles forming in the air and the dagger looks shot across the room. It was hinted to him once that his father had been besotted, but his mother had married for title. That was an even more ghastly idea. What if real love was possible and he fell prey to it? What if he put himself in the power of a lady? Only to discover too late that she'd only wished to be a duchess…

He sometimes berated himself for his high-flown ideas about love. It was no wonder at all that real people could not live up to it and would always disappoint. Though he hid all knowledge of it from his friends and understood it to be a fantasy, he could not forsake his volumes of Shakespeare. Many a school break, while closeted in his room as his parents raged below him, he'd lost himself in those volumes. Who could not be touched by Beatrice and Benedick or Rosalind and Orlando? If he were feeling particularly crossed, he might even thumb through Romeo and Juliet. Though, he'd only read the ending once and thought that was quite enough for one lifetime.

As for Miss Austen, well, those novels were even more hidden from view. Only LaRue knew of their existence. His friends would excoriate him if they ever discovered his appreciation of the lady. Though, who could not pray that Elizabeth and Darcy would come together? Who could not be utterly disappointed in Willoughby, no matter that one had already read the story and knew he would not come up to snuff?

Those stories were all dreams of what mankind aspired to, but in no way reality. Infatuation was fleeting, though it masqueraded as love. If real love as Shakespeare and Miss Austen wrote it *did* exist, it would be far too fraught with peril and he would steer well clear of it.

It suited him to ally himself with Dalton. Neither of them would marry for quite many years yet, and then only to get an heir. Romance was all well and good to play at, but one should not take it seriously. Fire brought warmth, but get too close and be burned.

He had lost his other friends to the altar, but he would not lose Dalton. At least, he hoped not. Dalton was the only thing between him and a flea-infested flat somewhere in Cheapside. Or even further afield.

"Look to yourself, Dalton," he said. "See that you do not

make the mistake with Miss Danworth. You and the lady of the flowing blond curls are frighteningly well-suited—you both swim in the same chilly sea."

"Do you imply we are both cold fish?" Dalton asked.

"Rather," Giles said, laughing. "You have said yourself that underneath her smiles she's as cold as ice. You might stare crossly at each other over a dining table for all your days and neither of you would wonder why the other one scowled."

"I can assure you Miss Danworth is no danger to me," Dalton said. "And *I* am even less of a danger to *her*. My father is her father's entailed heir and I believe it irritates the lady."

"Really?" Giles asked. "I didn't know."

"He is a distant cousin, and that side of the family has had a remarkable run of daughters. I do not wish to have anything to do with it and pray the old fellow will remarry and produce a true heir." Dalton paused, then said quietly, "Though I would pity the woman who married him, he is an unpleasant sort in public and I presume worse in private."

"There were rumors," Giles said, "when his wife still lived."

"Yes, there were," Dalton said briskly. "In any case, make sure Miss Dell remains only a flirtation. Now, we'd better go or we *will* be late, despite my planning."

CHAPTER TWO

KITTY HAD ARRIVED at the London house sans telescope. She supposed after all it was no great loss. The houses were so crowded together that she'd have to climb to the roof to see anything interesting. She *had* managed to smuggle her microscope in an oversized hat box. It had been a sixteenth birthday present from her father and was too precious to leave behind. What if there were housebreakers who perceived its worth?

On the day she had been given it, her father had pulled her into his study. He'd handed her a small book to go along with the microscope. In low whispers, he'd told her that the lenses in the apparatus were from van Leeuwenhoek's own collection and the book contained drawings of some of his earliest observations. Kitty had been stunned and asked how these things could possibly have been acquired. Her father would not say specifically, only that there were certain persons to be met in dark and low neighborhoods who traded in such things. He had requested that such a lens be located and brought to him. Three years and a large sum later, it had been.

It was an extraordinary piece of equipment and she would keep it with her always. She did not expect to see anything remarkable under it in town, though she could at least collect some local flora to examine.

She had not often been to the house on Berkeley Square and

when she had, she'd always stayed in the nursery, sharing a large old, creaky bed with her younger sister. Now, a room and attached sitting room had been prepared especially for her use.

Her dear mother had arranged everything just as Kitty would wish. The rooms had a soft look to them, filled as they were with rounded furniture and rich velvets in the deep blues and purples she favored. The sitting room had freshly painted white book-shelves, left empty for her to fill. An almost ludicrously overstuffed armchair in navy velvet with silver tacking was ready to accommodate her late-night reading. The thick carpet underfoot imbued the place with a hushed feel. Kitty had sometimes wondered if her love of softness was in some way a rebuke to her intellectual mind. Still, she could not be comforta-ble in anything over-austere.

Kitty was well aware that it had been her mother alone who had made all the arrangements. Her father, Lord Penderton, was perennially buried in his books and would not notice if the whole house had undergone a transformation, other than tripping over moved furniture. It was the baroness who was the beating heart of the house.

Lady Penderton was in the habit of entering a room where her family could be found, sizing the whole thing up, and issuing orders accordingly. On their first evening in town, she had come into the drawing room, stood for a moment, and said: "My dear husband, I can see your knees grow cold though you would not notice, being engrossed in a book as you are. I'll have a blanket fetched. Kitty, your eyes grow tired, do stop reading for ten minutes to give them a rest. Frederick, do come away from the window. Miss Crimpleton will not pass by for wishing. You'll feel better if you sit by me and tell me all about your last conversation with the girl. There, now. Have we all been sorted out?"

And of course, they *had* been sorted out. Lord Penderton's knees warmed, Kitty's eyes felt better, and Frederick relieved his feelings to his mother's sympathetic ear. After that was accom-plished, Lady Penderton wrote a long letter to Kitty's younger sister, so that she might not feel left out, though she stayed behind in the country.

Lord Penderton often said he would end up starving if his wife did not direct him to the dining room at the appropriate hour. Kitty thought that was right. None of them would get on very well without Lady Penderton. She was not at all intellectual. She only occasionally picked up a book and then only a novel filled with haunted castles and the poor maidens who attempted to survive them. One might think a scholar such as Lord Penderton and a lady uninterested in libraries would not be well suited. And yet, they were. As Lady Penderton often said, "Knowledge is an excellent thing, but somebody must keep us all alive."

Before Kitty and Frederick had left for the much-anticipated meeting of Mr. Lackington at Lackington & Allen, Lady Penderton had issued practical advice.

"Frederick, dear," she said, "do keep a close watch on your sister. I understand the place is vast and as it is a vast place filled with books, I do not like to think of our Kitty getting lost in there. Your father was once disappeared into the place for so long that I had to send a footman in after him. He was eventually located, buried under a pile of books about the Roman Empire. It is still not clear whether they fell on him, or if he'd been reading them one by one."

Since they'd set off, it had taken nearly an hour to reach Finsbury Square, though they would have easily covered the distance in half the time in the countryside. It seemed everybody in England was out in their conveyance and their own coachman had a time of it, weaving and dodging through the chaos.

Finally though, they had arrived. Lackington & Allen, Temple of the Muses. Frederick had helped her down to the sidewalk and Kitty took in the premises. Its arched windows and columns beckoned. She was nearly awestruck to contemplate what lay beyond its doors.

"Miss Dell! I say, Miss Dell!"

Kitty turned to the sound. To her surprise, Lord Grayson was at once waving and dismounting his horse. Kitty felt the familiar leap in her stomach at the sight of him, and then just as quickly dismissed it. It was one thing to look upon Lord Grayson's fine person, but another to converse with him.

"Who?" Frederick said softly to her.

"Grayson," Kitty whispered back.

"Miss Dell," Lord Grayson said, handing off his horse to a boy and hurrying to them. "You are in town!"

"Most apparently, Lord Grayson, as you can see," Kitty said.

"Yes, I see, indeed." Lord Grayson looked curiously at Frederick.

Kitty stifled a sigh. "May I introduce you to Mr. Dell, he is my brother. Frederick, this is Lord Grayson."

"Brother? Ah, very good. Of course, brother," Lord Grayson said.

The lord, having understood that Frederick was Miss Dell's brother, seemed to not require any more information about him. He turned back to Kitty. "May I escort you somewhere?" he asked.

"I am most obviously escorted by my brother, Lord Grayson," Kitty said. "And, we have an appointment with Mr. Lackington and would not wish to be late."

"Lackington?" Lord Grayson asked.

"Lackington," Kitty repeated.

"Oh! Lackington. The shop. The shop right here. Books, of course. I have not forgotten your penchant for them."

"And I have not forgotten your aversion to them," Kitty said in a pleasant tone. "Now, we'd best be off."

Frederick bowed to the lord and escorted his sister inside. "My God," he said to Kitty, "You told me he was a dandy, but he makes your average peacock look positively dowdy."

"That is Lord Grayson, Frederick," Kitty said, "he is like a prettily wrapped box that once opened is discovered to be empty."

"Wait a minute," Frederick said, "he is not the fellow that, well, how do I say it? The one that…leads ladies on."

"I would not be surprised," Kitty said. "There can be no gentleman that surpasses Lord Grayson in inventing ridiculous compliments and high-flown phrases. I imagine some females might be taken in by it."

"See that you are not one of them," Fredrick said in his stern older brother tone. "I would not like it said that my sister was the victim of disappointed hopes."

Kitty suppressed a giggle. "Frederick," she said, "nothing could be less of a danger to me."

Though Kitty might have said more of Lord Grayson, her thoughts were wholly captured by what lay before her. The massive circular counter with its high dome overhead, generously staffed, where anybody might pay for a book they had longed for, or perhaps had not even known existed. The bookshelves themselves, soaring toward the sky, their upper limits reached by rolling ladders. The people, everywhere, looking at a book or having an intense conversation about a book. Stairs leading to even more rows of books. It was glorious.

Frederick told a clerk their purpose and they were speedily escorted up those stairs and to one of the private apartments set aside for ladies and gentlemen requiring quiet.

Though it was a lovely room, with rare books carefully placed under glass and large bow windows overlooking the square, Kitty could settle her eyes nowhere. She was to finally meet Mr. Lackington.

Frederick had a cursory look at the books under glass, quietly sighed, and took himself to the window.

Kitty turned as she heard the door open.

Mr. Lackington was a smartly dressed gentleman in his middle age, only an ink-smudge on one of his cuffs giving away his profession. To Kitty's surprise, he was accompanied by a very tiny older lady in dark bombazine, her small head topped off by a frilled a lace cap. Kitty presumed it was Mr. Lackington's mother and supposed it was a particular honor that he should bring her.

"Miss Dell! Mr. Dell!" Mr. Lackington said, coming forward to greet them.

Kitty said, "How pleased I am to finally meet you in person, Mr. Lackington."

"The pleasure is mine, I can assure you," Mr. Lackington said gallantly. "I have received your letters with much eagerness over the past two years."

Kitty blushed, wholly unused to anybody beyond her father remarking that the ideas she'd written about so fervently were particularly interesting.

"Your visit could not have been better timed," Mr. Lackington said, "as I would wish to introduce you to this lady. She has been most interested in my tales of a learned young women from Devon. May I present Mrs. Caroline Herschel."

"Mrs. Herschel," Frederick said, bowing. "Delighted."

Kitty sunk into a curtsy low enough for the Queen, herself. Caroline Herschel! The famed astronomer. The discoverer of comets. The only female scientist to ever receive a royal pension. Caroline Herschel was being introduced to insignificant Kitty Dell. While the lady was shorter than Kitty by more than a foot, she was a veritable giant in astronomy.

"Miss Dell," Mrs. Herschel said, her English tinted with a slight German accent, "I am gratified to know that a young lady pursues scientific interests. Of course, we are all capable of it, but so few women dare to explore. Though, I am familiar with your father's work and so I should not be surprised."

"Mrs. Herschel," Kitty said, "I am honored, well, I am near overwhelmed, you are, well of course you know—"

"None of that, please," Mrs. Herschel said kindly. She held out her arm and said, "Now do walk with me and tell me how you confirmed the hemi-parasitic properties of Cornish eyebright."

As Kitty took the lady's arm, all thought of Mr. Lackington flown from her, she heard Frederick say quietly, "God, the eyebright again."

GILES REMOUNTED HIS horse and watched Miss Dell disappear into Lackington and Allen. He had been very surprised to spot her on a London street and his address to her had been exceedingly clumsy. How stupid not to have instantly noted that the lady so interested in books stood in front of the largest bookstore in town. Had he taken a moment to think about it, he might have casually strolled in and encountered her there. He might even have claimed she'd awakened an interest in books in him via their fascinating conversations at Newmarket. There was little a lady liked better than to believe she had affected some positive change in a gentleman. Men were never appreciated more than when they revealed themselves to be clay in a woman's hands.

But no, he'd been rash about it and had not even stopped to compose himself before throwing himself in front of her. And her brother. *That* person clearly took only the most cursory care with his dress. Giles supposed the fellow would think of himself as a man's sort of man—pretending to hardly care what he looked like. It was the height of posing, as absolutely everybody cared how they appeared. Dalton was of that devil-may-care ilk, but let him find a stain on a particular coat he was set on and very suddenly the devil cared very much.

Giles admitted to himself that he'd not been very clever on his first approach since their meetings at Newmarket. But then, she was so very pretty and when he'd seen her, that marvelous dark hair, those lively features. He could not help…well, there was no use analyzing the thing. He must just do better when he saw her next.

He began to get a sinking feeling as he trotted toward Destin's to meet Cabot. It was not only that he'd been rather uninspired in his speech. She had been downright dismissive! Lord Grayson was to be nothing in comparison to the shopkeeper that awaited her inside.

He attempted to cheer himself with the idea that she would not be so entranced by endless stacks of literature when the balls and parties began. In fact, the Bergrams' ball was on the morrow and certainly she would attend. He had it on good authority that Miss Dell's mother, Lady Penderton, was a longstanding acquaintance of Lady Bergram. That most of London was a longstanding acquaintance of Lady Bergram seemed beside the point.

He leapt off his horse in front of Destin's and strode inside to find Cabot.

THE CLUB WAS more casual than White's, and a deal more pleasant. Destin's was a young man's club and Marty Destin was a young proprietor. One might find any sort of bet to lay a wager on, take a room for the night, or have a good dinner when nothing else was on offer. However, what one would *not* find at Destin's was the old guard haunting its halls. Particularly the old guard that was just now engaged in a solemn pact to get their sons married.

Giles strode up to the table at the bow windows, Cabot already having commandeered it for them.

"So," he said to his friend, "here you are leaving your bride behind in the countryside already?"

Lord Cabot laughed. "Do not be ridiculous," he said. "I would not very well visit Tattersall's without Lady Cabot. Of course she has come with me."

Giles took the coffee Marty Destin had silently supplied the table with. "I do not see why she should have come. A lady cannot visit Tattersall's anyway. What does she do, stay in the carriage while you conduct your business?"

Cabot's brow wrinkled. "Grayson, my wife is not an ordinary lady. She is Mendbridge's daughter. She walks into the subscription room whenever she likes and nobody dares say a word about it."

Giles should have known as much. Miss Darlington, now to

be known as Lady Cabot, had never followed any particular rules when it came to horses. She'd always been given latitude as the daughter of the revered Lord Mendbridge. Giles remembered nearly unseating himself from his horse the first time she'd sailed by at an alarming pace, smartly driving her own Hooper High Flyer.

"I must know, are the rumors true that the lady rode your filly for the thousand guinea stakes at Newmarket?" Giles asked.

"What an idea," Lord Cabot said, staring intently into his coffee. "Where did you hear it?"

"Whispered everywhere," Giles said. "Females are near-swooning over the notion. The romance of it, you know."

"Kindly stop it when you hear it discussed," Lord Cabot said. "You were there and saw with your own eyes it was my groom who rode Bucephalus."

Giles took that as rather a confirmation than not. He'd seen *somebody* ride the horse, though it would have been impossible to confirm who it was at such a distance. Then, Cabot's groom had been ill afterward and carried away. Could his groom have been ill all along? That was the rumor, though he would drop the subject as he could see that his friend did not wish to discuss it.

"Talk of romantic rides to the finish aside," Giles said, "how do you get on with married life? I know it would not be gentlemanly to admit that you'd have been better to put the whole thing off for a few years, but we have known each other most of our lives. I would know the truth."

"Are you certain you *want* the truth?" Cabot asked.

Giles nodded and leaned forward. He was absolutely certain he wished to hear the truth. Just as certain as he was that all this talk of marital bliss from his recently married friends could not hold up long under scrutiny. Infatuation would fade and be replaced with he knew not what. He would hear the real case of it.

Cabot said, "I came very close to failing to win Lady Cabot, and if I *had* failed I would have regretted it for all of my days. I can no more imagine being parted from her than I can being parted with my right arm."

Cabot paused in the silence. "Recently, I have found myself at once wishing for a son, and not wishing for a child at all." His voice dropped to a near whisper. "What if she dies in childbirth? You see, that is the thing that haunts me."

Giles noted the hint of desperation in his friend's voice. If he had hoped to hear a tale full of regret, he would not hear it from Cabot. The man was besotted.

"God's will and all that, I suppose," Giles said, stirring his coffee.

"God's will can go to the devil," Cabot said. "In any case, my wife says I worry too much and she's as strong as a well-bred mare. I don't know though, she cries at the most unaccountable things. She says I am not to worry over it, it is only her temperament. Did I tell you I had to write it into the marriage contract? If I make her cry too much I go to the road and proclaim myself a beast. I've already done it once."

Giles had no wish to hear any details of the lady's weeping or Cabot's humiliation on the road. He said, "Lady Cabot compares herself to a well-bred mare? This is the result when you put two people who live for horses in the same house together. I can only imagine the metaphors of all things horse that must fly through your rooms."

"Never mind *my* house," Cabot said. "How do you get on in Dalton's house?"

"We are, for all intents and purposes, penniless. We can barely get things on credit anymore, as every tradesman in the world has heard of the pact. Dalton is as prickly as you might imagine over it. It is only his butler that does not seem to mind, as the wine cellar will last a few more years yet."

"No lady has yet presented an allurement sufficient to tempt you out of that Eden?" Cabot said with a sly smile. "I suppose you are eyeing Miss Dell for one of your ridiculous flirtations—you trailed her like a fox on a scent when we stayed in Newmarket."

"Miss Dell," Giles said. "I just saw her as a matter of fact. She looks as charming as ever. More charming, possibly. I will have enormous fun flirting with her."

"She does not strike me as a frivolous lady," Cabot said.

"She certainly is not," Giles said. "Miss Dell will be a contest, I do not delude myself on that score. At this moment, dusty books are more to her taste than anything I can offer, but what am I without a challenge?"

"Perhaps you might seek to accommodate the lady and actually read one of those dusty books," Cabot said.

Both gentlemen roared with laughter over the idea. After they had settled, Lord Cabot said, "I believe your pursuit of Miss Dell will come to nothing, and I am glad of it. She is my wife's particular friend and I would not wish to hear the recriminations after you have left a lady with disappointed hopes, as you always do. I would find myself standing on the road and shouting that I am a beast for even having known you."

"Nonsense, my lack of scholarship cannot put a lady off entirely. And by the by, there is nothing at all wrong with a season's flirtation. Not for myself, and not for the lady. It is all but expected for a first season, unless the lady is without sufficient means to return for a second round. It is the second season that is time for seriousness and by then I will have made my graceful exit."

"You view the thing from the wrong angle," Lord Cabot said. "It is not what Miss Dell thinks of *you* that will unravel your scheme, it is what Miss Dell will think of Sir John Kullehamnd. Lady Cabot is determined to introduce them at Lady Bergram's ball. She is certain it will be a match."

Giles felt a strange sense of outrage over this communication. Who was this Kullehamnd? Why should Lady Cabot be so keen on foisting the rogue in front of Miss Dell?

"And what is so extraordinary about the fellow?" Giles asked curtly.

Cabot folded his arms. "He is twenty-eight, said to be of

adequate means, and a fellow of the Royal Society. You see? He is eligible and he is a scholar. Lady Cabot says nothing else will do for Miss Dell."

KITTY HAD BEEN wrangled into her dress for the Bergram's ball as she read from a book, only having to switch it to another hand when Martha needed an arm for a sleeve. Her maid had chattered away about the evening and Kitty was certain Martha was more interested in it than she was. Kitty's life, always demarcated by two different poles, seemed as starkly contrasted as ever. One part was all intellectual curiosity, the other was dresses and pretty steps on a ballroom floor. One was meat and the other a summer trifle.

As the carriage was now making its way swiftly to the Bergram's door, she ought to be turning her attention to summer trifle, but how could she at such a moment? Only yesterday, she had gone to meet Mr. Lackington and had ended meeting Mrs. Herschel! Her thoughts had been so taken up with it.

The lady had been kind and had taken a real interest in her experiments on Cornish eyebright. It had been almost as if she debated with her father, though it was instead another lady.

After she and Mrs. Herschel had thoroughly discussed her experiments, and likely for far longer than Frederick had patience for, Mr. Lackington had ordered tea brought in. Kitty, Mr. Lackington, and Mrs. Herschel spoke of books and flew from one topic to the next. Mr. Lackington, who was turning out to be a dear and considerate gentleman, soon realized that the conversation had left Frederick far behind. After asking her brother a suitable number of questions to uncover his interests and quickly discerning his primary interest to be the management of his father's estate, Mr. Lackington spoke to him about how nitrogen in the soil affected harvests and how one might adopt the method of convertible husbandry to capitalize on it. Frederick was so cheered by the turn of conversation that he ended leaving with a book on the subject.

What society she'd kept yesterday afternoon! Everything had been stimulating and new.

That a particular encounter with a particular condescending gentleman kept intruding on these happy memories was unfortunate, but she did not allow them to linger long. Lord Grayson might have looked wickedly handsome on horseback, but as soon as he started talking the illusion collapsed.

"Kitty," her mother said, seated across from her in the carriage, "you seem a thousand miles away, and have done since yesterday."

"It's Mrs. Herschel's doing," Frederick said. "Though you would hope my sister's head would be turned by some single gentleman, it has been turned by the lady astronomer."

"No more than your own head turned upon meeting Tom Cribb," Kitty said. "You blathered on about it for months. Even poor Miss Crimpleton had tired of it."

"Cribb is a renowned pugilist!" Frederick cried. In a lower voice, he said, "Did Miss Crimpleton really complain of it?"

Kitty patted his hand, sorry she had dragged Miss Crimpleton into it. "No, she did not. I should not have said it. You might talk to Miss Crimpleton about Mr. Cribb's defensive stance for months on end and she would do nothing but admire."

Frederick appeared entirely mollified by this theory and Kitty hoped he would not actually take up the idea.

"Kitty, dear," the baroness said, "do remember that there are hours and hours in the day to think of Mrs. Herschel, but only the next hours to think of this ball. I know your rational mind will understand me."

Her rational mind *did* understand her mother. She must keep up her end of the bargain. She had been to Lackington and Allen. She would go many more times while she was in town. She and the baroness had been invited to call on Mrs. Herschel on

Tuesday. That was all lovely, but now she must turn her thoughts to the matter at hand.

It was no small matter, either. As much as she'd like to live as an intellect, she must marry. She was no Mrs. Herschel. She would not receive a royal pension. And, while she might have the means to live independently as a spinster, she did not wish to.

She wished to have children and had already mapped out their education, whether they be boy or girl. Especially for a girl. Though, even a boy would not be sent away to school. She had seen the result of that particular education well enough. Lord Grayson had done it all, right through Oxford, and left with nothing. Even her own brother, while not quite as empty-headed, had likely spent most of his school days on wagers and wine.

Aside from children, she wished to be of society, and spinsters were always forgotten. Though she liked to spend hours upon hours reading and thinking, a lively dinner at the end of it was always welcome. She would not like to imagine herself, sometime in future, ordering a tray to her room so as not to get underfoot of the mistress of Frederick's household.

To say that a lady was on the shelf was no exaggeration. A spinster became that piece of porcelain sitting in some corner cabinet that had been there so long that nobody really sees it anymore. If, one day, that porcelain is broken and swept away, people are left with only vague ideas that there used to be something there at all.

She wished to have her own house and had particular ideas of having a room dedicated to her telescope and her microscope.

All of this required a husband. The husband was necessary, though he felt somewhat superfluous to the whole scheme. She harbored some grand hopes, though. She might meet some gentleman who had her own penchant for exploring ideas and learning new things and might also be pleasant to look at. He need not be an Adonis, only pleasant in the middling way.

In any case, she could not deny that she liked dancing. There was nothing intellectual in it, society gained nothing from it, but she adored it all the same. Like the soft velvets and rounded corners in her bedchamber, some things just suited her. She ought not scold herself over it.

And then, she looked forward to seeing Penny this night, as her friend had written that she would attend the ball. Lady Cabot and her husband were in town on some sort of horse business and she had not seen her since their marriage. Kitty had been invited to Dorset more than once, but the baroness had forbid her to go. Her mother had said the first months of a marriage would set the tone for the rest of it and the couple should be left on their own to discover it.

Kitty was determined to enjoy herself this evening. Her mother was right, there were other hours in the day to contemplate Mrs. Herschel or any other serious matter. Now was a time for levity and enjoyment.

If a certain dashing gentleman insisted on putting his name down on her card, she was determined to appreciate his looks by studiously ignoring anything idiotic he might say. Her stomach might flutter all it liked.

"Ah, here we are," the baroness said. "It is to be the usual crush, I see."

CHAPTER THREE

THOUGH KITTY HAD been to a smaller ball at Newmarket, and several exceedingly small dances in private houses in Devon, this was her first encounter with a large London ball. In truth, it might well be the largest ball of the season.

The baroness had told her the Bergrams were an inoffensive kind of people. The sort one never thinks about until an invitation is delivered or one is composing the list for a large party. As they were neither reviled nor held in particular esteem by anybody, they were vague friends with everybody. And, as they had an enormous ballroom and gave very good dinners, all of London accepted their invitations.

They had finally entered the house, paid tribute to their host and hostess, and deposited their outer coats in the cloak room.

The crush of people already in the ballroom nearly overwhelmed Kitty.

"Never fear," the baroness said in Kitty's ear, "half these people will make their way to the card rooms when the music strikes up. As will I—Mrs. Cheldup insists I partner her at whist and goodness knows she needs somebody to hold up the other side of the table. I will not bet high, as I know I will lose every single pound of it."

Kitty smiled at the mention of Mrs. Cheldup. She was a sprightly and friendly lady who made up for her rather dim understanding of everything, including whist, by her charming joy in life. No amount of failures at the card table could dampen the lady's spirits.

Frederick said, "Jost is here. I will go and say hello."

"As you wish," the baroness said, "but do not leave your sister stranded for long."

Frederick nodded and set off winding round people toward his friend.

"Ah," the baroness said, "there is Penny. She brings somebody with her."

Kitty looked in the direction of her mother's gaze. Penny, now Lady Cabot, smiled and waved as she made her way over. Her looks were blooming, her cheeks pink, and Kitty thought only her happiness with Lord Cabot could account for it. Following Penny was a tall and serious-looking gentleman in rather somber-looking attire.

Penny kissed Kitty and said, "We have been parted too long, I am determined to come and see you on the morrow. However, just now, I would like to introduce you to Sir John Kullehamnd."

Kitty curtsied and the serious man bowed.

"Sir John is a fellow of the Royal Society, Kitty," Penny said with a twinkle in her eye.

Kitty was momentarily taken aback. The Royal Society! This gentleman must be exceedingly learned.

She suppressed a smile to note in herself a higher estimation of his looks than she had initially experienced. He was not dandified, he was not a Lord Grayson with the remarkably tied neckcloth. In truth, his neckcloth might have been tied by himself and possibly in a hurry. But a member of the Royal Society? Suddenly, his simple dress seemed far more attractive than any expensive coat could ever be.

"Delighted, Miss Dell," he said, in a deep voice devoid of cheerfulness.

"And this is Lady Penderton," Penny said.

Lady Penderton regarded the gentleman quizzically, though

not unfriendly.

"Kitty," Lady Cabot said, "I have taken the liberty of mentioning your proclivity for books and your recent conclusions about…" Penny paused, as if searching her mind for information. "Well, it was a plant, or two plants, I remember that much."

Kitty smiled. "You refer to my study of the hemi-parasitic properties of Cornish eyebright," she said.

Sir John nodded. "On gorse, I presume," he said.

Kitty nodded, fascinated by this person.

Penny looked back and forth between them indulgently. "So," she said, "as I think you will have much to discuss…Sir John? Perhaps you might take supper?"

Sir John nodded, as grave as a vicar, and put his name down. He bowed and walked away.

"What do you think, Kitty?" Penny asked. "Have I not done a bit of brilliant matchmaking? I met him at a dinner a few nights ago and did not understand half of what he said. I instantly thought of you. What Lord Cabot is to my love of horses, he is to your love of books."

"It is far too early to speak of matchmaking, Penny," Kitty scolded. She relented and said, "Though I will be most interested in a conversation with the gentleman."

Penny smiled knowingly and then said, "What say you, Lady Penderton?"

The baroness smiled. "I've not much to say this moment. I have seen him last year at some rout or other, though did not know anything of him before then. I believe his title and his money spring from the continent. Somewhere north, Denmark, perhaps? Though his accent would point to his being born here."

"Not a ringing endorsement," Penny said laughing, "but not a condemnation either. I suppose we may count on the Royal Society to be his primary recommendation."

Before the baroness could answer, Lord Grayson had pushed his way into their circle.

"Miss Dell, Lady Penderton, Lady Cabot," he said bowing.

"May I, Miss Dell?" he asked, holding his hand out for her card.

Kitty could not help but note the difference between gay Lord Grayson and the serious gentleman who had just departed. And, though she thought she ought to disdain it entirely, she could not help but appreciate his careful dress. He always looked so…wonderful. It was a pity that she could not wave a wand and put Sir John's intellect into Lord Grayson's person or vice versa.

She handed over her card.

Lord Grayson peered at it. "Alas, you are already engaged for supper. Sir John…" Lord Grayson trailed off and then his head snapped up. "Sir John? Sir John Kullehamnd?"

"The very one," Penny said. "Are you acquainted with our new friend?"

"I certainly am not," Lord Grayson said stiffly.

Kitty looked at Lord Grayson in some surprise. He'd denied the acquaintance with rather more vehemence than would be required.

Penny seemed to find his answer all too satisfactory. She said, "The gentleman is of a serious turn of mind and not a very practiced flirt, and so I would doubt you had much in common."

Lord Grayson smiled thinly and wrote his name down for the first. He bowed and strode away.

Lady Penderton looked at Penny curiously. "You were quite sharp with Lord Grayson. Do you harbor antipathy toward him? I understood him to be a particular friend of Lord Cabot."

"He *is* a particular friend of my husband's, Lady Penderton," Penny said. "And while I do not despise the gentleman, I am cautious of him in regard to any unmarried ladies in his vicinity. He is a collector of hearts, I am afraid."

"He is quite ridiculous, Mama," Kitty said.

"Yes, I see," Lady Penderton said thoughtfully. "He seems rather fun, though. He is handsome and has a certain charm to him."

Before Kitty could explain to her mother that handsome and charming was precisely the problem with Lord Grayson, gentlemen began to approach. Lord Burke was known, as he'd often been to their neighborhood in Devon. Others were not, but took advantage of Penny and the baroness standing nearby to make the introduction.

Kitty's card was filled before a half hour had passed.

GILES PUT HIS name down on a series of eager-looking lady's cards. He was not particularly discriminating about it—it felt more of a job than it ought. He joined Cabot on the far side of the ballroom.

"I see Lady Cabot has accomplished her aim this evening," he said to Cabot.

"Has she?" Lord Cabot asked. "I quite lost sight of her in the crowd."

"She is over there," Giles said, indicating the direction with a nod. "She stands with Miss Dell and Lady Penderton. Sir Gloomy has put himself down for Miss Dell's supper."

"If you mean Sir John, I told you she meant to make the match," Cabot answered.

"But have you seen him?" Giles said heatedly. "I had him pointed out to me. There, over there, that fellow who looks like an undertaker!"

Lord Cabot looked where he was bid. "Yes, I see what you say. I suspect Lady Cabot was not wrong in describing him as an overly keen scholar. He'll be the type who hurried to dress and threw on the first clothes he encountered as he'd lost track of time in his library."

"Scholar, indeed," Giles said dismissively.

"He may not bring any joie de vivre in his dress," Cabot said, "or in his manner as far as I can tell from here. But it is my understanding that Miss Dell is not at all moved by a well-cut coat." Cabot suddenly laughed and said, "Perhaps she is one lady who will not fall for your charms, such as they are."

"Certainly, she will not be bowled over by anything *that* person will have to relate from his ridiculous library," Giles said.

"Good God, Grayson," Lord Cabot said, sounding out of patience. "Move on. The room is filled with adoring young ladies who will swoon over your compliments. Do not attempt to climb a mountain when a hill will do."

Giles did not answer, but silently fumed. As it happened, a hill would not do. He'd set his sights on Miss Dell at Newmarket and he'd never failed at a conquest. He did not see why he should be felled by the morose Sir John. He would not be.

Oh, Miss Dell liked to tease him for his shallow font of knowledge. However, she only teased and he was certain she liked dancing with him. As he had her first, and Sir John must wait until supper, he thought he might cement her opinion of the fellow. He would make Sir John appear tedious and that would be the end of Lady Cabot's schemes in that direction.

The idea cheered him immensely as he gazed across the ball-room at the lovely Miss Dell. She really was marvelous in her dark blue gown, surrounded by a sea of pastels. Tall, slim, her intelligent dark eyes flashing. She was in no way suited to the awkward Sir John. Certainly not.

THE BARONESS HAD gone off to the card room and her predicted disasters at whist with Mrs. Cheldup. Frederick, though he was meant to keep a sharp eye on Kitty, was still deep in conversation with his friend, Jost. Kitty well knew that her brother would not pursue putting his name on any particular lady's card. Rather, he would wait to see who had not been paired and gallantly step in. He would ensure that every lady wishing to stand up danced at least one set. He had always done so in Devon, as he was of the opinion that when he could not claim Miss Crimpleton, he should make himself useful to his hostess. As a result, hostesses everywhere adored Frederick Dell.

While Kitty and Penny waited for the musicians to strike up, Penny chattered on about her new life as Lady Cabot. Kitty was vastly amused to hear of how they enjoyed long romantic dinners, where they spoke of equine bloodlines over excellent wine. She found herself rather *relieved* to hear that Lord Cabot was now fully acquainted with the real Penny. Not the always happy and bright lady presented to society, but the Penny who Kitty knew well—so easily hurt and bruised. Penny claimed she'd wept a dozen times already and that her poor lord only wrung his hands and asked if it was his fault until she could not cry longer for laughing. She'd had a particularly long cry over the news that Miss Austen had passed, not because she so loved the lady or her books, but because she had once compared herself to foolish Marianne Dashwood. She'd tried to explain it to Lord Cabot, but he had been completely mystified.

While Kitty was delighted to hear of her friend's happiness, she could not wholly put her mind to it. There was a small part of her thoughts that would keep drifting to Lord Grayson. He'd taken the first and so she could not be many more minutes away from his florid compliments and empty phrasings. She was loath to admit it, but she was also not many more minutes away from his skill at dancing. She'd experienced it at Newmarket at the club ball—there was an expert ease to it that had thrilled her.

"In any case," Penny said, bringing her back to the present, "he is a darling to me and we are having enormous fun expanding the stables and buying horses. We shall be the premier horse breeders in England, you shall see. My own father will come to us. Ah, here comes Grayson."

Penny squeezed her hand and whispered, "Resist all suggestions that your eyes are the night sky and your flowing locks throw shame on Aphrodite."

"I have never heard anything so ridiculous," Kitty said.

"But you are likely to hear the ridiculous very soon," Penny said, laughing. "I will go and find my husband, we are to dance together though I am sure we will be scolded over it. We do not much care, it is a silly rule."

Kitty watched her friend depart, surprised that she would dance with Lord Cabot. She was certain Lady Bergram would note it, and note any single lady who sat out when Lord Cabot should have stepped in. After all, Frederick could not dance with them all. But, as Penny said, she and her lord did not much care about a censure.

It seemed rather wonderful to be a united force such as that. It spoke of secrets and decisions between them and the world's opinion held at arm's length.

"Miss Dell," Lord Grayson said, holding out his hand. Kitty allowed herself to be led, *and* she allowed herself to give credit to the lord where he had earned it. There was a confidence to him that could only be pleasing. Whatever off-putting thing he might say, he would not fumble in his steps.

They joined the three other couples that would form their square and to Kitty's surprise, Sir John was to her right. He'd stood up with Miss Blessy, a lady Kitty had been briefly introduced to as one who also came for her first season.

The music began and Lord Grayson led her through the pantalon. His movements were graceful and Kitty thought he was the sort of dancer who might easily rescue a lady who'd momentarily forgotten the steps. That she might do so was one of the ideas that had kept her up at night while the preparations for London had marched forward. She'd had a dancing master for years, but though she'd practiced, her mind was so often on other things.

"How do you find London so far, Miss Dell?" Lord Grayson asked, as they returned to their side and passed round each other.

Kitty was very much relieved that he had not led with her moonbeam eyes or her grace of Athena. It seemed he was determined to have a conversation in the sensible realm and she welcomed it.

"I find the town invigorating, Lord Grayson," she answered. "Especially the people in it. I have recently had the great good fortune to be introduced to Mrs. Herschel."

"Mrs. Herschel? I do not believe I know the lady," Lord Grayson said.

Kitty pressed her lips together. Of course he would not even have heard of the great scientist.

"Mrs. Caroline Herschel is an astronomer and has discovered a number of comets," she said.

"Comets. Those stars that fly through the night. Charming."

Kitty nodded, not bothering to expound on what was known of comets, though Sir Isaac Newton had come to more particular conclusions than stars flying through the sky.

"Though, how does one have interest in such things when there are stars brighter than any in the night sky right here on earth?" Lord Grayson said gallantly.

Kitty suppressed a sigh. They were back to the florid phrasings.

They had completed the pantalon and returned to their place as the opposite couples took the floor.

Kitty watched Sir John lead Miss Blessy and she blushed ever so slightly for them. Miss Blessy was short and plump and had a look of vague confusion, as if she were not over-familiar with where the dance was going. Sir John was upright and stiff, looking as if he led his partner through some sad occasion, though he at least seemed to have better command of the steps.

Next to her, Lord Grayson said softly, "One really ought to employ a dancing master before engaging oneself at a ball."

Kitty turned her head sharply. "Do you insult a lady, my lord?" she whispered.

"Certainly not," Lord Grayson said, louder. "The fault is always to be laid at the gentleman's door."

Kitty fumed. Perhaps Sir John had not the smoothness or skill of a Lord Grayson, but that did not mean there was anything positively wrong with him. Or his dancing. Though it be a bit stiff. She supposed *Sir John* was not under the illusion that comets were stars flying through the night.

"My sympathy goes out to Miss Blessy," Lord Grayson said quietly.

"Sir John Kullehamnd is a member of the Royal Society," Kitty whispered heatedly.

"Then I suppose they do not do much dancing there," Lord Grayson said.

"I suppose they do not," Kitty said, having heard quite enough from Lord Grayson. "They are far too busy making discoveries to benefit mankind."

"And yet," Lord Grayson persisted, "mankind dearly loves to dance."

Kitty had reached the very end of her patience. Lord Grayson might be dashing and a splendid dancer, but that was all. It was the height of conceit that this fool thought himself above a member of the Royal Society just because he had memorized some steps.

"Mankind," Kitty said, "was informed in 1543 that the sun does not revolve around the earth. Perhaps a gentleman might infer from that information that the world does not revolve around *him*."

Kitty felt a vast relief in saying so, though she was aware she'd been shockingly rude and therefore not very ladylike. The baroness always said that you must be kinder to the people you dislike than you were to your friends, as too much honey was as poisonous as nightshade but nobody could ever fault you for it.

For his part, Lord Grayson did not reply. Nor did he say anything for the rest of the set.

At least she had stopped his insults against poor Sir John.

GILES HAD FELT a temper rising in him ever since he had squired

Miss Dell through the first quadrille. He did not often have a temper, as he was so rarely displeased with life. Even finding himself near-penniless at the present time had not dampened his outlook.

Just now, though…

How had the conversation gone in such a bad direction! When he'd had a look at Sir John's bumbling through the steps, he'd thought his work had been done for him. All he need do was point it out. It was not as if he'd invented anything against the fellow. He was a terrible dancer!

But Miss Dell had not cared anything about it. No, she was only impressed by the man's membership in the Royal Society.

What could she mean by it? He understood the lady to be a bit of a bookworm, but how was that to affect who she preferred? Did she somehow imagine that if she were to contract herself to a dry thing like Sir John, that he would consult her on his readings or experiments or whatever he did that had not left time for dancing lessons?

He could not believe it to be so.

As his rare tempers were wont to do, eventually his consternation began to fade. It was replaced by his naturally buoyant optimism. Certainly, Miss Dell did not *really* prefer the likes of Kullehamnd. Perhaps she only toyed with him to increase his ardor.

Well, if that was the lady's game, she was skilled indeed. He'd never been so determined to win a lady's favor.

He had thought it unfortunate that Sir John was to take Miss Dell into supper, but now he began to think differently. A man like that would only expose his dullness over a protracted encounter.

Giles was determined to be nearby as it happened and had been hurrying Miss Danworth toward the supper room to accomplish it.

Miss Danworth, never very carefree anyway, came along with him, but not without staring at him annoyed.

CHAPTER FOUR

Kitty had quite regained her spirits over the course of the evening. Lord Burke had been his ever-charming self, though he seemed somewhat wistful these days. She had noted it at Newmarket and it was with him still.

She had also danced with other gentlemen who she had not known prior. Frederick, apparently believing it was his purview, had attempted to signal his approval or otherwise as each partner led her to the floor. Sir Allen was a yes, though Kitty found him tedious. Mr. Weymouth was a no, though he was good-humored and made her laugh.

Frederick had only shrugged at Sir John.

Kitty knew that Sir John was not the most exemplary partner, having viewed him with Miss Blessy, but she was confident they should get through well enough.

They *had* got on well enough, though it was not particularly inspired. Sir John was still stiff, but improved now that he did not have to keep track of which direction Miss Blessy was heading off to.

They'd had a fascinating conversation on the nature of hemi-parasitic plants. Kitty was looking forward to what else they might discuss over supper.

All was as it should be, until Lord Grayson practically rushed the table and sat Miss Danworth and himself across from her and

Sir John. The parties were quickly, albeit reluctantly on her end, introduced.

Aside from her aggravation at Lord Grayson pushing in, Kitty was leery of Miss Danworth. She was a lovely lady, with a mass of sunshine blond curls fighting to escape her hair combs. Her dress was exceedingly elegant. She was everything a lady should be, but there was a coldness in her manner. It was not in her words, which were commonplace enough, but something in her manner. She reminded Kitty of a neighbor in Devon who looked coolly upon all the world as an enemy, until they were proven otherwise.

"Sir John," Lord Grayson said, "I understand you are a member of the Royal Society."

Sir John nodded. "I have the honor."

"What do you fellows do all day?" Lord Grayson asked. "I presume fencing and shooting are not the thing, else I'd join myself."

"We conduct research and present our findings," Sir John said curtly.

Kitty was incensed. Lord Grayson was going out of his way to mock Sir John and there was no doubt that Sir John knew it.

"Have you discovered anything noteworthy, Sir John?" Miss Danworth said pleasantly.

"I am working on a paper that I hope will have some merit," Sir John said, "though I would not advertise it as such until rigorous testing of my theory has been completed."

"I am certain it shall have great merit," Kitty said.

Lord Grayson appeared surprised by the endorsement. "It sounds dreary, though," he said. "Spending all one's time in one's mind. I'd much rather *do* things, than think about things."

Sir John looked at Lord Grayson with cold eyes. "Our ability to think deeply is what separates us from the animals. Apes and dogs can *do* all manner of things."

Kitty pressed her lips together to hide a smile. Lord Grayson might be able to parry with a sword, but Sir John's words were sharper than any metal.

Lord Grayson's hand tightened on his fork. "Do you imply, sir, that I am an—"

"I never imply, Lord Grayson," Sir John said. "I am very particular in my speech. I did not call you an ape or a dog, I merely pointed out that they can do many things. My apologies if you did not understand me, the fault is always to be laid at the door of the gentleman who has spoken."

Kitty was delighted with Sir John. His phrasing was certainly meant to mirror Lord Grayson's comments on Sir John's dancing—*the fault is always to be laid at the gentleman's door.* Sir John had overheard the comment and he would not be browbeat by such a one as Lord Grayson.

She watched with satisfaction as a faint tinge of pink crept across Lord Grayson's cheeks. It did not, however, stop him from talking.

"Perhaps Sir John will allow Shakespeare's opinion—*things won are done, joy's soul lies in the doing,*" Lord Grayson said, his voice giving away his irritation.

"Miss Dell," Miss Danworth said hurriedly, "I understand from Lord Grayson that you are exceedingly learned yourself."

Kitty smiled, just imagining what Lord Grayson had said about *that.* "I would not claim to be exceedingly learned, Miss Danworth, but I do have a curiosity for the knowledge the world has to offer."

"You must call on me, then," Miss Danworth said. "Lord Childress's library is becoming well known for its interesting volumes—my father has recently acquired the Palaskar collection."

Kitty took in a breath, as did Sir John. The only person in the conversation who did not appear to understand the significance of the Palaskar collection was Lord Grayson.

Mr. Palaskar, now long-deceased, had traveled the world in search of rare and unique volumes. The gentleman was gifted with languages and it was said he had been fluent in seven of them. He'd spent the majority of his career translating his treasures into English.

"Miss Danworth," Kitty said, "is it true that for each volume there is a translation?"

"For most," Miss Danworth said. "Mr. Palaskar's own works are all bound in red leather and they sit side by side to the original work. We have employed a librarian, a very skilled and multi-fluent gentleman, to organize it all and translate the ones that were missed. I am certain Mr. Crackwilder would be happy to show you about."

"You are most kind, Miss Danworth," Kitty said.

"And you too, Sir John," Miss Danworth said pleasantly. "You are welcome to come and have a look. I am at home on Wednesdays."

"A rare and important honor, Miss Danworth," Sir John said gravely.

"Wait a minute," Lord Grayson broke in. "Crackwilder? Jeremy Crackwilder of the tenth?"

"I believe he was a soldier, Lord Grayson," Miss Danworth said, "but I would know little further. He walks with a cane, if that identifies him."

"Of course it must be him," Lord Grayson said. "He was my lieutenant."

Kitty found herself frustrated that Lord Grayson would manage to make the conversation about himself. She very much wished to hear more of Palaskar's library. She was also hard-pressed to imagine Lord Grayson charged with a lieutenant. How on earth had the man located pressed shirts and snowy cravats in a war?

The conversation moved on to speculation over whether Lady Lilith was truly to travel to America. Kitty did not care if Lady Lilith threw herself off a roof, though she worked to pretend interest. Sir John appeared to wish Lady Lilith *would* throw herself off a roof to be done with the debate. It was only Lord Grayson and Miss Danworth who appeared to find it at all interesting.

Kitty purposefully ignored Lord Grayson's attempt at a penetrating gaze when he'd said, "Sometimes a lady may seem even more distant than America, though she still be in England."

As she studiously ignored Lord Grayson, Kitty thought with trepidation of calling upon Miss Danworth. The lady had been courteous to extend the invitation, and Kitty would certainly go as she could not miss a visit to Palaskar's books, but she thought the lady somehow off-putting. Miss Danworth smiled, she was polite, but cool. She was not the sort where one felt an instant friendship spring up. But then again, she *did* have possession of Palaskar's books and that must go a long way in her favor.

The discussion over Lady Lilith eventually faded and Miss Danworth engaged in a conversation with Lord Grayson about Kitty did not care what. It left her free to speak to Sir John about her recent encounter with Mr. Lackington and Mrs. Herschel.

"Mrs. Herschel was so kind as to invite me to call on Tuesday," Kitty said.

"Ah, yes, her weekly salon."

"Salon?" Kitty said. "Do you mean an intellectual salon?"

"Such as we are, I suppose," Sir John said. "Those of us who pursue various interests attend. We often have members of the Royal Society come to present findings before they do so to a wider audience more formally."

Kitty was delighted. She had thought the call to Mrs. Herschel would be quite usual, but not it seemed not usual at all. An intellectual salon!

Though she found herself delighted, she wondered what her mother would make of it. She doubted the baroness would find the idea as invigorating.

Sir John had excused himself from the table and Kitty turned to Mr. Walker to her right. She was well aware that Lord Grayson kept trying to catch her eye, but she would not indulge him in it.

When Sir John returned, he seemed more relaxed than he had been. He spoke on a variety of topics and Kitty wondered how he'd suddenly become so much more voluble. She noticed his eyes had grown darker somehow; she could hardly see where the irises stopped and the pupils began. It struck her as slightly odd, until she speculated that he'd gone off to have a thimble-full of brandy in the library. She must not fault him for not being so naturally outgoing as Lord Grayson. Some gentlemen needed some liquid help in that direction.

Finally, the evening came to an end and Frederick arrived to collect her. She ignored Lord Grayson's look of outrage when Sir John bowed and said, "Until Tuesday, Miss Dell."

GILES TROTTED HIS horse through the empty streets in the direction of Crackwilder's apartment. He knew his old lieutenant would be awake still, the man never went to bed until at least three and it was just past two.

Though he'd been in the habit of dropping in, he'd not seen Crackwilder in some months. If he'd been more diligent, he'd have already known the fellow had taken employment with Miss Danworth's father.

What had that Sir John fellow meant by *until Tuesday*? Were he and Miss Dell to meet somewhere? Were they to meet to view Miss Danworth's library? But Miss Danworth's at-home was Wednesday. If not there, then where? What happened on Tuesday?

Perhaps they were to convene at Lackington and Allen. That would suit the two of them. Sir John could wax on about nonsense nobody cared about while pretending to have read every book in the shop.

Sir John was pathetic.

And what of Miss Dell's brother? Certainly, he could not approve of the milquetoast Sir John.

Ah, there was the building, and a candle still burned in Crackwilder's window.

Giles dismounted and knocked on the door, preparing himself to face the landlady and her horde of unwashed children.

It was not many minutes before the sounds of a lock turning reached him. Mrs. Radish, pronounced Ra-deesh if one wished to stay in her good books, filled the doorway. Peeking around her rumpled and stained skirts was one of the Radish offspring.

"Go on, Arfur," she said to the imp, adjusting her nightcap, "go hold the gentleman's horse until he comes back out again."

Giles silently made the guess that the boy's name must be Arthur, which had been mysteriously transformed into Arfur. The unfortunately named Arfur Radish yawned but did as he was bid.

His horse dispensed with, Giles had only to get past the landlady.

"You'll be wantin' Mr. Crackwilder, I reckon?" Mrs. Radish said.

"Indeed, Mrs. Ra-deesh," he said smoothly. He stifled his laughter over the rather foolish question. Who else could he possibly want in her establishment?

"I don't fancy the hours he keeps and neither does Mr. Ra-deesh," Mrs. Radish said with asperity. "He walks, you know. Back and forth, back and forth." She dramatically looked toward the ceiling of the run-down little foyer. "We can hear 'im. Walkin.' With that cane clack-clack-clacking across the floor."

Giles waited patiently for Mrs. Radish to conclude her complaint. As it was always the same complaint, he did not feel compelled to answer her. It was his understanding that aside from the clacking of his cane, Crackwilder was an exemplary tenant. It was also his understanding that Crackwilder had thrown a book at the lady's head the last time she'd mentioned his clack-clack-clacking, leading her to only mention it to her tenant's visitors.

Seeing that *this* visitor appeared insufficiently outraged by the cane-walking, Mrs. Radish sniffed and stepped aside to let him in.

He bowed low, as if she were a duchess, well-knowing it was the only thing that could possibly appease the woman.

"Get on with you, then," she said, mollified. She turned and marched into her own apartment to face her ill-named collection of children.

Giles took the stairs two at a time and found Crackwilder's door ajar on the upper landing.

He pushed it open and said, "Have you no care for thieves and reprobates? Anybody might just walk in."

Jeremy Crackwilder was a man somewhere in his early thirties, though a military career and an injury made him appear older and more careworn than his years. He was the son of a tradesman, though had he been dressed in expensively tailored clothes, his manners might have passed muster anywhere. He was as erudite and refined as he was hardened by war.

His rooms were little more than libraries, any pictures having once hung on the walls disposed of to make room for bookshelves. A desk tucked into a corner was piled high with papers.

"You are right," Crackwilder said, turning from the fireplace. "As anybody *has* just walked in. And no, I do not usually leave it open, but I heard Arthur whistling outside and saw him holding your horse."

"You mean, Arfur. Fancy a drink?" Giles said, helping himself to the sideboard. He would not have made himself so free with his friend's brandy, had he not purchased it himself. After Crackwilder had saved his life at Waterloo, Giles had asked him what he could do to repay his savior. Crackwilder had said, "Keep me in brandy." And so he had, and then some. Even now, with limited funds, he had not shirked that responsibility. He never would. The world might view him as careless and carefree, but he was reliable to anybody that depended on him. He had even offered Crackwilder a room in his house, when he'd had the funds to pay for a house. His lieutenant had claimed he'd rather hang himself from the highest tree, rather than have to look upon Lord Grayson's dandified person day after day.

For all his insults, Giles thought his lieutenant was rather fond of him.

Crackwilder nodded to the brandy and limped to the nearest chair. "So? What's the problem?" he asked.

"Why should there be a problem?" Giles asked, pouring out two glasses.

"You always come here with a problem," Crackwilder said, taking his glass. "Always late at night, and always with a problem."

Giles should have had the good grace to blush, but he was too used to his friend's rather insulting manner. He did not mind it, and in fact thought he might prefer it. He imagined it to be similar to having a brother one has squabbled with since the nursery. He might have the loftiest titles in the world but it was all for naught with Crackwilder.

"You happen to be right," he said, "though I am not even certain how to explain this particular problem. You see, there is a lady—"

Crackwilder roared with laughter. "I knew it! Some father finally came at you with the dueling pistols! And no, I don't know how to get you out of it, nor will I be your second. I will say, though, I told you so."

"Nothing of the sort has happened," Giles said quickly. "It is just…well, first—I understand you have been employed by Lord Childress to manage a collection of books. Palkar or Palsar or something like it."

Crackwilder set his drink down and stared at him. "Palaskar. If you are even thinking of making his daughter, Miss Danworth, your latest flirtation, I advise against it. Childress would carve out your heart and eat it as soon as look at you if it did not end with a proposal. Do not ask me to assist in what would be a foolhardy venture concluding in your early demise."

"I have no interest in Miss Danworth. It is another lady. A lady who is interested in those books and I think she will visit to see them. A Miss Dell."

"And what does this Miss Dell have to do with me?"

"I don't know," Giles said. "I am not sure how to approach

the whole thing. You see, she is mad for books. Really quite mad for them. I thought she might put them aside for the season, but now there is this Sir John Kullehamnd who belongs to the Royal Society…"

Giles had trailed off, well aware he was not being particularly coherent. There was little chance that his words *could* be coherent, as his thoughts were not.

"It just seems improbable that he should be preferred," he said. "I mean, why does she go on with all the reading? That is what I do not understand."

Crackwilder picked up a volume from the side table and hurled it at Giles's head. "Because she likes it, you idiot!"

As this was not the first time his friend had thrown a book in his direction, Giles ducked and it hit the wall behind him, falling to the floor with a thud.

"I suppose you mean to point out that she is not likely to change her interests," he said.

"Sharp-witted as ever," Crackwilder said, draining his brandy.

Giles poured him another and said, "I should like to have something to talk to her about, though. She seems keen on comets, perhaps you might summarize what you've read about them."

"I might, and you would not remember a word I said. You are many things, but you are not a scholar. I am acquainted with Sir John and he will run rings round you intellectually. Do not attempt a competition in that area, you will be trounced. My advice is, *buy* the lady a book."

Giles sat up straight. "Of course! Why should I torture myself with listening to you drone on about comets when I could just buy her a book?"

"My other advice is, set your sights on a lady who does not so particularly value knowledge."

"Where would the challenge be in that?"

"This situation is less a challenge and more a drowning man at sea," Crackwilder said drily.

"If I am drowning, you have thrown me my first rope to grab hold of to keep my head above water," Giles said. "Let us see if Sir Gloom thinks of buying Miss Dell a book. He will not, I'm sure. A man like that has no originality of thought."

"And neither did you, until I suggested it."

KITTY HAD OFT noticed that when one wished for time to pass quickly it would insist on passing slowly and when one wished it to slow it felt as if it sped along. A holiday or a treat took forever to arrive, and yet an interminable church service arrived every week with remarkable rapidity.

While she knew time to be a reliable thing and the perception of its changes merely an oddity of the human mind, that did not help Tuesday to come any faster.

The tedium of waiting had been relieved only briefly by a visit from Penny. Lady Cabot had wished to hear her opinion of Sir John. Kitty had, of course, related Lord Grayson's rude behavior and Sir John's nimble set down.

As she spoke, it was all *for* Sir John and *against* Lord Grayson, which pleased Penny exceedingly. As she spoke, Kitty worked to convince herself of Sir John's superiority. He was not as dashing as Lord Grayson and had not the lord's easy manners. Sir John might be just a bit too stern and serious. But what could one expect from a learned mind?

Kitty really felt herself foolish in thinking that it would be wonderful if Sir John were a tad more cheerful. She'd spent months wishing to encounter a gentleman who would discuss serious matters with her and now she had. That her heart did not beat faster at the sight of him was nothing compared to that.

Penny was certain that Sir John was an excellent match. Kitty was determined to be certain of it too.

Finally, Tuesday had come and now she and her mother

entered Mrs. Herschel's residence in Bedford Square. Aside from the other luminaries she might encounter, Sir John would be there. She was determined to like him.

Kitty had prepared her mother with the information she had received from Sir John—this was not to be a usual call, but more an intellectual salon.

The baroness had not been any more intrigued by the idea than Kitty thought she would be. Still, her mother was a naturally cheerful person and accustomed to the intellectual pursuits of her husband and so was confident she would get on well enough.

They were led into the drawing room by a sprightly old butler not much taller than Mrs. Herschel herself. Kitty hesitated near the door, hardly knowing what to do or where to look. The room was filled with people. Books were scattered on every surface. A pianoforte that must have come with the house had been unceremoniously pushed into a corner and piled with more books.

Mrs. Herschel spotted them and made her way over.

"My dear Miss Dell," Mrs. Herschel said. "And this must be the baroness, your mother."

"Indeed, I am, Mrs. Herschel," the baroness said. "Very kind of you to extend the invitation."

"The kindness lies in your coming," Mrs. Herschel said. "I only hope we will not bore you, we are all abuzz about a letter that was recently received. Do come in."

Kitty felt put at ease at once by Mrs. Herschel's friendly manner. In any case, she could not have spared a moment for her nerves, she was far too intrigued to hear of an important letter. Surely, it must be some historical document, recently found. She was eager to hear the details and then communicate them to her father.

"My dear guests," Mrs. Herschel said loud enough to capture everyone's attention, "we are fortunate to have new additions to our weekly gatherings. May I introduce Lady Penderton and Miss Dell. Mr. Lackington, Sir John, I believe you are already acquainted."

Kitty smiled at Sir John, meaning to encourage him. At least, she supposed that was what one did to encourage. She ought to have asked Miss Crimpleton about it before she left Devon. Whatever that girl had done, Frederick had been very encouraged by it.

Sir John inclined his head in her direction and gave her a small smile. One encountering the smallness of the smile for the first time might have been put off by it. But Kitty thought she understood one thing about Sir John—smiles of any sort were not given out freely. She must feel the compliment of it. After all, there must be more value in a small smile rarely given than a wide smile coming as freely as raindrops.

Mr. Lackington bowed kindly in her direction and she was cheered to see a person in attendance who she knew to be disposed toward her.

Mrs. Herschel proceeded to introduce the rest of the company. Most were gentlemen, some Kitty might have met at a ball and others who were recognized on their achievements alone. All but the women were members of the Royal Society. Of the women, Kitty took them to be far more illustrious.

Just as Mrs. Herschel had done, these ladies had gained fame in certain circles, *despite* being a woman. The great explorer, Lady Stanhope, only recently returned from her adventures in the Middle East, and botanist Mrs. Acton were among them. What minds were contained in this room! They were those who made the pursuit of knowledge their life's work.

Kitty was intrigued to find that one of the men was named Mr. Crackwilder. Surely he was the man employed by Miss Danworth's father to organize the Palaskar collection. It must be so, he stood with a cane just as Miss Danworth had described him.

Kitty was in awe to be in such company, and not for the first time wondered why society gave so much credit to those who had been born in a bed that had a title dangling over it, but so little credit to those who made their mark through their own efforts. She loved her brother dearly, but what had he ever done?

Kitty and her mother were shown to a sofa recently vacated to accommodate their arrival and Mrs. Herschel poured them tea. That was the only thing that resembled a usual call. Rather than conversations taking place in small groups, the company had surrounded Mrs. Herschel and clearly waited for her to speak.

"As you all know," Mrs. Herschel said, "Sir John has received a mysterious letter that threatens the very foundations we stand on. The scientific community has fought long and hard to leave the embarrassing days of John Hill behind us. Sir John, do read the letter again for the edification of those who have not heard it."

Sir John nodded and took a folded sheet of paper from his pocket. He opened it with a snap and read: "The Royal Society continues to act in a frivolous and dilettante manner, inducting the worthless and excluding the worthy. One would not expect a society whose sole aim is the pursuit of ever-expanding knowledge to be blinded by such mundane attributes as title and money. This pandering to fools with worldly goods will not go unpunished. Even now, there is a John Hill in your midst. As I pen this, there is a paper published by the society that will be revealed to be a hoax. John Hill may not have gained a total revenge, but a reckoning is coming. May you practice blushing for yourselves now, as it certainly will become a habit when all is revealed."

Sir John paused and said, "It is signed, *Veritas*—Latin, meaning truth."

Mrs. Herschel said, "We must root out this Veritas. The Royal Society cannot be allowed to fall."

CHAPTER FIVE

KITTY'S HEAD SPUN. Mrs. Herschel had just charged the party that they must save the Royal Society. Who threatened it? Why?

Whatever was unfolding before her, it was fascinating.

"I implore all of you," Mrs. Herschel continued, "to examine what has been published by the society in the past two years. We must uncover the paper that contains the hoax. Lean upon your own expertise and give close examination to those papers relating to your field."

The company was energized by Mrs. Herschel's directive and began moving off and forming small groups. Kitty was entirely mystified. Who was John Hill and why would anybody wish to threaten the Royal Society? Why was Mrs. Herschel leading the charge when she was not even a member?

Mrs. Herschel turned to Lady Penderton and Kitty. "I do apologize for the oddness of this drawing room, but as you have heard, we are in the midst of an emergency."

"Do not apologize to *me*, Mrs. Herschel," the baroness said good humoredly. "A mysterious letter? A plot? It is the most interesting thing I've heard in a drawing room in ages."

"But Mrs. Herschel," Kitty said, "at the risk of exposing my ignorance, who is John Hill? What did he do that could be so very damaging to the society?"

Mrs. Herschel took a sip of tea and put her cup down. "In the mid-fifties, there was a fellow who was excluded from the society, though he felt strongly he ought not to have been. A botanist, among other things. He *did* contribute to our understanding of plants and was even knighted by the Swedes. However, he was a prickly sort and so did not have enough friends to pave the way for him."

"Ah," Lady Penderton said. "A man who considers himself deeply wronged is always dangerous."

"Just so, Lady Penderton," Mrs. Herschel said, nodding. "As a revenge, John Hill wrote a preposterous paper called *Lucina sine concubitu* and submitted it to the society—a ridiculous piece of work proposing that…"

Mrs. Herschel trailed off, though both her listeners leaned forward. "Well, perhaps it is not suitable to go into details as it relates to human anatomy."

Lady Penderton laughed. "I do not think you could say anything to shock me, and my daughter has read widely enough that little will be a mystery to her."

Mrs. Herschel nodded. "It proposed that a female might get with child without help from a man. From the air, as it were."

Kitty stifled a giggle. "That is preposterous, indeed. Who would believe such a thing?"

"The society did not publish the paper, but they *did* debate it," Mrs. Herschel said. "That fact was reported everywhere when word got out about it. The paper was signed Abraham Johnson, but was in fact John Hill. Mr. Hill set out to embarrass the society as a punishment for being excluded, and so he did. It seems we are facing the same situation now. Though, back in those times Mr. Hill did have a point, there were far too many gentlemen inducted who were not particularly intellectual. Those days, fortunately, are long over."

"I wonder why this Veritas, as he calls himself, should give a forewarning to his plan, though," Kitty mused.

"I believe it to be a torture of the members," Mrs. Herschel said. "The worst part of a bad outcome is the anticipation of it."

"Speaking of the members, Mrs. Herschel," Lady Penderton said, "how do you come to lead the effort to expose the rogue? Ladies are not even admitted to the hallowed halls of Somerset House."

"Not technically," Mrs. Herschel said, "though if one has discovered enough comets, one may be admitted to a certain curtained balcony to hear the occasional lecture. In any case, I expect I will someday be a recognized member and would like the society to still stand when we finally arrive at that hoped-for day. I am not alone in that prediction or that wish. I suspect Miss Dell will feel the same."

"I most certainly do," Kitty said. "But Mrs. Herschel, if the society has become more rigorous in its membership, what can this person have against it?"

"That is the *real* question, to my mind," Mrs. Herschel said. "What is the actual motive of this person?"

The conversation about John Hill and what ought to be done went on throughout the room. Kitty and her mother remained on the sofa and Sir John approached and gave his thoughts on the mystery. They must only discover two things—which papers hinted they might contain a falsehood, and which of those had been written by a man likely to be disgruntled over some matter. Kitty listened and worked hard to be impressed by Sir John's reasonings, though she thought he rather stated the obvious. She had a great urge to rise and approach Mr. Crackwilder. She very much wished to hear of the Palaskar collection.

As Sir John wound down his conclusions, Lady Penderton signaled that it was time to take their leave. Despite the unusualness of the gathering, the baroness was not so eager to ignore the usual rules of a social call. She had, though, invited both Mrs. Herschel and Sir John to call on them.

In the carriage, Lady Penderton said, "Goodness, that was amusing. Your father shall be entirely diverted."

Kitty supposed her mother was right. Her father, though well qualified to be a fellow of the society, refused to have anything to do with it on account of its president, Sir Joseph Banks. Sir Joseph had spent a lifetime bringing foreign flora into England and her father thought it the height of foolishness for its unpredictability. Lord Penderton was certain England would be taken over by bamboo or some other invasive species and they'd had a public falling out about it years before. Her father was very much of the opinion that the Royal Society had not had a sensible president since Martin Folkes, in his own father's time.

"I shall be vastly interested in how the mystery unfolds," Lady Penderton said. "I propose we make regular visits to Mrs. Herschel as I cannot think where else we'd hear anything about it."

Kitty was surprised and pleased. "I am gratified, mama, that you should take such an interest in defending the reputation of the sciences."

Lady Penderton's peals of laughter filled the carriage. "No, child," she said, recovering her breath, "I am only interested because it will amuse your father. I dearly love to make him laugh."

GILES HAD NO particular idea where the ridiculous Sir John hoped to encounter Miss Dell on Tuesday, but as he *did* have the idea of buying Miss Dell a book and thought Lackington and Allen a likely place to encounter them, he'd set off in good time.

Aside from encountering Miss Dell, he had planned to be introduced to Mr. Lackington. Miss Dell appeared to hold him in some regard and Giles supposed Mr. Lackington could select a book the lady would find riveting.

He had been disappointed to see no sign of Miss Dell, though he had loitered for hours. Mr. Lackington was also not on the premises. Giles wondered if he ought not come back another day, but then decided against it. He was determined to see that a book be delivered to Miss Dell before the sun had set. The morrow was Wednesday, and he would lurk outside of Miss Danworth's house until he saw Miss Dell arrive to look at that collection of books that were to be so notable. Then he would casually arrive and reveal that he had been the mysterious sender of Miss Dell's book. He and Miss Dell would be put on better footing instantly, and Sir John could do what he liked about it.

It had occurred to him, after much mulling, that Miss Dell had been irritated with him because, all along, he'd not paid the proper respect to her interests. That had been a mistake. A very stupid mistake. Why had he been so arrogant as to dismiss her proclivities, and why had he been so very sure she would throw them over?

He'd been very highhanded!

Well, he would rectify it. He would purchase some valuable volume and lay it at the feet of her scholarly heart. It was not a typical purchase for him, and certainly now in his penury it would not seem logical. But what were shops for, but to pay accounts at one's convenience? Though tradesmen of all sorts had been inconveniently demanding payment from Dalton, he doubted a bookshop would be as miserly as a butcher.

The clerk, who'd been attempting to convince him for the past hour that Mr. Lackington would not return that day, stared hopefully at him.

"My good fellow," Giles said, "I need a book about comets, or stars, or the sky in general. An expensive one. Show me the way."

The clerk's eyebrows raised ever so slightly. "This way, my lord," he said, "to the section on astronomy."

Giles followed the fellow up a set of stairs and past rows and rows of mile-high shelves of books. The clerk turned a corner and pointed to a section. "Just here, my lord," he said. "Might I help you select something?"

"No, quite all right," Giles said. "I shall know what I seek when I see it."

The clerk bowed and left him alone to contemplate his purchase.

"My God," Giles said softly, "who wrote all these books?"

The stack rose in front of him, a veritable mountain of literature. Most of the books were bound in the usual way with black or brown leather. There was one slim volume though, that was a delicate cream shade with gold embossed print. It was on the highest shelf, as if put there so only the most determined treasure hunter might find it.

Giles rolled the ladder over, climbed up, and pulled it from the shelf. Jumping down to the floor he turned it over. *An Examination of Geocentric Cosmology and a Defense of Aristotle's Theory* written by Reverend H. Bête.

He was delighted with it. It sounded wonderfully obscure, just the sort of thing that would strike Miss Dell as worthy. As well, while he'd not paid much attention to his schooling, one could hardly get through it without hearing the name Aristotle more than once. The old fellow had written no end of things, though who would wish to plow through them all…

Miss Dell, that was who. Certainly, this must be the book for Miss Dell. After all, one could hardly go wrong with Aristotle and the binding on the book was magnificent.

He tucked the volume under his arm and jogged past the endless shelves and down the stairs. Seeing his clerk, he held the volume in the air like a hard-won victory.

The clerk hurried over.

"I will want this delivered," Giles said. "It is to go to Miss Dell, in Hanover Square. I believe Mr. Lackington will know the precise address. A note too, to say: in admiration of your scholarship, may this new information add to your already noteworthy amount of knowledge and enlighten you on a subject of interest."

The clerk's brows slowly drew together, like two caterpillars warily approaching one another.

"I will leave it unsigned and inform the lady of its sender

myself."

"Unsigned," the clerk said softly.

Giles paused. "No, that will not do," he said. "What if she decides to give the credit to Sir John?"

"Sir John?"

"Never mind him, he is useless," Giles said.

"You wish to purchase *this* book, my lord? With *that* note?" the clerk asked.

"Certainly," Giles said, handing the book to the clerk. "If I wished for another, I would not have chosen this one. Can you not see how fine the binding is?"

"It is very fine, my lord," the clerk said. In a much lower voice, as if he told a secret, he said, "This particular volume is four pounds. The value lies in the binding, which *is* very fine. Otherwise, it is a curiosity, you see."

Giles did think it curious that a book could run four pounds. It seemed a ridiculous amount for paper and leather, but then it *was* the great Aristotle and it *was* for Miss Dell. No expense must be spared.

"Put it on account," he said. "And see it is delivered first thing on the morrow. That is absolutely vital. You must have some stack of papers somewhere, in which you keep your customers' addresses?"

The clerk nodded. "We know well enough where to find Lord Penderton's house, he's one of our best customers. If you are certain—"

"It is to be signed mysteriously," Giles said. "Sign it simply with 'G.'"

"G, my lord?"

"Yes, of course G," Giles said. "That cannot be confused with K for Kulle-whatever-his-name."

"G," the clerk said.

"And write it all down for me—the title, author, and my note. I would not care to forget any detail when Miss Dell wishes to thank me for it."

"As you wish, my lord," the clerk said.

Giles was thoroughly satisfied. The past hours had been well spent after all. Miss Dell could not fail to be gratified upon receipt of such an exquisite volume.

Sir John could not hope to compete. Oh, the fellow might run to the shop and attempt to buy something, but Giles had already purchased the superior volume. In any case, he doubted the fellow could afford four pounds for a book.

That he himself, at this moment, could not afford it either seemed not worth thinking of.

KITTY RAN DOWN the stairs to her father. He had sent word that he wished to see her in his library. She hurried down the corridor to the door of his study, a sense of foreboding growing with every step she took. It was just after breakfast and her father's habit was to closet himself in that room with his studies until after two o'clock. He would come out at that hour, only because he began to get hungry. The last time he had broken with the schedule had been because a blackbird had flown in through an open window and could not be convinced to leave. He'd finally sought out the baroness to complain of a *member of Aves having the unmitigated gall to install itself in my study.*

Kitty pushed the door open with trepidation, lest she find a bird in flight or some other disaster in the making.

"Come, Kitty," her father said, motioning to a seat. He was behind his desk amidst an array of papers and books. Lord Penderton was a dashing sort of middle-aged gentleman, but for the inevitable ink stains on his hands and cuffs. Both the baroness and the lord's valet ensured that he was perfectly presentable at breakfast, though both knew he would not be in his study an hour before his person resembled that of any government clerk.

Aside from his scholarship, the lord was known as a particularly skilled master of his estate—Kitty's dowry was sizable, as was her sister's, and Frederick would be left exceedingly comfortable. This financial success, Kitty knew, was a result of him leaving his affairs to an experienced steward and having no interest in gambling away any profits. Over a dinner long ago, Frederick had asked his father for the secrets to the successful management of the estate. Her father had no secrets to relay, and only said *sometimes the best thing to do is get out of the way.*

Now, Lord Penderton studied her gravely. Kitty could not imagine what had happened.

"It seems," he said, "that you have an admirer."

"Surely not," Kitty said reflexively, her mind racing. Had Sir John spoken to her father? No, it could not be so, they were too little acquainted. Though, she could not think who else it might be. She had danced with several gentlemen who had seemed to find her agreeable at the Bergram's ball. But she did not really know any of them.

She was at a complete loss. There was nobody she even knew well enough to ask for an interview with her father.

Her father picked up a book and handed it to her. "This arrived for you. Naturally, Hidgson brought it to me to examine."

It was very finely bound, and Kitty laughed as she read the title—*An Examination of Geocentric Cosmology and a Defense of Aristotle's Theory.* She assumed some poor fellow had paid richly to have it published. She supposed the author was a gentleman who was convinced that modern scientific theories were an abomination to the church. Who else would argue Aristotle's now very outdated and disproved geocentric theory of the heavens revolving round the earth?

Could Sir John have sent it? Perhaps he had some notion that they could discuss the arc of advancement from ancient times to modern day?

"You will notice the author's last name?" her father asked.

Kitty had not in fact noted anything particular about it, it was some reverend or other. Her father, however, had a keen eye and no detail escaped him. Once he'd pointed it out, it jumped out at her as the most obvious thing in the world. The Reverend H. Bête. Bête was foolish in French. The whole volume was meant as a jest.

"It is the note that accompanies the book that I find particularly striking," Lord Penderton said. "It hints that you have either caught the eye of a gentleman with an elaborate and keen sense of wit, or you have caught the eye of the stupidest man in London."

"May I see it, papa?" Kitty asked, entirely at a loss as to what sort of note might accompany this strange gift.

"I shall read it to you, dear," Lord Penderton said, picking up a single sheet of paper with Lackington and Allen's embossed header on it. "It says: *in admiration of your scholarship, may this new information add to your already noteworthy amount of knowledge and enlighten you on a subject of interest.*"

"Certainly, it is meant as a jest," Kitty said. "Though, the one person I might have thought would send me a book is not the type of gentleman to jest. At least, I did not think so."

Though Kitty had not thought so, and had wished Sir John to be more lively, perhaps she had been wrong? Perhaps his stiffness had only been on account of an early acquaintance? Perhaps Sir John was not so stiff after all. Perhaps he was learned *and* liked to laugh.

"It is only signed as 'G'," her father said.

"G?" Kitty said. Good Lord. G? No, it could not be from Lord Grayson. As soon as she thought it could not, Kitty realized that it could, and that it in fact must be.

"I perceive you make a guess on the sender?" Lord Penderton asked. "Who is the gentleman and is he a wit or the dimmest man in creation?"

"I believe, though I cannot be certain," Kitty said, "that G stands for Lord Grayson. And, I am sorry to say that I do not believe the gentleman will have any idea that the book is meant in jest."

"My God," Lord Penderton said, "where do people send their sons to school these days?"

"I suspect it matters little where gentlemen are sent if they fail to listen when they arrive," Kitty said.

"Well, I do not like it. You may have the book, we will keep it as a joke between us. But Kitty, my dear, do not encourage this fellow."

Kitty made to stand and deliver a forceful rebuttal to the very idea, but her father waved her back into her seat.

"I imagine," Lord Penderton said, "that the fellow is comely or dashing or handsome or whatever young people call it these days. Nobody ever requires much of men like that, it has always been so. But it will not be right for you, Kitty. You need not marry a scholar, in fact I urge you not to. There is benefit in a marriage between persons of differing temperaments. I should have been miserable having married a lady similar to myself. Your mother balances me, as you may have noticed. However, *stupid* is another matter entirely! Your mother may not share my love of research, but when I discuss it with her she understands me. You see? We are of equal intelligence and of varying interests."

Kitty nodded, though she *did* harbor hopes of marrying a gentleman of precisely similar interests. If only the book had been from Sir John as some entertaining jest!

"In any case," Lord Penderton said, "you may keep the book and read of how the Reverend Foolish attempts to resurrect Aristotle from the ashes. I expect it will be amusing."

KITTY HAD FLIPPED through the book's pages and indeed it *had* been amusing, though she also blushed for Lord Grayson's empty-headedness. She would have liked to believe that the gentleman understood the volume to be a jest, but she did not have a shred of hope that it was the case. She had not long to consider it, though, as it was Wednesday. Miss Danworth's at-home day, and that particular home was the current residence of the vaunted Palaskar collection.

The baroness had been surprised to hear that Kitty would call on Miss Danworth. Lady Penderton had become acquainted with the girl the season before and had not singled her out as somebody her daughter would naturally gravitate toward.

In the end, she'd said, "As you wish, Kitty. Miss Danworth is perfectly respectable and perhaps I have misjudged her temperament. There are those persons who strike one as cold who are only shy. In any case, her companion, Mrs. Jellops, will be a scrupulous chaperone. Take Martha in the carriage." The baroness had paused, then said, "In any event, I do not suppose Lord Childress will be at home."

Kitty had been relieved that her mother did not choose to accompany her on the call, as she had not said a word about the collection or that Sir John would likely call as well. It was not that either of those things were wrong, it was only that Kitty could imagine her mother's frown to discover the call was to be about books and not the usual social meeting. As for Sir John, the baroness had said nothing about him, though Kitty was well aware that her mother viewed him as too serious. Perhaps even tedious, though she had not said so.

The carriage had arrived to 42 Grosvenor Square in good time and Kitty had been shown in. The outside of Miss Danworth's house was as one would expect, large and of pale stone with oversized windows. The inside, though, had an unexpected gloominess to it. There was a heavy feeling, as if there were not enough light or not enough furnishings and carpets to soften the sounds of walking on the marble floors. The frighteningly stern butler did little to warm the coldness of it.

Kitty felt uneasy as she was led through the front hall, having the strange feeling of being watched or unwelcome.

She was very much relieved when she entered the library. It

was vast, but carpeted and its endless rows of dark wood shelves warmed it. Its air was one of comfort, though she supposed she would always feel so when surrounded by books.

Miss Danworth rose. "Miss Dell, how good of you to call. I have had tea set up in here rather than the drawing room in anticipation of your arrival."

"You are very kind, Miss Danworth," Kitty said.

"Nonsense," Miss Danworth said. "I do not have so many callers as a regular thing. There are those who…well, my father is a rather stern gentleman."

Kitty did not know how to answer. She hardly knew what Miss Danworth meant by it. Did she mean that Lord Childress was feared in some manner? Her mother had made some mention of assuming the lord would not be at home but she had not thought anything of it.

"This is Mrs. Jellops, my companion," Miss Danworth said.

Mrs. Jellops was a round and amiable-looking sort of woman. The kind one imagines indulges in cakes and biscuits on a regular basis and never regrets having two when one would do. Her cheeks were plump to fit her person and she smiled pleasantly at Kitty.

A man walking with a cane entered the room. "Ah, Mr. Crackwilder, this is Miss Dell," Miss Danworth said. "The lady I mentioned as having an interest in the Palaskar collection."

As Kitty had noted when she'd seen him at Mrs. Herschel's, Mr. Crackwilder was not dressed richly, but exceedingly neat. There was not a crease to be found on his person.

He bowed and said, "I was fortunate to be introduced to Miss Dell at Mrs. Herschel's salon. I was just now going to pull some of the more interesting works for her perusal.

"That is most appreciated, Mr. Crackwilder," Kitty said warmly.

He smiled kindly at her and went to the shelves. The door opened and the stern-faced butler announced Sir John.

Before Sir John could say anything, a loud knocking could be heard from the front hall. The butler hurried off to let in whoever was doing the banging.

"Mrs. Jellops, this is Sir John Kullehamnd," Miss Danworth said. "Who else may have arrived, I have not the faintest, though I presume we shall soon see."

The party looked toward the door with some anticipation. Kitty hoped it might be a scholar come to examine the Palaskar collection.

"Heavens, Lord Grayson," Miss Danworth said, as the lord entered the room.

CHAPTER SIX

K ITTY WAS BOTH astounded and embarrassed that Lord Grayson had arrived to Miss Danworth's house. Of course, he had been aware of their plan to meet with Mr. Crackwilder and examine some of the Palaskar books, but it had nothing to do with him! Further, there was the ridiculous book he'd sent to her that must be acknowledged.

Kitty had assumed she would see Lord Grayson again at some ball or dinner. She'd planned to thank him and delve no more deeply into it than that. She was certain he did not know the volume he'd sent her was a jest and she had no intention of pointing it out. He rather deserved it, she was certain he'd not looked at the volume for a moment before buying it. Always, the intellectually incurious would seek out shortcuts and easy ways, and that was precisely what he must have done to have fallen for the literary ruse. For all that, she would not intentionally embarrass him—one should never point out a fault that another could not rectify and she was certain that Lord Grayson's mind could not work any harder than it currently did.

For all her consternation at seeing him, Kitty could not ignore the little flutter that went through her. How could he look so dashing absolutely all of the time?

"I am pleased you have come, Lord Grayson," Miss Danworth said pleasantly, "though surprised to find you interested in my father's library. Here is Mr. Crackwilder, is he the same that you knew in the war?"

"Indeed, he is," Lord Grayson said, nodding to Mr. Crackwilder. "And I consider him a friend, as he does me."

"Such as he is," Mr. Crackwilder said.

Kitty looked with some surprise at Mr. Crackwilder. It was not so usual for a person of his standing to speak to a lord in such a manner.

Lord Grayson seemed to take no notice of it and said, "As for your surprise in my interest in the Palkar collection, Miss Danworth, I cannot account for it. Naturally I am interested. Who would not be interested?"

"Palaskar," Sir John said. "It is the *Palaskar* collection."

Lord Grayson ignored Sir John's correction. He said, "Miss Dell will comprehend my interest in literature, having just received a volume of some note."

Kitty felt her cheeks pink and prayed Lord Grayson would go no further. To end the topic, she said, "Very kind, Lord Grayson."

"Lord Grayson has sent you a book, Miss Dell?" Miss Danworth asked.

Before Kitty could answer, Sir John muttered, "Some dreadful French novel, I presume."

"Indeed not, Sir John," Lord Grayson said, staring him down. "It was in fact an examination of geocentric cosmology and a defense of Aristotle's theory written by Reverend H. Bête, a book I am certain you've never heard of. And, it was magnificently bound."

"A jest?" Sir John said derisively. "I would not have thought Miss Dell would be interested in satire. It is rather a waste of paper, in my opinion."

"Jest?" Lord Grayson said, rather more loudly than was called for.

"I do enjoy that sort of thing, as it happens," Kitty said, working to stop the conversation from going further.

Lord Grayson, seeming oblivious to the ghastly direction he

was headed, said, *"Satire?"*

Mr. Crackwilder hurried to Lord Grayson's side and gripped his shoulder hard. "Hah! You see, Lord Grayson is such a wit that even now he plays along with the game. Everyone knows how he adores those sorts of books. It is the cleverness, you see."

Kitty thought she *did* see. Lord Grayson had not suspected for a moment that the volume was anything less than a scholarly reflection on Aristotle's theory. As he would not have the first idea of what that theory had been, he would not understand the ridiculousness of a person wishing to defend it. Now his friend, Mr. Crackwilder, had perceived the situation and attempted a rescue.

Lord Grayson looked enquiringly at Mr. Crackwilder. In a low tone, Mr. Crackwilder said, "Just as we discussed the other evening. A magnificent jest."

"It sounds amusing, Miss Dell," Miss Danworth said. "You must tell me how you find it. Now, Mr. Crackwilder, if you would select some books from the collection, I will pour the tea."

While Kitty had not found Miss Danworth to be the warmest of persons, she was grateful beyond measure that her hostess had the presence of mind to change the conversation.

Mr. Crackwilder nodded to Miss Danworth and then requested Lord Grayson accompany him to the table to assist him. It was the silliest thing in the world, on its face. However, Kitty had the notion that Mr. Crackwilder intended to warn his friend to avoid saying another thing about Aristotle's theories.

If it were so, then Mr. Crackwilder was indeed a good friend.

Sir John, of them all, was not so eager to leave the topic behind. "Did you indeed find the tome amusing, Miss Dell?" he asked.

Kitty had no intention of revealing any opinion at all and only said, "I am afraid I have not had a moment to look at it, Sir John."

"I do not have the facility for such lightheartedness myself," Miss Danworth said, "though I admire the ability in others. Lord Grayson has that sort of happy temperament that always seems to find the sunny side of things."

Sir John appeared disdainful of a happy temperament and Kitty was sorry for it. Lord Grayson might be an intellectual buffoon, but he *was* always pleasant-natured. She would wish to see some of that pleasantness in Sir John at this moment.

Mr. Crackwilder called them to the table and Kitty left her seat with alacrity. This was what they'd all come for—an examination of the Palaskar collection.

AN HOUR LATER, Kitty made to take her leave. She could have listened for days at a time to Mr. Crackwilder describe the Syrian collection of short stories, or the difficulties of translating a book of poetry written in Swahili, or the surprises contained in the Persian book of herbal remedies, or the early mathematical theories of the Greeks. However, she knew she must not overstay her time and tire Miss Danworth.

Miss Danworth had invited them all to come again, and that must be enough. Though, Kitty did wonder if Lord Grayson would go on with it. He'd been decidedly bored with their extended discussion of mathematics. He *had* become animated when they discussed the book of poetry, and he and Mr. Crackwilder had debated the likelihood that it must have originated from the island of Lamu. Still, she did not think the lord would turn up for a scholarly discussion again.

It was just as well, as Sir John seemed intent on exposing Lord Grayson's lack of an education on every topic. Why had he argued so hard against Lamu, anyway? She could not like it of Sir John. One who was superior in knowledge need not set about to prove it. Still, she supposed Sir John *was* superior in that regard and she could see how the gentleman might be aggravated by the likes of Lord Grayson. It must grate that there were such lords fanning about, being given every consideration and having every advantage in life, though they came with nothing in particular to recommend them.

SIR JOHN LET himself into his house nearby St. George's church. It was by no means a large house and contained no servants but for a charwoman who came in during the day, but it had come with some furnishings and the address was good enough to pass as unremarkable.

He had spent the past two years carefully cultivating the society around him. He was not unaware that he did not have the easy manners or impeccable dress of a Lord Grayson and did not attempt to compete in that realm. What he *did* have was a sharp intellect, and that must be his entrée into the ton.

He had become, to his satisfaction, one of those gentlemen who was always included on the larger guest lists and even some of the more intimate soirees such as musical evenings, card parties, and dinners. He was not conceited enough to conclude that this was a result of any personal charm, but that he had the most shining endorsements a man could have—a title, though it was foreign, the ability to speak creditably on a variety of subjects and, most importantly, he was unmarried.

He bent down to start the fire the charwoman had laid. Once the flames began to lick the kindling, he settled himself into the chair in front of it. He picked up the small book that lay on a side table and thumbed through it. Its binding was worn and soft, and it was the only book in the house. It was the only book he required—the remarkable diary that outlined every outrage that had been done to men like him.

As he read this page and then that page, all of them as familiar as his own hand, he contemplated the future. Soon enough, he'd find himself very comfortable. He would be the master of his own house, and the master of servants so plentiful that he would not blink without something being fetched for him. Most interestingly, he would be the master of his wife and the bane of his father-in-law's existence.

That he knew who that wife would be had been settled before he'd even arrived to town. It had been no great decision, it was as if the gods had arranged it all for him. He had studiously laid the groundwork over the past two years. Now, he was approaching the crucial months and nothing must get in his way.

As he understood his faults fairly well, he reviewed all that had occurred since the start of the season. He was prone to prickliness and not very skilled at hiding it. Grayson had provoked him and he had provoked back, though it did not particularly serve his purpose. He was all but certain that book of poetry originated on Lamu, but he found he could not allow Grayson to claim the victory. He must not be so self-indulgent!

As well, he was not naturally a romantic and he did not think he had fared very well in those efforts so far. In truth, he could not even measure those efforts they had been so little. He must try harder.

There was work to be done, refinements to be made. He would make them. His plan would not fail.

He would succeed, where another had not. A certain old man would smile down from the heavens when all that Sir John Kullehamnd had accomplished was revealed. That it was likely that nobody else would be smiling was not Sir John's concern.

IT WAS TO be a night in for the Dell family. The baroness had insisted that, as busy as the season was, there must be one night a week when they all gathered together. She was of the opinion that a weekly dinner would be the glue that held them all together.

Kitty had not been surprised by it; her mother liked nothing more than to have her flock gathered round her. Nor was Kitty surprised by her father's acquiescence to the plan—he counted on his wife to be the sensible dictator of he and his children and would never think to imagine he knew better than she on such a matter. He might prefer to be left on his own with a book in one hand and port in the other, but he knew that it was not prudent to always be left to his own devices. His wife's instincts on these matters were always more reliable.

In truth, nobody was opposed to the dictate of a weekly night in, not even Frederick. As much as he loved his club, Dell family dinners were invariably interesting and often jolly.

The wine had been poured and the first course had just gone round. Lady Penderton said, "Kitty and I happened upon an interesting bit of news while calling on Mrs. Herschel the other day."

"Mrs. Herschel?" Lord Penderton said. "I would not have thought the learned lady one to engage in idle gossip."

Kitty hid her smile, her father thought absolutely every piece of news was idle gossip. Unless it interested him, in which case it was simply news.

Lady Penderton did not bother to hide her smile. "It's to do with the Royal Society, my love. Apparently, there is a viper in their midst."

Lord Penderton laid down his fork. "A viper, you say? Now that is something worth knowing. Who is the fellow? We'll have him to dine."

"*That* is the amusing part of the story," Lady Penderton said. "Nobody knows who he is, they are at sixes and sevens over it."

"They say, papa, that he is another John Hill," Kitty said. "Mrs. Herschel told us that, long ago, a man called John Hill embarrassed the society terribly."

"Hah!" Lord Penderton cried. "Another John Hill. That is famous! He was a thorn in everybody's side."

"You know the story, then?" Kitty asked.

"What story?" Frederick said, looking back and forth at his father and Kitty.

"Do I know the story?" Lord Penderton said in an incredulous tone. "How could I *not* know the story? It was my own father and

Martin Folkes who opposed the induction of John Hill."

Lord Penderton paused, then said in a quieter voice, "Though in the end, I think they regretted it. More trouble than it was worth, as it turned out."

"On account of *Lucina sine concubitu*," Kitty said.

"On account of what?" Frederick said, completely lost.

"Just so," Lord Penderton said.

"But what is Lucina-whatever-you-said?" Frederick asked.

"A ridiculous paper proposing a woman can get with child from the air," Lady Penderton said.

"That is outrageous!" Frederick said.

"So it was," Lord Penderton said, "though some fellows thought to make themselves look intelligent in debating it. Trouncing the idea is what I think they meant to do. Only they made themselves look foolish."

"What I mean, sir," Frederick said, "is it is outrageous that anyone should mention such an idea to Kitty! You know, having to do with…"

"My dear Frederick," Lady Penderton said, "I do not see how Kitty would have understood the story if that part had been left out."

"And now you say, my dear," Lord Penderton said, ignoring his son's indignation, "that there is a new John Hill in the mix? Very amusing, you must keep me informed."

"It is not very seemly…" Frederick said, trailing off.

Kitty felt some amount of pity for her brother. He was a stickler for propriety, and she knew he was genuine in his opinion that a lady should not hear of such things. Ladies were to remain ignorant of how the species, or any species, kept producing more of the species. Where he'd got such notions, nobody knew. Miss Crimpleton lived on a working farm just as they did and must have seen all sorts of breeding, though Frederick would combust into flames to think of it.

Lord Penderton seemed to recall something and motioned the footman for more wine. "That reminds me, my dear, Kitty and I have an amusing tale for *you*. Eh, Kitty?"

Kitty looked down at her plate. She wished her father had not thought to divulge the arrival of the book from Lord Grayson.

"Our Kitty has an admirer, a peculiarly dull-witted admirer," Lord Penderton said. "He sent her a book that proposed to defend one of Aristotle's old theories, geocentric cosmology of all things. The book was a jest, you see. However…no, I will not ruin it, you tell it Kitty," her father said in high good humor.

Kitty sighed. "It was a book from Lord Grayson and he did not realize it was written in jest."

"You see, my dear?" Lord Penderton said, laughing.

"Poor Lord Grayson," Lady Penderton said.

"Now you cannot mean it," Lord Penderton said. "A block-head is no match for Kitty, even though he be a duke someday."

"That is right, mama," Frederick said, seeming to feel they had finally landed on a subject he knew something about. "Kitty is too clever for a dolt. I, myself, would not prefer a lady who was too dissimilar to my own temperament. A mismatch such as that has no hope of success."

"Nonsense, darling," Lady Penderton said. "While you have the soul of a poet, Miss Crimpleton might be depended upon to manage the accounts better than Shylock. I have seen her negotiating for a ribbon as if a life were at stake. Not a farthing will escape her notice—she will do very well for you."

"Shylock? Miss Crimpleton?" Frederick said, his tone all outrage. "I say, mother, I must object…"

"Never mind it," Lady Penderton said kindly. "She is a lovely girl."

Frederick, appearing mollified, said, "*That*, of course, I can agree to."

And so the Dell family dinner went on, Lady Penderton working to keep her lord amused and Frederick protesting when he felt things drifted beyond the mark. Kitty enjoyed herself well enough, but for the niggling discomfort over the discussion of Lord Grayson's idiocy.

It was true, he had been foolish. She did not think he'd taken even a moment to really consider his gift. He had gone into Lackington and Allen and, like a magpie, settled upon the shiniest object.

For all that, though, it had been kindly meant.

GILES HAD DINED at Lady Montague's house. He would avoid the place and its hostess if he could, but just now he was forced to find places to eat. If there was anything complimentary to say of Lady Montague, it was that she had food. That was probably all he could credit her with. She was a gossip and a schemer. Still, there had been no other invitations in the offing, and so he had availed himself of her roasted meats.

It had been the usual Montague affair. Her table was filled with those who were too afraid to refuse her and so the compliments to the hostess ran sickeningly thick on the ground.

The only bright spot, which had not seemed so bright at first, was finding himself seated by a lady named Mrs. Hemmings. He soon discovered she was the new Lady Ashworth's aunt and had been at the center of all that had gone on with Lord Ashworth last season.

Giles did not know if half of it were true, as it sounded as farfetched as possible, but it had been wildly entertaining.

He had excused himself from the house as soon as he decently could and made his way to Crackwilder's apartment.

Having greeted Mrs. Radish/Ra-deesh in a suitably gallant manner and cut short her complaints about her tenant, he'd gone up and found his friend at work at his desk.

"The prodigal gentleman has arrived," Crackwilder said upon seeing him. "I sent you to buy the lady a book and somehow you buy her a satire or some nonsense. As if that were not bad enough, you were not even in on the joke!"

Giles threw himself into a chair. "How was I to know? The binding was particularly fine."

"How were you to *know*?" Crackwilder asked, closing a book on his desk. He went to the sideboard and poured two glasses of brandy. Handing one to Giles, he said, "You were to know by opening the book and reading some of the pages. Anybody would have realized that a defense of the sun revolving round the earth was a jest."

Giles stared at his glass. "So that was Aristotle's theory, was it?"

"And the author's name was French for foolish!"

"Was it?"

"My God, man, what did you do at school? Hold your hands over your ears?"

Giles willed himself not to flush at the suggestion. He knew well enough that it had been close to that. He had been too taken up with horses and races and bets and wine to attend to his studies. When he did take up a book, it was meant to be history or Latin but somehow ended being poetry or a play. He was well aware that if his father had not been a duke he would have been pitched out with the rubbish at the end of his first term.

"I was not as attentive as I could have been."

"An understatement for the ages," Crackwilder said drily.

"All right," Giles said, "you've had your fun with insults. The question is, does Miss Dell know that *I* did not know the book was written in jest?"

"Of course she does," Crackwilder said. "The truth was written well enough on her face. Sir John knew it, too."

"Kullehamnd," Giles said derisively.

"Miss Dell was kind in not condemning you outright, but she is not your sort, Grayson," Crackwilder said.

"She *is* kind, is she not? And she's precisely my sort," Giles said. "But for the small difference between us of...collections of facts."

"What you call a small difference, I call the distance of here to the moon."

"What am I to do, then? To shorten the distance?"

"Why should you want to?" Crackwilder said eyeing him. "Are you only being perverse? Do you pursue the lady because she is so ill-suited to appreciating your charms, those alleged charms having nothing to do with intellect?"

"I do not know, precisely. Perhaps it is perverseness, perhaps it is my winning spirit. I do not like to accept defeat is all. Now, what shall I do?"

"There is nothing you can do. Miss Dell appreciates a scholar, and that you are not."

"Then I will become a scholar," Giles said, feeling a sense of resolve settling over him. "And you will help me. I'll pay you for lessons. Naturally, I cannot pay you at this very moment, but you can keep a record of accounts and I will pay you someday."

Crackwilder was looking more and more amused as Giles spoke. Finally, he snorted and said, "Where would we even start?"

"I do not know," Giles said, "*you're* the tutor. Just pick somewhere and start. Pick something I might throw into a conversation with Miss Dell. Do not bore me with things that would never come up. I want science and stars and such."

Crackwilder downed his brandy. "Science and stars. I never heard anything more ridiculous."

"And yet, you will do it?"

Crackwilder set down his glass and folded his hands, regarding them thoughtfully. "Miss Dell seems to have a particular interest in the Royal Society. She attended one of Mrs. Herschel's gatherings and appeared most keen to hear of the recent goings on."

"I cannot imagine that anything *goes on* at the society, but all right," Giles said. "Teach me some of it and take me to Mrs. Herschel's next gathering."

"No, absolutely not, you will not set foot inside that lady's doors. Mrs. Herschel's crowd would make mincemeat of you and you'd be worse off than when you started. I have a better idea. Just now, that particular group of men is reading all of the papers published by the society in the last two years. You will read them too. It is not too big a piece of cake for you to bite off, assuming you can read, and it is a subject Miss Dell is interested in."

"You know full well I can read. Excellent notion!" Giles said. "When can we begin?"

"Considering your lack of academic rigor, we'd best start tomorrow. Though, we must fix a place to meet. It cannot be here, it is too loud during the day. Mrs. Ra-deesh has a lot of children, you know."

"Destin's," Giles said. "There are a few private rooms. I will arrange it. Two o'clock?"

"Two? I suppose you do not rise any earlier?"

"Of course I do. But then LaRue takes his time, and there is breakfast, and somehow I am often running behind. We should make it two so that I am not late."

"Two it is," Crackwilder said, almost as a sigh.

CHAPTER SEVEN

SIR JOHN KULLEHAMND had just been shown into the drawing room. Kitty smoothed her skirts, having made her curtsy, and sat on the sofa next to her mother. Sir John seemed nervous and the baroness said kindly, "How good of you to call, Sir John."

Sir John nodded. An awkward silence followed and was mercifully broken by Hidgson bringing in the tea tray.

The baroness poured the tea. Seeming to realize that the two younger people in the room had absolutely nothing to say, or if they did, chose not to say it, she said, "My daughter and I were most amused to hear of the mystery of Veritas threatening the Royal Society. Have you discovered anything further?"

Sir John took his cup, looking very grave. "I cannot say that I am myself amused by the plot," he said. "I believe the man to be dangerous to the continuation of the society. But no, nothing new has been discovered."

Kitty felt the tension in the room as if it were a thing that might be seen. Sir John and her mother were of such different temperaments! Where the baroness found levity and amusement, he found none.

"Goodness, though," the baroness said, "can the society really be taken down by one disgruntled individual?"

"Possibly," Sir John said. "It has only regained its footing in recent years and therefore remains weak and vulnerable."

"Then you must do everything you can to stop Veritas," Kitty said, hoping to give Sir John the sense that at least one person in the room took his concerns as seriously as he did himself.

In truth, Kitty *did* take his concerns seriously. As much as it frustrated her that the society did not allow women, it could not be permitted to fall! The progression of mankind's understanding would be delayed and stymied and nobody could wish for that. In any case, Mrs. Herschel was confident that the day would come when the society would see sense and admit females. Kitty dearly hoped to be among them.

Sir John appeared approving of Kitty's directive. "Indeed, I will do everything in my power to unmask the culprit, Miss Dell. I am diligently reading through all the society has published in the last few years, looking for any sort of clue."

"Oh, how I wish I could be a part of it," Kitty said wistfully.

Sir John's expression went through several changes and Kitty thought she might have somehow stepped out of bounds.

He said, "Naturally, a lady cannot be a member of the society, but I know of no rule that dictates that a lady cannot read the papers published by us. Mrs. Herschel has been known to comment publicly on them and the more noteworthy often appear as excerpts in the newspapers. As well, I believe Lady Stanhope has engaged herself in the task."

Kitty brightened. All of that was true. She had read various bits of research here and there. Usually things that had been passed along to her father. She had only never considered that one might order copies.

"Though, Sir John," she said, "how would one go about getting the copies?"

"I will see to it, Miss Dell," Sir John said gallantly. "In the usual case, I would say that these papers are not suited to the female intellect. However, I believe *your* mind quite up to the task."

Kitty could not help but be flattered. Sir John was not the most lively and amusing fellow, but he saw her mind. He really saw what she was capable of. Further, how exciting it would be to engage in the hunt for the mysterious Veritas!

The distant sound of the door knocker reached them and Sir John rose. "You will have other callers and so I will take my leave."

Kitty and the baroness rose. "Thank you for your call, Sir John," the baroness said pleasantly.

"And thank you for your offer," Kitty said. "I can hardly wait to begin reading."

"Though we will have many other things to attend to," the baroness said firmly.

Sir John made his bow and left the room.

Kitty heard Penny out in the hall. "Sir John," she said, her voice all enthusiasm. "How charming to encounter you here."

Kitty did not hear his reply, as his voice was deeper and did not carry as well as Penny's. It was not a moment before her friend was in the room.

Penny curtsied to the baroness and skipped to Kitty's side. "I see he has wasted no time in calling," she said.

Kitty blushed and studiously ignored Penny's hint.

"And what say you, baroness, on further acquaintance?" Penny said.

The baroness smiled. "He seems a pleasant enough gentleman," she said.

"Yes," Penny said, "I think so as well. He is so like Kitty."

"In some regards," the baroness said softly.

GILES HAD ARRIVED to Destin's in good time and secured a private room. He had told Dalton he would go there to meet Crackwilder, as Dalton might very well turn up there himself at some hour. It had become a more and more favored spot, as Marty was one of the few people they owed money to that did not constantly point it out.

Giles had not told Dalton the reason for meeting his lieuten-ant. Dalton would have thought him gone mad and locked him above stairs.

Dalton might have been right in the assumption. Really, it was one thing to chase a lady, but what was he doing now? He'd hired himself a tutor so that he might become learned. It had never been one of his ambitions to store great collections of uninspired facts in his mind. Give him Byron over Aristotle any day of the week. Give him tales of love and adventure, highs and lows, foibles and redemptions. It was those things that were the stuff of life, not dry measurements and dusty theories. And yet, here he was, preparing for a lecture on he knew not what sort of tedium.

Perhaps it would not be so bad. After all, he supposed he was reasonably intelligent, his downfall had only ever been a lack of interest and effort. And, would it not be a delight to spring his improvement upon Miss Dell? Would it not be a delight to spring it upon the puffed-up Sir John as well?

In any case, he supposed learning something of the sciences would not kill him.

Crackwilder came in, his hands full of a stack of papers. Giles eyed them with trepidation. There seemed to be far more than he had anticipated. Did these fellows spend their entire day writing?

"You are on time," Crackwilder said. "It is a miracle."

Giles shrugged as Marty Destin came in with the coffee tray. "It is only miraculous that I hurried LaRue," he said. "My valet was entirely out of sorts and is certain my neckcloth is not as it should be, but I refused to allow him to start over."

Crackwilder sat down and said, "You describe it as a battle hard fought and won. I really do not know how you survived an actual war."

"You certainly do," Giles said, "as it was you who saved me."

After Marty Destin shut the door, Crackwilder said, "I have never told anybody that I pulled you down to the ground as you were straightening a cuff while bullets sailed over your head. Nor will I ever. It does not do either of us credit. You are an excellent swordsman and a crack shot, but neither of those attributes would have saved you from yourself."

"Never mind my idiocy on a battlefield," Giles said. "Today you are to rectify my idiocy in a drawing room."

Crackwilder laid the stack of papers on the table. "Here are the papers published by the society for the past two years. Read them, and I will clarify anything you don't understand and quiz you on the contents. That should prepare you to have a reasonably literate conversation with Miss Dell. Further, if you stumble upon anything that seems suspect, point it out. The society has reason to believe there is some sort of counterfeiter in the mix and he must be discovered."

Giles pulled the papers toward him as Crackwilder helped himself to coffee. The task did not sound difficult. Only read some dusty papers on dusty subjects and he would be able to go toe to toe with Sir Gloom. As he knew that the knowledge contained in the papers was the *only* thing Sir John had over him, the man would be easily defeated and got out of the way. As for any counterfeiter in the mix, he could not care less. His aim was to impress Miss Dell, not become one of the society's Bow Street Runners.

He thumbed through the papers, reading the titles, to get an idea of precisely what he would be tackling. As he did so, he became more and more suspicious.

He laid them down. "Very amusing," he said. "I see your purpose—point out to your stupid friend exactly how gullible he is. Now that we have got past that, where are the real papers?"

Crackwilder stared at him. "Those are the real papers."

"They cannot be," Giles said.

"But they are," Crackwilder said. "What did you imagine they would be?"

"I cannot say, but really, Crackwilder?" Giles said. He pulled a paper from the stack. "Look at this one," he said. "An account of the feet of those animals whose progressive motion can be carried on in opposition to gravity."

"Yes," Crackwilder said. "What of it?"

"It is about how house flies land on walls without falling off! And this, the formation of fat in the intestine of a tadpole! Or how about, an examination of fossil remains of a rhinoceros at Plymouth! Or a description of the teeth of a dolphin!"

"The society's members have varying interests," Crackwilder said, shifting in his chair.

"And this is the sort of thing Miss Dell is interested in?" Giles asked, incredulous.

"Apparently so," Crackwilder said. "In any case, it is of no importance whether or not you are interested in a subject, only that you have read the latest research on it."

"So you are telling me," Giles said, "that there are fellows who spend their days contemplating such things? Staring at a house fly and wondering why it does not fall off the wall? And that these gentlemen are respected for their observations?"

"Yes."

"That is the stupidest thing I've ever heard! What a waste of life! This author, this fool, Everard Home, had been better to call a footman to kill the fly thereby giving him some time to read Shakespeare! *I wasted time, and now doth time waste me.*"

"Richard II?" Crackwilder asked.

"Indeed," Giles said. "And why are some of his papers signed Mr. Home and some signed Lord Home? Is he a recent?"

"Very recent. Titled less than two years ago. In any case, I did not think these papers would suit you," Crackwilder said. "If there were a Royal Society of reading Shakespeare or the romantics, or even Miss Austen I suspect, you would be its president. But scientific observations will never be for you. Therefore, Miss Dell will never be for you."

Giles crumpled the corner of the paper in his hand. "Nonsense, Crackwilder. I can learn all about flies walking on walls if I must."

✥

KITTY HAD DRESSED in her most subdued gown—a pale blue organza with simple trimmings. This evening was the Countess of Thornbridge's ball and the baroness had thoroughly briefed Kitty on what was certain to be a very odd affair.

The countess had a peculiar interest in the ton's lineage. It was said she even employed a genealogist to document histories and that she had no interest whatsoever in people she termed *recently arrived*. She was determined to make matches between suitably old families and held the ball every year to accomplish just that. As her idea of suitably old was very, very old, the ball would be exceedingly small and awkward.

The baroness said it was only their own bad luck that Lord Penderton's family had been barons since the fifteenth century and the baroness' own family reached just as far back. While it would be an affair happily skipped, the countess was known to hold a grudge for as long as the ancient histories she admired.

Frederick had sent a note claiming a serious illness the season before, and this year he wriggled this way and that with every excuse he could think up, to no avail. Both he and Kitty would attend, and console themselves that it was only one evening.

As they waited in the line of carriages proceeding to the lady's door, that line being short as so few people qualified to attend, Frederick said, "My friend Jost is always forced to come. He told me there is a lady named Miss Blaise who turns up every year, has alarming fish eyes, and will swim toward a gentleman like a carp after a minnow."

"Frederick," the baroness said scoldingly.

"It is true, though," Frederick said. "Jost says he was lucky the past two rounds as Miss Blaise had her sights set on Lord Ashworth, but now that he's married, nobody knows who she will turn her big eyes to."

"Aside from your terror of Miss Blaise, does Jost say anything of the gentlemen who will attend?" Kitty asked.

She was certain she would not see Sir John at the ball, a foreign title would not do for the countess. What she was not certain of was whether she was disappointed over it. On the one hand, she enjoyed conversing with the gentleman and could only be satisfied with his recognition of her scholarship. *He* did not treat her like an empty head. On the other hand, he did not set her heart fluttering or her palms or cheeks warm. How she wished that he did! He was precisely what she looked for—comely enough, learned, and willing to engage her intellectually.

"All I know about the gentlemen who will come," Frederick said, "is there is never enough of them. I shall be on my feet all night. At least, that's what Jost says."

"Perhaps Jost," the baroness said, "might keep his thoughts to himself from time to time. The evening is not likely to be filled with merriment, but one does one's duty."

"Father does not," Frederick said. "He's home snug in his library with a book."

"Your father," the baroness said sternly, "has his own duties to accomplish. Considering the prosperousness of the family's estate, you can have nothing to object to."

Kitty hid a smile. Frederick should have known better than to complain of what Lord Penderton chose to do. His wife would defend him to her dying breath.

"Good God," Frederick said, peering out the carriage window. "There's Grayson just getting off his horse. It is a miracle he arrives at all—his neckcloth appears to have taken a thousand years to compose."

Kitty sat stock still. She did not look out the window or show any outward interest in the news.

The baroness smiled at her indulgently. "Perhaps the evening will not be so dull after all."

GILES HAD ARRIVED to Lady Markham's ball in good time. It was one of the very last places he would like to be, but his mother was a stickler on it, he must attend.

He supposed the duchess was charmed by the idea that he might encounter a girl from a very old and storied family, but he also supposed that was because his mother had never bothered to attend. It was always dreary, and now he had not even the company of Ashworth to entertain him.

One thing he did know about this evening—one must be always alert to who might be creeping toward him. Out of the corner of his vision, he noted Miss Blaise drifting in his direction.

He turned to avoid meeting her very alarming eye.

As he turned toward the door, he felt a momentary breathlessness, as if he had ridden after a fox for some miles over rough ground. Miss Dell stood at the entrance to the ballroom.

She was marvelous! Amid the jewels and lace and ribbons and net overlays surrounding her, Miss Dell stood simple in an elegant organza gown of the most charming pale blue.

Of course, a lady like Miss Dell had no need to pile on mounds of sparkle and fountains of fripperies. A lady of Miss Dell's caliber had no need for shopped-for distractions.

And her demeanor! She did not simper and peek under her eyelashes as if she hardly knew how she got there or where she was supposed to look.

She was all elegance.

As Miss Blaise crept every closer, Grayson defeated her plans. He strode away from her with all vigor. He must secure Miss Dell at once.

"LADY PENDERTON, MISS Dell, Mr. Dell," Giles said, bowing.

"Lord Grayson," the baroness said, "how charming to see you here. I should have realized you spring from ancient stock."

"Ancient enough, I suppose. My ancestor fought alongside Henry Tudor," Giles said. "Though in retrospect, perhaps it was not his finest hour."

The baroness laughed and said, "It *was*, according to the countess."

"Miss Dell," Giles said, holding his hand out for her card. "May I?"

The lady handed over her card, and he was delighted to see that her supper was still free. Of course it would be, Sir John would not be invited into this hall if he tried to beat down the door. He wrote his name down with alacrity.

Before he could say anything further, he was slapped on the arm by a fan. He turned to find Miss Blaise.

"Lord Grayson," she said, tittering, "you are very bad!"

Giles might have been nonplussed over what he'd said or done that was so very bad, but for knowing Ashworth's experience with the lady. Somehow, a whack on the arm and condemnation of being very bad was some sort of compliment.

"Miss Blaise," Giles said smoothly, "allow me to introduce you to Mr. Dell. He was just inquiring who that lady might be who so elegantly wielded the gold fan."

"Inquiring!" Miss Blaise nearly shouted. She cracked her fan across Frederick's arm and said, "Very bad, indeed! Do not be so bad as to take my supper, Mr. Dell!"

KITTY HAD SAID nothing at all on Lord Grayson's approach. She'd done nothing but hand over her card. She had not been able to ignore her feelings in the carriage when Frederick had noted Lord Grayson getting off his horse.

It had been pleasant, and yet unnerving. Almost as if she'd had a great shock. It felt very like the time she'd lost her footing at the top of a steep hill. In the moment before she'd tumbled, every inch of her skin had prickled.

She scolded herself for being so easy to sway. A handsome face should not send a shiver. But then, he'd come to her so quickly and he *did* look so charming. Frederick might complain that the lord's neckcloth took a thousand years, but the result was so very pleasing to the eye. A frivolous thing to notice, but there it was.

Perhaps she should not mind that she found some sort of attraction in him. After all, it was only a dance and a supper. In truth, it was likely to be the most pleasant dance of the evening. Since Lord Grayson had taken himself off, she'd been led to dance by nothing but callow youths and aging lotharios.

As well, she could not deny that Lord Grayson was amusing. How could she help but smile over his devilishness at handling Miss Blaise? That lady was now engaged for supper by Frederick, her brother having been boxed right into it. Frederick was irate, but the baroness had laughed behind her fan all the way into the card room over it.

Just now, aging lothario Lord Bradford was listing all of his various accomplishments as if he applied for a position. Kitty was to know that he was a keen birder—*watching* birds, not shooting them. He had already expounded on his theories of cooking meat. Apparently, when the lord's cook deemed a roast exceedingly done, the lord ordered it roasted an hour more. Meat should be dry, as God intended it. This had been coupled with his ideas of drinking wine—a half-glass on Sunday, in honor of our Lord God.

Kitty stifled her laughter over imagining what the future Lady Bradford would face on a usual day—meat as dry as a desert, accompanied by weak lemonade. That is, if there ever *were* a future Lady Bradford.

No, Lord Grayson might be foolish and might have sent her a ridiculous book. But he was dashing and amusing. She could not fault him for that.

GILES HAD SUCCESSFULLY gained Miss Dell for supper and avoided

Miss Blaise for the same. He could not, however, avoid the lady entirely. He'd taken her first, thinking it was well to clear that fence earlier, rather than later.

She did not do too much fan-hitting, as she was less interested in his own very badness and wholly focused on Frederick Dell's very badness. The lady interrogated him mercilessly about Dell and what he did not know, he invented. According to Giles, Dell was the catch of the century. He thought that would keep Miss Blaise off his trail for many seasons to come.

Giles assumed Dell was furious, but that could not be helped. When it came to the Countess of Thornbridge's ballroom, it was a battlefield. Everyone must seek to survive any way they could.

Now, finally, he led Miss Dell to the floor.

She'd blushed when he took her hand. Certainly, that was a very good sign.

Giles was also cognizant of the various looks of envy on gentlemen's faces. Lord Bradford, in particular, seemed put out. The fellow was absurd, always talking about how one ought to cook meat and how he rarely accepted dinner invitations because all too often the meat was not sufficiently dry.

Miss Dell's brother was not so much looking envious as he was throwing him daggers. Perhaps he should not have foisted Miss Blaise upon him. He did not wish to make an enemy of any of Miss Dell's relations.

As the dance began, he said, "I am afraid your brother is not pleased with me, Miss Dell."

The lady smiled and said, "I think he is not, though I believe my mother was amused."

The baroness was amused? That was good news, indeed. Let Frederick Dell stew in his juices, what matter *that* if Miss Dell's mother was amused by his recent gambit?

"I would also like to mention," Giles said, "that I hope you do realize that I sent that book as a jest. It occurred to me that perhaps I am too much jesting and forget that others are not in the habit."

Miss Dell's brow wrinkled, but then cleared. She said, "Of course, Lord Grayson."

"Excellent. What I mean is, I own that I do not spend all my time with my nose in a book. But that does not mean I don't read at all. In fact, I am just now examining a pile of papers that have recently been published by the Royal Society. The past two years, as a matter of fact."

Miss Dell looked at him, her expression seemed full of wonder. "Do you say, Lord Grayson, that you have joined in the hunt to unmask Veritas? I am also reading the papers for that purpose."

Giles was entirely nonplussed. He had thought only to read those dull and ridiculous sheets to impress Miss Dell with his knowledge. He had completely dismissed Crackwilder's mention of the counterfeit, but he got the feeling that the counterfeit and Veritas were one and the same.

"Naturally," Giles said smoothly, "the situation cannot be allowed to stand."

"Just as I think!" Miss Dell said with enthusiasm. "Any right-thinking person must wish to defend the society."

"Consider me engaged," Giles said solemnly, all the while wondering how he might find out more about what he'd engaged himself in. He supposed Crackwilder would know.

Miss Dell appeared thoughtful. Quietly, she said, "I did you a disservice, Lord Grayson. I would not have thought you would take such an interest in the effort."

Giles had not had the *slightest* interest in it. Until now.

"Regardless of a man's proclivities," he said, "that man must always exert every effort in defending what is right no matter where it takes him."

"That is very well said," Miss Dell said, smiling. "I am looking for any clue as to who the villain might be. Sir John was kind enough to deliver me copies."

At the mention of Sir John, Giles stiffened. Was that man to dog him everywhere?

"Perhaps we might speak more about our findings over supper?" Miss Dell asked.

Giles nodded, though he could not help recalling Crackwilder's comment that he was a man drowning at sea. It would take all his skill to keep his head above water during *that* conversation. He had absolutely no findings to discuss.

But what if he *could* unearth some findings? What if he could unmask the villain, as Miss Dell called him. It would be the most ridiculous effort of his life, but Miss Dell would not think so. It was of vital importance to her adorable scholarly heart.

He must be as Miss Dell wished him to be. Gone were the amusing compliments he was so skilled at and in were the dusty papers of the Royal Society that he was most certainly *not* skilled at.

CHAPTER EIGHT

IN THE CARRIAGE on their way home, Frederick had been complaining for some minutes.

"I swear my arm is bruised!" he said. "The lady wielded her fan like any knight of old at a joust. Jost says I am doomed, because Miss Blaise pronounces me very bad."

Lady Penderton looked indulgently at her son. "Miss Blaise does not mean to injure you, my son. She is only nervous and fan whipping is the result of that energy she does not know what to do with. One of these days, Miss Blaise will hit a fellow and he will see the charm of it, and the charm of her generous dowry, and that will be that."

Frederick, ignoring his mother's sympathy, said, "And Grayson! What does he mean by throwing me at the lady's feet like meat to a lion? It was bad form."

"It was excessively amusing," Lady Penderton said. "If you would stop a moment to think, you might look forward in anticipation to the moment when you might repay the lord for his kindness. I am sure some opportunity might present itself."

"Yes," Frederick said, rubbing his hands together, "perhaps I will. Perhaps Grayson will some night find himself stumbling through a dance with Miss Blessy. I have stepped in to rescue the lady enough times lest she sit out, I can attest to her diabolical ability to go the wrong way."

While Kitty heard the conversation, she did not pay much attention to it. The night had been too filled with other diversions.

Lord Grayson joined in on the hunt for Veritas!

It was extraordinary. She would not have guessed in a thousand years that he would show the slightest interest in such a venture. In truth, she would have thought he'd deride the very idea of it. She'd even had the notion he would have laughed at it. She had been wrong!

They'd had a lively conversation at supper. Kitty did not yet have any theories of who the troublemaker was but had been in the process of taking copious notes. She planned on cross-referencing every claim she read, to see if it could be supported in some way by prior writings. If it was not built upon prior discoveries, then it would go on her list of suspicious items warranting further investigation.

Lord Grayson had posited that they might want to look more closely at Lord Everard Home, on the theory that nobody rational sat around thinking about houseflies on walls. For that matter, Lord Home seemed to write an excessive amount of papers on bizarre subjects *and* he was only recently titled. Who really knew where the man had sprung from?

Kitty was able to put his mind at ease regarding Lord Home. It was true he seemed a quixotic individual, but he was also a recipient of the Copley Medal, the highest honor given by the society.

Though Lord Grayson had seemed incredulous over the idea, he had put aside his suspicions of that particular gentleman.

They had agreed to keep one another informed of any discoveries.

After they had exhausted all ideas relating to Veritas, they spoke of the more usual things. Kitty talked of Penny and her happiness with Lord Cabot. Though, she had been shocked when Lord Grayson had countered by inquiring if it were true that Penny had ridden the lord's horse at Newmarket.

She had been shocked, and not entirely sure she could be certain it was *not* true. It would be just like Penny to dare such a thing. Still, she denied it vehemently.

To change the subject, Kitty had inquired into Lord Grayson's family. In retrospect, she wished she had not. Of course, he did not mention the dukes' pact, though he could not have helped but think of it. As for the state of his mother and father, he did not go into any detail, but she was not led to believe it was a happy union.

But then, his musings had led him to talk of Shakespeare. Just as when he'd spoken of poetry from the island of Lamu, he seemed to have a depth of knowledge of the subject. Kitty had, of course, read all of the great bard's plays, but long ago in the schoolroom.

In retrospect, she found herself silly for attempting to cover her lack of understanding of the subject by proclaiming that uncovering Veritas must take precedence over plays and poetry.

Lord Grayson had looked amused and said: *And this, our life, exempt from public haunt, finds tongues in trees, books in the running brooks, sermons in stones, and good in everything.*

She had been completely lost and he had laughed and said, "It is from *As you like it.* What I mean to say is, if you must put the mystery above all else, it must be as you like it."

It had been the first time that it had been the *lord* who had run intellectual rings round *her.* She could not decide if she admired it or was irritated by it.

Perhaps the most extraordinary aspect of the evening was Lord Grayson himself. Stripped of his usual florid compliments, he began to seem a real person.

She knew very well that his claim that he had sent the book as a jest was not true. He'd only sought to recover his pride. She could not condemn him for that. After all, how many times had Frederick pretended to know something he most certainly did not? Frederick would die a thousand deaths before owning an error of understanding. It was a strange aspect of the male psyche, but evident all the same. And for all that, she must admit, she had done just the same in attempting to veer the conversation away from Shakespeare, it being a subject she was not so well-versed in.

So, while Lord Grayson certainly did not know anything of Aristotle's theories or recent advancements in that arena, was it not admirable that he sought to defend the society's honor?

"Kitty, dear," the baroness said, "you seemed very engaged at supper."

"She could not possibly have been, mama," Frederick said. "She was stuck talking to Grayson. Though, I hardly had time to observe anybody else as I was too busy ducking Miss Blaise's weapon of choice."

"I *was* engaged, as it happens," Kitty said. "Much to my surprise, Lord Grayson has taken up the search for Veritas and is reading all the papers to discover the culprit."

"Is he?" the baroness said.

"I was also gratified that he chose to talk sense and not fill the air with impossible phrasings," Kitty said, though she did not know why she felt she must defend her opinion.

"Well," Lady Penderton said, leaning back with a satisfied smile, "Lord Grayson may not be a scholar, but he is no dullard."

HAVING GOT PAST Mrs. Radish/Ra-deesh with only a few minutes of complaint about her tenant, Giles paced what little floor there was in Crackwilder's apartment. "It is vital that I discover this Veritas, whoever he is. Tell me all about it."

"Good Lord, Grayson," Crackwilder said, amused. "Why on earth should you involve yourself in it?"

Giles stopped and stared at his friend. "I really do not know why everybody thinks *I'm* the one who is stupid. Is it not obvious enough? Miss Dell is working on the mystery, therefore I must solve the mystery."

"If I cannot solve it, I do not see how you could," Crackwilder said.

"Tell me everything you know so far," Giles said.

Crackwilder heaved a sigh. "There is not much to go on," he said. He sipped his brandy and related the history of the original John Hill and how he'd managed to embarrass the society.

When Crackwilder had done, Giles poured himself a generous glass of brandy to settle his temper. These scholarly people were absurd! All along, they'd posed as deep thinkers intent on unraveling the world's mysteries. They'd advertised themselves as having capabilities beyond the average man. The truth was, they lived in a strange little world where the most ridiculous thing was held vital. It was very like one of his old great aunts who spent every Christmas telling him of the goings on of her neighbors. At the last, he was meant to be riveted by the tale of a certain Mr. Johnson who'd given up cows and had gone to sheep. Mr. Johnson, if his elderly relation were to be believed, had shaken the entire county with this shocking development.

"So you are saying," Giles said in a controlled tone, "the fellow wrote a paper about a woman conceiving *from the air* and a bunch of idiots debated it. And now, there is likely another fellow setting out to do the same thing?"

"In a nutshell," Crackwilder said.

"And you do not find this ridiculous?" Giles asked.

"Somewhat," Crackwilder admitted. "However, the society is not what it once was. There was a time they'd have even let *you* in—it was more a distinction than any real scholarly attainment. John Hill's complaints were not unwarranted."

"The society needn't bother inviting me," Giles said derisively. "I would poison myself were I to find I'd taken an unnatural interest in houseflies or the innards of a toad."

"Yes, yes," Crackwilder said, waving his hands, "but you understand my meaning. The society is more rigorous now, despite various papers you find unworthy."

Giles shrugged and wondered what in the world they were

rigorous about, though he did not say so.

Crackwilder leaned forward. "Grayson, we are on the cusp of something, though we know not what. The world will not stay as it is. Changes will come, and they will come through science. It is not the housefly that is notable, it is understanding what the housefly can do and how it does it."

"Very well," Giles said, though he was not convinced, "far be it for me to hold back the marches of progress. However, my only interest in this mountain of absurdity is uncovering the fellow that seeks to disrupt it. Miss Dell wants him found, and so I want him found."

"We *all* want him found."

"I suspect it is Sir John," Giles said, the notion just having come to him. He did not have any particular evidence to support the claim, but it would be very convenient if that villain actually *was* the villain.

Crackwilder snorted. "It is not Sir John. I realize he is a thorn in your side, and he is not the most engaging fellow, but he is not your man."

"How can you be certain?" Giles said. "Nobody seems to know much about him. Where is his title from, exactly? I have heard both Denmark and Sweden, but nobody seems to be sure."

"Sir John, for all his awkward manners, is no mastermind," Crackwilder said.

"I think I will make inquiries," Giles said. "I have distant cousins all over Europe, I will write them. Perhaps they will know from where his title springs."

Crackwilder laughed heartily over the idea. "If you do have such relations, I suspect you have never graced them with a single letter."

Giles did indeed have distant cousins across Europe. His grandmother, and now his mother, were meticulous in documenting the family tree, which was old and vast. He, and everybody else in the family, received a Christmas letter documenting all the joyous recent additions and unfortunate to-be-mourned subtractions. And no, he had never written to any of them. He had not congratulated on marriages or births, nor condoled on illnesses and deaths.

But that did not mean he could not write now. He must just hope LaRue had put the latest letter somewhere safe. He'd not even opened it this year.

As he thought of it, he was becoming more and more certain that Sir John was the man he sought. He'd come from nowhere. Crackwilder said the original John Hill had been knighted by one of those northern European countries too, though he could not recall which. Was that not coincidental? And, did they not share a given name, both were Johns. Further, was it not Sir John who'd received the mysterious letter? Why him? Why not Banks—he was the president of the Royal Society. Why would a person who sought to discompose the society write to a nobody like Sir John?

Giles stood up and drained his brandy. "Well," he said, "I have no time to lollygag around here with you all night. I have an imposter to catch."

KITTY POURED TEA for Penny, they having arranged between them to have a cozy morning in her drawing room. Penny and Lord Cabot would return to Dorset in a fortnight and, with the season so busy, neither were certain how often they might see each other before then.

"But you will come to Dorset soon?" Penny asked. "I would wish that you had come already—you will be most impressed with our improvements to the stables."

Kitty smiled over the idea that she would be enamored of the stables. "Of course I wished to come all along, but my mother was certain that those who are newly wed should be left on their own."

Penny blushed prettily and said, "I suppose she was right. We have had rather a glorious time in our own company. Now, you are not to think we've set the house up as my father's cottage in Newmarket. It is not all dusty floors and no carpets."

"It is not?" Kitty asked in some surprise.

"Well, it is," Penny admitted. "But just as in Newmarket, I have made certain there is a room you shall like very well. It is stocked to the hilt with velvet and pillows. My lord took one look at it and said it might suit the most delicate princess and so I know you shall like it."

"I hardly think myself a delicate—"

"You know what I mean, though."

And of course, Kitty did know what her friend meant. Penny might fall asleep on the back of a horse, but she preferred a deal more softness.

"Now, do tell me how the season progresses for you," Penny said. "I am all hope that it runs a deal smoother than my own."

Kitty sipped her tea to delay. She was not certain how to express her thoughts on the last few days. But then, it was Penny. Her dear friend forever, and holder of her secrets since they were small children. Nothing should be held back from Penny.

"A great deal has happened, actually," she said. "First, Lord Grayson sent me a book. It was kindly meant, but made him look foolish. It was written in jest, you see, but he did not know it. I believe he was charmed by a rather fine binding."

Penny giggled. "That sounds very like him."

"Yes, I know," Kitty said. "Though, I could not like that Sir John was intent on mocking him over it. The subject came up while we were visiting the Palaskar collection of books."

Penny's brow wrinkled. "I will not even ask what the Palaskar collection is or why Lord Grayson should be visiting books of any sort. But Kitty, can you really fault Sir John for his disdain of Lord Grayson? He may be my husband's friend, but he is a bit of a scoundrel. He toys with ladies' feelings for his own amusement. Should he not be disdained?"

"That I cannot say, only that Sir John was particularly unkind about the misstep. And also, Penny, I sat at supper with Lord Grayson last evening and he has heard of the rogue who is intent on embarrassing the royal society and has engaged himself to catch the man. He was quite sensible, and I really did enjoy our conversation. Perhaps he is not as bad as you think."

Now Penny's brow was truly knit. "I do not claim to know of any rogue who wishes to embarrass anybody, but I am truly worried now. Of course I knew that Lord Grayson had singled you out for his attentions at Newmarket. I suspected he might continue with those attentions. But Kitty! You cannot allow yourself to be taken in by him! Really, you are too clever for it."

Kitty felt her heart skip a beat. Naturally, she knew of Lord Grayson's reputation. She had even experienced his absurd flattery. But the conversation they'd had between them last evening had not been that.

"I am no fool," Kitty said. "I would not be so silly as to fall for false compliments. But Lord Grayson has seemed to have ceased that ridiculous gambit. He did not try it with me last night. Our conversation was full of good sense. It was interesting and intelligent. I could not help but be charmed by the circumstance."

Penny stared into her teacup. "He is more diabolical than I took him for," she said quietly.

"Why do you say so?" Kitty asked.

Penny set her cup down. "I say so because he has modified his advances to suit you. Do not you see? He has realized that the stratagems he has employed with others will not work on you. So instead, he has changed his approach."

Kitty felt as if her heart had hit the ground with a thud. Could that be true? Was it all just a game? Could she really have been such a fool?

If it were true, how he must laugh over it today! He would have seen that she was such in earnest, entirely taken in with this new ruse. *If* it were true, it would make him more than a rogue, it would make him a devil.

Could it be true? She did not know. She did not *think* so.

"But he even spoke of Shakespeare and quoted from him," she said. "I was led to believe that possibly he was not entirely a dolt. He might be learned in his own way, though his interests differ from my own."

"Oh yes, he often does throw Shakespeare around," Penny said derisively. "I used to wonder if he kept quotes written down on slips of paper to be brought out when convenient. I remember a particularly tedious dinner when he went on and on about words in the trees and something in the water and everything in the forest."

"From *As you like it*," Kitty said softly.

"I suppose so. Kitty, do not be as foolish as I once was with Lord Cabot. Do not turn from someone who so well suits you."

"Sir John," Kitty said.

"Of course, Sir John," Penny said. "I cannot express to you the wonder of marrying a man who is suited to you. It is everything, Kitty. Absolutely everything."

Kitty nodded, though she was not certain she meant it. She was not certain of anything. Her opinion of Lord Grayson had changed so much in the last day and now it was to swing back in the other direction? It was like staring at a pendulum until one felt dizzy.

Had she been led down a merry path by a handsome rake? It was too ridiculous. Sensible Kitty Dell, of all people!

And then, she could not deny that her feelings were hurt by it. Did Lord Grayson have no regard for her whatsoever? He must not, if he would seek to draw her into one of his notorious flirtations. That he would risk that she would be gossiped about and pitied!

And yet, was he really so skilled that she could not detect the falsehood? Could someone that devious make such a silly mistake as Lord Grayson had made with the book he'd sent? That seemed incongruous.

Was Penny so ranged against the lord that she suspected him without merit?

Or worse, was she, herself, attempting to rationalize away Penny's opinion for reasons she had not yet examined?

"All I say, my dear friend," Penny said, squeezing her hand, "is be careful of Grayson. Very, very careful."

GILES HAD DRAGGED LaRue from his bed at an ungodly hour, determined to actually read one of his grandmother's Christmas letters. The valet was all irritation and mumbled quite a lot of French. Giles was certain he'd been painted an ungrateful mongrel, though he pretended he did not comprehend it. LaRue dug through some trunks and found the still-sealed sheet.

Giles had torn it open and scanned it. It was pages and pages of people nobody knew. My God, if the count already had four sons, why must it be of note that he'd had a fifth? Why must he care that baron so-and-so's daughter had married some fellow in Kristianstad? Oh, and here, he was to know that Count De la Gardie had married for a second time, wife number one having expired five years ago.

There were plenty of entries from England, too. Some he knew as relations and some he'd never heard of. None of it was interesting reading.

Well, he supposed his grandmother must spend her time some way. At least it gave him a convenient list of people to write to.

"LaRue," he said, "creep down to Dalton's library and steal all of his writing paper. And pen and ink. I shall write a letter, and then you will copy it dozens of times. This must be done at once."

LaRue stared down his nose. "J'étais autrefois valet et maintenant je ne suis plus rien!"

"You know I do not understand half of that," Giles said.

"I was valet, now I am nothing," LaRue said. "No more than

the clerk!"

"When you are finished copying letters," Giles said drily, "you may be a valet once more. Now go!"

LaRue did go, though slamming the door as he went. Had the other inhabitants of the house not imbibed far too much wine the night before, they would all have awakened. As it was, Giles thought LaRue would be safe to make off with writing paper until at least noon.

A HALF HOUR later, Giles had written a letter begging his dear relations to forward anything they knew of either John Hill from the 1740s or '50s, or Sir John Kullehamnd of lately. Any information would prove vital and no detail would be too small.

As LaRue started copying, and complaining in French all the while, Giles began to think of other methods of exposing Sir John as the fraud he must certainly be.

It would be convenient to hire an investigator, but hire him with what? He had not the funds. A bookshop or some creditor that did not understand precisely how penniless he was might extend him credit, but an investigator? No, they would demand a retainer, and a retainer he did not have.

He supposed he could sell off some of his coats.

No, he'd have to sell some of them as it was to keep Crackwilder in brandy and to pay for all these letters about to rain down on the continent. He could not sell all of his coats. Not yet, anyway.

He would have to be his own investigator. And LaRue could be his assistant. The valet would moan bitterly over it, but he would do it. What choice did the fellow have, anyway? Who else would put up with such a servant?

In any case, he'd made a good start. In the meantime, he and Dalton were to dine at Lord Milton's this evening, and he had every hope of seeing Miss Dell there. Milton was friendly with her brother, and so certainly the sister would come?

That is what he hoped, anyway.

He would apprise her of the letters he was sending all over Europe. He could not yet accuse Sir John, he was astute enough to know that Miss Dell would dismiss that out of hand without solid evidence. However, he could claim he suspected a connection between John Hill and Veritas. He sought information about John Hill, as that fellow had been knighted by the Swedes or somebody else in that neighborhood, and God knew where else the man had hung his hat. That would show his interest and effort in the matter. In time, when he had the information he sought, he would condemn Sir John as being Veritas. Or knowing Veritas. Or in a cabal with Veritas.

For now, he must just be certain Miss Dell knew he was in earnest.

CHAPTER NINE

KITTY HAD FOUND her thoughts going this way and that over Penny's warnings. At one moment she was convinced that she'd been taken in by an expert scoundrel, and then the next minute questioning if it could be true that she was that gullible. Or that Lord Grayson could be that scheming.

By the afternoon, she had determined that she must know the truth. Penny had claimed that Lord Grayson quoted Shakespeare as a method, a means to impress. If that were so, he could not be intimately acquainted with all of the texts. He would only have collected a few phrases he might throw into a conversation.

She'd gone to her father's library, found a selection of volumes, and taken them to her room. If Lord Grayson was a fraud, he would not know the origin of the quotes she unearthed and planned to throw at him the next they met.

She felt hurried, as she thought she might meet him again this evening, though she could not be certain of it. She might have an equal chance of meeting Sir John. A dinner was to be hosted by Lord Milton. Kitty knew him to be a member of the society, but then she also knew him to be a member of the Jockey Club, having encountered him at Newmarket. Both Sir John and Lord Grayson may have been invited, or neither of them.

If Lord Grayson were to attend, she would discover the truth.

She had laid the volumes across the desk in her sitting room and took up *Measure for Measure*. She could not recall ever reading it and was certain it had not been done recently on the stage.

After flipping through the pages, she was more than certain. The plot was almost obscene and she certainly could not bring it up in a conversation. What an idea!

She moved on to *Timon of Athens*, *Pericles*, and *Troilus and Cressida*. If Lord Grayson were such an avid reader of Shakespeare, he would know them. If he'd merely written down some phrasings he found pleasing, he would not.

Kitty began reading *Troilus and Cressida* and promptly laid the book down. There on the page—*Things won are done, joy's soul lies in the doing*. Lord Grayson had said that precise thing to Sir John. It might very well be a coincidence that she happened upon a phrase he had put in his pocket.

She would focus her attention on *Timon of Athens* and *Pericles*.

SOME HOURS LATER, having listened to Lady Penderton's advice on dining at Lord Milton's table, Kitty and Frederick were in the carriage. According to Lady Penderton, Lord Milton's footmen were over-attentive and would fill a person's wine glass before it was half empty. Lord Milton thought it made for a jolly gathering. Lady Penderton said that was no doubt true, but she did not care to hear of any of her offspring having *too* jolly a time.

"Dalton will be there," Frederick said, as the carriage rumbled over cobblestones, "and so I assume that means Grayson, too. I have heard those two are keen to attend any dinner that will have them as they don't have a guinea between them."

Kitty felt a little shiver at the mention of Lord Grayson. She scolded herself over it. She was not gullible and she had thoroughly prepared herself. If Lord Grayson's spouting of Shakespeare had been a ploy, she would find it out. She had practically memorized *Timon of Athens*, tedious as it had been. And, if she unmasked Lord Grayson as a rogue, she would make sure he understood he'd been found out.

"And what of Sir John?" Kitty asked. "Will he attend?"

"Possibly," Frederick said, "Milton finds him particularly intelligent."

Kitty only nodded and peered out the carriage window, pretending an interest in the people on sidewalks as she passed them by. Penny's words came back to her over and over—the wonder of marrying a man well-suited. Penny said it was everything, absolutely everything. Sir John *was* well-suited to her. He had everything to recommend him. She must keep that idea in her thoughts. It would be foolish to dismiss a man out of hand, only because he did not make her heart beat faster.

"Is it down to them, then?" Frederick asked. "Dandified Grayson or dry as toast Sir John?"

"Nothing is down to anything!" Kitty said, turning away from the window. "Why should you say so?"

Frederick shrugged. "Those seem to be your admirers. At least, the ones you've appeared to take an interest in. Why not Jost, though?"

Kitty could not help but laugh. "Frederick, Mr. Jost has only been introduced to me and barely said a word. He has not even bothered to secure me for a dance."

"He is…reticent, is all. With ladies. He's a fine fellow, though!"

"I am sure he is," Kitty said, smiling. "Though I would not know."

"All I say is, there are plenty of gentlemen you might consider."

"I am not considering anyone at this moment," Kitty said, not entirely sure that was true.

Blessedly, Frederick's inquiries came to an end, as they had arrived at Lord Milton's house. His pressing questions had discomposed Kitty. Surely she was not seen as preferring anyone? That could not be. She did not know her own mind, why should anybody else presume to know it?

She comforted herself with the idea that Frederick had launched the conversation to introduce the idea of Mr. Jost. He was Frederick's oldest friend and according to her brother, a very amusing fellow. Kitty thought he must be one of those gentlemen who was comfortably loquacious in the company of his own sex, but mute in the vicinity of a female. Poor Mr. Jost had so far had absolutely nothing to say to her and she very much doubted he ever would.

MUCH TO DALTON'S surprise, Giles had been ready to leave the house early rather than late. Though he would not tell Dalton for the world, he was intent on having a moment with Lady Milton to make any necessary adjustments to the seating arrangements at her table.

He had thought the conversation with his hostess would be smooth and quick. After all, was it not a usual thing that a single gentleman requested to be seated next to a particular single lady? At least, he had done it himself enough times. He had been more than surprised, irritated even, when he discovered from Lady Milton that Miss Dell was proving very popular. It seemed that two gentlemen had called earlier in the day to ask about the very same thing.

It was outrageous! Who were the scoundrels?

Lady Milton did not say, but drifted off to greet a recent arrival.

Giles had at least accomplished the second best—he would be seated across the table from Miss Dell. Milton's table was not over-wide, not like some others where the distance rivaled the English Channel. Perhaps it would not be the most regular thing in the world, but he thought he would find his opportunities to speak to her across the divide.

This gain did come with a loss, though. He was to take in Miss Blessy. He must only comfort himself that there was to be no dancing. Miss Blessy could not go the wrong way while she was sitting in a chair. At least, he hoped not.

Giles had kept himself facing the drawing room door, waiting for Miss Dell's arrival. He had barely noted the other guests arriving. Most of them he knew and he had already heard their most amusing stories many times over.

The one who had just come in, though, he *did* note. Sir John. Why should he be here? Giles was aware of Milton's involvement in the Royal Society, but why should he be dragging in all sorts from his silly club?

He wondered if Sir John had been one of the gentlemen to call on Lady Milton earlier.

That devil!

⇛⇚

KITTY ENTERED LADY Milton's drawing room and instantly noted both Lord Grayson and Sir John. Most alarming, both gentlemen seemed to be coming toward her with remarkable speed, as if they were in some sort of footrace.

"My God," Frederick muttered next to her.

"Miss Dell," Lord Grayson said, reaching her first. He nodded to Frederick. "Dell."

Sir John was not a moment behind. "Miss Dell," he said.

Lord Grayson shifted so that he was nearly standing in front of Sir John. "Miss Dell, I would wish to acquaint you with an investigative action I have taken to uncover Veritas."

Kitty was taken aback. Had Penny been wrong, after all? She could not be certain, but it seemed extraordinary that Lord Grayson would have actually done anything to solve the mystery if it were just a trick to gain her attentions.

"Certainly, I would wish to hear of anything you have done regarding the matter," Kitty said.

"We would *all* like to hear it," Sir John said crossly.

"Keep to your own investigations," Lord Grayson said over

his shoulder. He held out his arm.

Kitty allowed herself to be led. *If* Lord Grayson had truly done something, she must know what it was.

To Lord Grayson's apparent annoyance, Sir John followed at a discreet distance. It was the most absurd situation in the world. As evidenced by Frederick's raised eyebrows and smirk when Kitty glanced behind her.

Not wishing to call attention or in any way appear silly, Kitty said, "Lord Grayson, I am sure Sir John should hear of your endeavors as well. We must all work together, I think."

Lord Grayson was less than gracious about it, but he did not absolutely refuse. Sir John joined them in their circle.

"If you will recall, Miss Dell," Lord Grayson said, "all of this mystery springs from John Hill those many years ago. Whoever is Veritas seeks to call back to those days, perhaps as some sort of revenge. John Hill was knighted—Mr. Crackwilder thinks probably by the Swedes. I posit that he must have spent a significant amount of time there, and perhaps other places on the continent."

"A logical leap, I think," Kitty said, not entirely following wherever Lord Grayson was going.

"It occurred to me that Veritas must have some connection to John Hill. If not, why mention him at all? The note that was sent was not long, and yet he specifically links himself to John Hill."

"I had not thought of that," Kitty said softly. In truth, she had not given a moment to consider why or how the two might be connected. It was a clever suspicion and one that had merit.

"There must be a connection somehow," Lord Grayson said.

"The connection is only in the idea of what John Hill repre-sented," Sir John said. "As was made clear in the letter."

"If only there were a means of discovering if such a connec-tion existed," Kitty said, ignoring Sir John's dubiousness.

"Though a connection surely does not exist," Sir John said.

"I believe there is a way to discover it," Lord Grayson said, as if Sir John had said nothing at all. "My grandmother is an ardent genealogist. She has kept contact with our distant relations, a fair number of them located in Sweden, Denmark, France, Portugal, and Spain. Of course, Sweden and Denmark would be of interest. If you see what I say."

"I think I do!" Kitty said, all enthusiasm. "You will make inquiries with your relations to see what anybody may have heard of John Hill. There may be some family stories, some remembrance of him, just as my father remembers the story from my grandfather. Perhaps Veritas is even a relation of John Hill!"

"Exactly," Lord Grayson said. "Any bit of information may provide a clue as to the connection of the old to the new."

Kitty hoped she contained at least some of her astonishment. Here was a real action to be taken. So far, at least from what she gathered from Mrs. Herschel, nobody had thought of anything to do that might solve the mystery beyond reading recently published papers.

"A ridiculous goose chase," Sir John said gravely.

Lord Grayson turned sharply to Sir John. "I see," he said. "And what, pray, are *you* doing to unmask the culprit?"

A faint bloom of pink arose and made its way across Sir John's pallid cheeks. "I, sir, am examining the papers recently published. As all of us with sense are doing. It is in words that truth may be found, if only one is equipped to read them."

Kitty took a breath in. Sir John was running dangerously close to an insult that must be answered. And, though Lord Grayson was most certainly a dandy, she suspected the lord to be no stranger to a pistol.

Lord Grayson laughed. "You speak an infinite deal of nothing, or so Shakespeare would say of you. And *Sir* John, take note that I am not a sir, I am a lord. Address me as such or you will find we have a most unpleasant meeting some early morning."

Kitty watched in alarm and prayed Sir John would make his apologies. Though she prayed it, she was not certain he would do it. His breath came quick and his eyes had taken on a strangely cold and distant, almost dead, aspect. His pupils were unnaturally small, and his dark irises seemed pools of black.

As if it were a hundred miles away, though it was only the other end of the drawing room, Lady Milton said loudly, "Everyone, let us go through."

GILES HAD LED Miss Blessy to her seat and the lady had only managed to step on his toes once. Lady Milton had been as good as her word, Miss Dell was seated across the table from him. What Lady Milton had not revealed was who the gentlemen would be to have the honor of being seated next to Miss Dell.

Though he was infuriated, he was not surprised to see that one of them was Sir John. He *was* surprised to see Dalton was the other gentleman.

Were he such an unsuspecting man as Lockwood or Hampton or Cabot or Ashworth, he might have idly wondered why Dalton had made an effort to secure Miss Dell to his right. As he was not any of those innocent-minded gentlemen, he did not wonder. Dalton had taken great pains since the inception of the Dukes' Pact to insert himself and cause trouble between any couple he feared might make their way to the altar.

Apparently, Dalton's fears over Miss Dell had grown to such a degree that he was once again sticking his nose in.

It was ridiculous, of course. How many times must he explain to his friend that he only engaged in infatuations? That he had become a bit single-minded about this particular enchantment did not make it any different whatsoever.

The hard outer layers of his heart were all for Miss Dell. The inner layers, though, would never be for anyone. The deep recesses where Shakespeare and Byron lived were theirs alone.

As for Sir John, Giles was more determined than ever to reveal him as Veritas. Of course, he'd not mentioned his suspicions to Miss Dell. Not yet, anyway. Though he wondered if Sir John did not seem exceedingly uncomfortable with the whole idea of gathering information from the continent? He supposed the fellow would be even more uncomfortable if he realized the subject of Giles' inquiries was not only John Hill, but Sir John Kullehamnd as well.

As the dinner wore on, it was proving difficult to insert himself in the conversation across the table. For one thing, Miss Blessy had a lot to say. She was a regular Gratiano—words and words adding up to nothing. If he was not mistaken, it was a good ten minutes of talking before she managed to convey that she had a brother still in the schoolroom.

Lady Philippa on his other side provided little relief from the onslaught of Miss Blessy. The lady was recently married, which had surprised everybody, as her temperament was very like Lady Montague's—always seeking to find fault and condemn. Among other things, Lady Philippa related the shocking story she'd been told, by one who had been told, by one who knew someone who had been there, of Lady Cabot driving a phaeton at scandalously excessive speeds. At the end of each story, Lady Philippa would narrow her already narrow eyes and say, "What do you think about *that*?"

Giles thought absolutely nothing about *that*, except to think it was well that Lady Philippa had not heard the rumor of Lady Cabot riding her lord's horse at Newmarket.

Finally, he saw his opening. Miss Blessy was telling the roundabout story of her brother to Mr. Fister and Lady Philippa was relaying the shocking story of Miss something-or-other who'd worn a delicate silk to a picnic to Lord Macendray. Dalton was turned away, as was Sir John.

Miss Dell's eyes met his.

Before he could speak, she said, "Every man has his fault, and honesty is his."

Giles knew the quote perfectly well, though it seemed apropos of nothing at this moment. "Timon of Athens?" he asked.

Miss Dell nodded, though she appeared surprised that he should know it.

"But what does it mean?" Giles asked.

Miss Dell inclined her head toward Lord Dalton.

Giles knew in an instant that Dalton had been up to some sort of trickery. "Whatever he has said, do not believe a word of it!"

Miss Blessy turned to him. "Who should we not believe, Lord Grayson?"

Miss Dell's brows raised ever so slightly, as if she dared him to say more.

Both Sir John and Dalton had turned away from their dinner companions at the sound of his raised voice.

"I only say, Miss Dell, that there are those lords who will prevaricate for their own purposes," Giles said.

"As I understand it, Lord Grayson," Miss Dell said, her voice as cold as ice.

CHAPTER TEN

IN THE COUNTRY, Kitty had sometimes gazed through her telescope and watched a murmuration of starlings at dusk. As they dropped from towering heights and broke apart and came together and swooped up again, her logical mind said they were specially built for such activity. Her less than logical mind said they must be sickeningly dizzy.

She felt sickeningly dizzy at this moment. Curled up on the soft velvet chair in her sitting room, she grasped the armrests lest she lose her balance. She had come upon too much information for one evening, and she knew not what to believe. Like a starling, she could not easily determine which way to go. *Unlike* a starling, she did not have close neighbors in flight who would signal the direction.

Her sole aim that evening had been to test Lord Grayson on his knowledge of Shakespeare. She wished to discover if Penny was right—did the lord only keep a few phrases in his pocket to use for effect?

It did not seem so. He had accused Sir John of speaking *an infinite deal of nothing.* If her memory served her, that was from the *Merchant of Venice.* Then, when she'd said, *every man has his fault, and honesty is his,* he'd recognized it instantly from *Timon of Athens.* It was an obscure line to have recognized. She supposed she could at least conclude that if Lord Grayson thought to use

Shakespeare as a means of flirtation, he had memorized a vast amount of it.

She wished that were the only thing she must think of.

There had been the conversation between herself, the lord, and Sir John. Lord Grayson was actually doing something to solve the mystery of Veritas. At least, he said he was. Could she be sure of that, though? And even if he were not doing anything, if it were only some strategy to slip into her good graces, why had Sir John been so perspiring and angry over the notion?

All of that had been only a lead-up to what she would be informed of at dinner.

She had not been enthused to find Lord Dalton on her left. She found him a rather frightening sort of person and had not the first idea of what they might talk about.

It would have been well if they had gone down the road of usual subjects, but Lord Dalton would not have it so. In fact, he had been far more direct than one was used to experiencing at a dinner. His words were burned into her memory.

"Miss Dell, forgive me if I overstep, but I would warn you off Grayson."

Kitty had not quite known how to answer, only that she longed to hear his reasons. Would they tip the scales on her wavering opinion?

"How so, Lord Dalton?" she'd said. "I understood you to be Lord Grayson's friend. Do you say something against him?"

"He *is* my friend, Miss Dell," Lord Dalton said. "As are many other gentlemen I would not introduce to a sister."

Kitty was both shocked and wishing for more. Why would Lord Dalton say such a thing as that? Why would he condemn his friend as not fit for refined society? It was true that Lord Grayson was known as a terrible flirt, but she had not heard anything more dreadful against him.

"As you have spoken plainly, and strongly," Kitty said, "I think it my prerogative to ask you to be specific in your charges."

Lord Dalton had seemed irritated by the notion, as if he were not in the habit of being questioned. Kitty did not fill the silence, however. She only waited for him to answer.

Finally, he said, "I had hoped to avoid shocking what I am sure are your delicate sensibilities. At least, I am told that all young ladies have delicate sensibilities these days. However, if you insist on knowing—he has laid bets at his club that he can engage your affection. He does it every year with some girl or other. I thought to warn you off as I am growing tired of the game. It does not do him credit to injure a lady's reputation. Now, I find it does not do *me* credit, as he is living in my house."

Kitty had been dumbstruck. Whatever she had thought of Lord Grayson, she had not thought that. Her name was mentioned in a gentlemen's club? It was *written down* in a club book? And in such an outrageous manner?

"By the by," Lord Dalton said, "I have bet against him. I think, this time, he may have set his sights on a lady too intelligent to fall for his amorous gambits."

"I was never in the slightest danger, my lord," Kitty said.

Had she meant it though? Or had she allowed herself to believe that Lord Grayson was somehow different from what everybody said he was? She had believed that he'd taken up the challenge of unmasking Veritas and that had made such a difference!

Then, there was the source of the condemnation to consider—Lord Dalton. She did not know him well, but there was something she did not entirely trust about him. For that matter, Penny had not said much about him, but she did not seem to love him. At least, not as she did other of Lord Cabot's friends. She was very approving of the Lords Hampton, Ashworth, and Lockwood.

Was Lord Dalton to be trusted? Or was he also playing at some game? If he were, she could not fathom what it was.

As well, if it were all true, why did Lord Grayson engage in such behavior? That, of all questions, burned in her the most.

"Lord Dalton," she'd said, "while it is of no concern to me, I am curious. *Why* does Lord Grayson behave so badly? *Why* does he seek to injure any lady?"

"He does not imagine he injures, it is only meant to be a bit of fun," Lord Dalton said. He paused, as if he were parsing his thoughts. "Grayson, if I understand him, is not capable of falling in love, therefore, he falls in infatuation. His pursuits are rather like a meringue—wonderful in the moment, but an hour later one has forgotten all about it. Despite the poets' high-flying phrases, I think it a rather common condition."

"Is it a condition you suffer from yourself?"

"I am even less likely than Grayson to be slayed by love," Lord Dalton said with a rare smile. "Though I do not see that deficiency as suffering."

Kitty would have liked to press on. She was not sure she had ever had a gentleman speak to her in such a frank manner. And yet, her mother's training and good example overtook her. She merely nodded and turned to Sir John.

And what of Sir John? Over dinner, they'd had a perfectly acceptable conversation about the various papers from the Royal Society they'd both read. Sir John had been kind enough to mention other papers that had been published earlier than her current collection and point out particularly interesting studies.

She was very sure she should have been more fascinated by an examination of the head of a platypus. And why could she not pay proper attention to the description of the gizzards of a cassowary?

These sorts of conversations were just what she'd most wished for. A gentleman who would discuss the findings of the day, and she his equal.

Perhaps it had not been to Sir John's credit that he had seemed over-smug at Lord Grayson's outburst across the table. Though he could not know the circumstance, he seemed to take too much pleasure in another's apparent distress.

But then, he had allowed himself to be guided back to scientific discoveries and had informed her of the properties contained in the tusk of a narwhale. In any case, did not every person have their faults?

Sir John might be, on occasion, a bit unkind. But he was learned, and he recognized that she was too.

But why did he not have a greater effect on her? Why did her heart not skip a beat in his presence? Perhaps it would, but it had not done yet. And, if it never did, was that so terrible?

Her mother might say so, but she was not her mother.

Kitty gazed around her sitting room. The bookcases that had been empty upon her arrival were now filled with books. She was safe here, she understood this room. As for what went on outside of this room, she was entirely lost.

"You are in over your head, Kitty Dell," she said quietly, "and you'd best get out of the water before you drown."

GILES GALLOPED HIS horse through the streets, determined to catch up with Dalton. The devil had studiously avoided his stare over port at Lord Milton's table and then promptly joined a card game in the drawing room. Giles had turned his attention to Miss Dell. It was urgent that he speak to her. She must know that Dalton was full of tricks and nobody should believe him if he claimed the sun was out or the day was Wednesday.

Miss Dell had been no easier to reach than Dalton and had seemed to adopt the same evasions. She partnered at whist with her brother and there was no getting near them. It would be difficult enough to strike up a conversation in a card game one was not a part of, but then there was Dell himself. What had at first seemed a neutral stance had seemed to have hardened somehow. Giles got the distinct impression that Dell did not care for him. He supposed the fellow was still sore over having been thrown in the vicinity of Miss Blaise's fan.

Giles had hoped to bide his time, waiting for Miss Dell to

leave. He might depart at the same time and have a moment to speak to her in the foyer as she waited for her cloak.

That was not to be, she'd been surrounded by her brother, Mr. Fister, and Sir John—all wishing to be the first to hand over her garment.

If Giles had not been in such earnest, he might have laughed at the near-wrestling between Sir John and Fister, before Dell settled the matter by demanding the delicate velvet wrap be handed over.

Somehow, Dalton had slipped out when he was not looking, though he did not think the man could be too far ahead of him. In any case, he knew where Dalton was going, as they lived in the same house.

He would demand to know what Dalton had said. Then he would demand that Dalton retract his words the next time he encountered Miss Dell.

But first, he must catch him.

He reined in his horse and trotted down a narrow alley. It was a shortcut and would bring him to the avenue that was Dalton's likely route.

He hurried over the wet cobblestones, not caring to think what they were wet from as it had not rained all day. He turned onto the better lighted street. Dalton was trotting toward him.

Giles blocked his path, forcing Dalton to rein in his horse.

"Well?" he said. "What lie did you tell Miss Dell?"

Dalton yawned, as if he had been expecting to be waylaid. "Is it a lie to say that there are bets laid all over town about whether you can win the heart of a particular lady?"

"I have nothing to do with that!"

Dalton examined his glove. "You have everything to do with that, my friend. If you had not spent season after season pursuing one lady after the next and then nothing comes of it, there would not be any bets. There would not be any amusement in it. As it is, you have created this situation. You, and no other. By the by, I have bet against you. I do not believe Miss Dell is so foolish as to fall for your stratagems."

"I demand you retract it, Dalton! You must tell Miss Dell you did not mean what you said."

"I did mean it."

"Say you didn't."

"I will not," Dalton said. "Further, it is for your own good. When I said Miss Dell is not foolish enough to fall for you, I did not say *you* were not foolish enough to fall for *her*. We have a deal, Grayson, keep up your end of it."

With that, Dalton urged his horse and cantered down the road.

SIR JOHN PACED his sitting room, only stopping to occasionally stab at the fire. Such an evening! He had expected it to be rather dull, just one more necessary step in his plan. Instead, it had been one of distinct highs and lows.

He must not spend too much time thinking over the highs. He need not congratulate himself too much over his successful dinner by the side of Miss Dell. He had come prepared to speak of the things that interested her, and so he had.

He was certain she was growing fond of him. Why else would a lady ask so many questions about the head of a platypus? And then, he was certain there had been some sort of falling out between Miss Dell and Grayson. He did not know the cause, but he'd overheard Miss Dell ask Dalton what he had against Grayson. Then, she had been decidedly cool when Grayson had attempted to engage her across the table.

That was all well and good, but he must turn his attention to the lows of the evening. He must consider the lowest point in the night in particular. Grayson claimed he would make inquiries on the continent. *That* was not at all convenient.

Had he been in earnest, though? Grayson was a flighty and

self-indulgent sort—far too interested in the fall of his cloth to have time for such tasks. Grayson had not the means to pay for an investigator at the moment, of that he was sure. Contacting distant relations seemed a flimsy effort. Should he really concern himself with that fop's pronouncements? Even if the idiot were intent on doing something, how much would he actually get done? Men like that did a lot of fine talking, but very little doing. He knew all about them from the diary—they were idle, pointless, and useless.

Grayson might write all the letters he liked inquiring after John Hill. Were he to receive any replies, they would likely be complimentary. The only real danger was if Grayson somehow mentioned his own name. Especially to a Swede. Perhaps he had been self-indulgent in inventing such a name. It had amused him and that had likely been a misstep. However, what was done could not be undone.

He supposed he should not worry overmuch at having such a one as Grayson making inquiries. Though, it was never a good idea to dismiss a threat entirely.

Perhaps he would see what he could discover about Grayson's real intentions. It would put his mind at rest if he could confirm that the lord only spouted off for the benefit of Miss Dell.

Miss Katherine Dell, granddaughter of Lord Charles Penderton, would not waste a moment in disabusing Grayson of his alleged charms. For a lady like Miss Dell, the dandy had no charms.

IT WAS TUESDAY, and that meant a trip to Mrs. Herschel's salon. Kitty had worked to put aside her own troubled mind and think of the matter at hand. She might hear of some development in the pursuit of Veritas.

When Lord Grayson had laid out his plan to write letters all over Europe to inquire about John Hill, Kitty had almost been tempted to tell him of Mrs. Herschel's gatherings. She had thought she might even ask Mrs. Herschel to invite the lord so that he might speak of his suspicion that there must be a connection between John Hill and Veritas.

She was glad she had not, considering what had come after.

As they drove through the London streets, Lady Penderton reached across from her seat and grabbed Kitty's hand. "You are becoming pensive as a habit, my dear. I do wish you would share whatever thoughts you may have. And please do not tell me it is all about the Royal Society! We shall hear enough on that subject very shortly."

"It is not that," Kitty said, not certain how to explain herself, "it is only that town is so different than I imagined. In Devon, everyone is as they appear to be. There are no surprises. I cannot say the same for London."

"Have you been surprised by someone?" her mother asked.

"Yes. No. I do not really know," Kitty said. "You see, that is what I mean. I am not certain I understand gentlemen at all, outside of Frederick and my father."

"I see," Lady Penderton said. "You are afraid you will make a mistake that will follow you all of your life."

Kitty had not thought of her roiling ideas in that way, but she suspected her mother had gone right to the root of it. If she could not depend upon her own judgment in regard to Lord Grayson, how could she depend upon it to judge anybody? How was she to know that she'd made the right choice? That she'd not been deceived?

Last evening, somebody had lied to her—was it Lord Grayson or Lord Dalton? Had she been a fool?

She really did not know. Further, she had a large dowry and she was not so innocent as to ignore that attraction. There might well be those who feigned interest in her because of it. How would she know?

Her large dowry attracting less than honorable gentlemen

had been understood by her well enough before she'd come to town, but it had not discomposed her. She had been so confident in her ability to judge correctly.

Now she was not so confident in her abilities and a misjudgment might have terrible consequences.

Then, there was her wish that Lord Grayson was not as Lord Dalton painted him. Was she allowing her wishes to persuade the facts?

It all made her very unsure of her footing, as if she treaded over rocky ground in ballroom slippers. It was not a feeling she was at all used to experiencing.

"I will not shower you with comforting platitudes, Kitty," Lady Penderton said. "Your fears are valid, I'm afraid. I have been lucky, but there are those women who have not been so fortunate. Of those, not a one of them understood what they were really walking into. It is a grim reality."

Kitty looked at her mother in some surprise. She *had* thought Lady Penderton would shower her with comforting platitudes. It was rather alarming that she did not.

"That is what your family is for, my dear," Lady Penderton said. "When you find you have a real interest in a gentleman, and I think it is far too early for any of that yet, your father, brother, and I will find out everything there is to know about him. If the gentleman once kicked a cat in his youth, we will discover it."

Kitty could not help but to smile over the idea. Kicked a cat, indeed.

"Do not torture yourself with these worries, you are surrounded in the safety of your family. Commit to nobody until you have consulted with us," Lady Penderton said. "Now, let us proceed into Mrs. Herschel's house. I have high hopes of hearing something delightfully absurd that will amuse your father."

MRS. HERSCHEL'S DRAWING room was as crowded as it had been the last time Kitty had been there. For all the people in attendance, there was surprisingly little talking. There seemed be a tension or an anticipation in the air, as if something momentous was about to occur. Kitty was certain there was news about Veritas.

Kitty and Lady Penderton were shown to a sofa in front of the tea tray. Kitty was certain they were given the consideration on her mother's account—she was a baroness, not a scholar, and Kitty suspected nobody knew what to do with her other than honor her title with a choice seat.

A few other people came in and Mrs. Herschel rose. The room quieted, and she said, "Welcome, my esteemed guests. I will get right to the point as I know you would wish it. We are in dire need of a new direction for our inquiries. Our initial idea of combing through the papers recently published by the society has led to..."

Mrs. Herschel paused. Kitty could not imagine what looking through the papers had led to, if it were not the unmasking of Veritas. As so many of the people in the room appeared uncomfortable, even abashed, she did not think it could be so. Only Sir John and the ladies in the room did not appear struck.

"It has led to a number of unfortunate incidents," Mrs. Herschel finally said. "Sir Joseph, while eager to detect the interloper, has asked us to cease this particular avenue of inquiry so that there are not any further...mishaps. Sir Joseph has even suggested that the idea of a paper having been published that would embarrass us all may have been a ruse to sow discord. If that is the case, it seems it was all too successful. Now, I suggest we use this meeting today to arrive at some other things we can do. There are great minds in this room, certainly we shall arrive at a new idea."

Mrs. Herschel sat down next to the baroness. The people in the drawing room moved off into groups, speaking quietly amongst one another.

"Baroness," Mrs. Herschel said, refilling her teacup, "you must think us odd, indeed. I hardly dared hope you would come again."

Lady Penderton took the cup and said, "I would not miss it, Mrs. Herschel. I am finding all of this quite fascinating, and I am certain Kitty feels the same."

Kitty nodded, and her mother went on. "Do tell me, though, what particular mishap was the result of reading a pile of papers?"

Mrs. Herschel glanced round the room, and then said softly, "It was enthusiasm, you see. One fellow would think he'd spotted something suspicious in a paper and then question the fellow who wrote it. It eventually ended in fisticuffs in Covent Garden. Mr. Nackery interrogated Lord Home over whether he had actually examined the innards of a tadpole and made valid conclusions on its aggregation of fat, or whether the paper was meant to hint that the society itself had run to fat."

Kitty stifled her laughter. The baroness was not quite so successful at it. "Surely not?" she said, her shoulders shaking.

"I am afraid so," Mrs. Herschel said. "And it was just as absurd as it sounds—neither gentleman is particularly skilled at fisticuffs. I understand it was a ridiculous rolling around in the dirt more than a pitched battle."

Mrs. Herschel was silent for a moment. She said softly, "I really do not know what we are to do. I have even paid an investigator and he's come up with nothing."

Kitty had entirely given up any intention of mentioning Lord Grayson and his ideas. Now, though, the investigation seemed to have come to a standstill.

"Mrs. Herschel," Kitty said, "it was recently suggested to me that there might be an actual connection between John Hill and Veritas. Lord Grayson has made some effort to discover it. He writes to his relations on the continent to inquire. At least, he says that he has. But even if he has not, might that not be a worthy avenue?"

"Grayson?" Mrs. Herschel asked, her eyebrows slowly coming together across her forehead. "I do not know him."

"No, of course you would not," Kitty said. "He is in no way engaged in the society's business."

"Then why should he pursue the man we seek?" Mrs. Herschel asked, appearing very puzzled.

"Well," Kitty said, stammering, "I do not know that he really has. He may have been only talking. Though I did think the idea had merit."

"I suppose it may," Mrs. Herschel said. "After all, we have no place to start and there is as good as anywhere."

Mrs. Herschel turned in her seat and called, "Sir John, do join us. Miss Dell has an interesting idea for us to consider."

Kitty felt her face flame. Sir John was already acquainted with the idea and did not think it worthy at all. She should have told that to Mrs. Herschel at the outset!

"I am afraid," Kitty said, "that Sir John has heard Lord Grayson speak and did not find it a very compelling notion."

Of course, it was entirely too late for the claim to do any good, as Sir John had already made his way over.

CHAPTER ELEVEN

"Miss Dell has told me of this idea that the man we seek might have a connection to John Hill," Mrs. Herschel said. "As I have not heard any other promising ideas, perhaps we ought to look into it."

Sir John nodded, and Kitty thought he hid his disdain for the theory better than she'd have thought he would.

"Perhaps Miss Dell would consent to walk with me and expound on the suggestion, so I may better understand where to begin," Sir John said gravely.

A demur was on Kitty's lips, but it was too late. Sir John held out his arm. She looked to her mother, who nodded though she did not appear overly enthused by the idea. Kitty had no choice, she rose and took Sir John's arm.

He led her round the various groups huddled together and talking of what ought to be done, to a bow window at the far end of the room.

"I did not realize, Miss Dell," Sir John said, "that you were intent on pursuing Lord Grayson's rather wild and unlikely ideas."

"I am not pursuing anything, Sir John," Kitty said hurriedly. His tone sounded rather scolding and she felt herself stiffen. "It was all well and good to read the papers from the Royal Society, but I can go no further than that."

"No further but to suggest Grayson's idea to Mrs. Herschel?" Sir John asked.

Why was he speaking to her as if she were a naughty child? Kitty said, "I do suppose, Sir John, that I am free to suggest anything I like to anybody I like."

Sir John seemed taken aback by her challenging tone, but he speedily recovered. "Of course, naturally," he said. "I did not mean to imply you should not."

Kitty nodded, as if she understood that he had not meant to imply such a thing, though she was not certain she really did understand it.

"It is only," Sir John said in a contrite tone, "that I do take a particular interest in your welfare, Miss Dell. Surely, you do not remain unaware of it."

Kitty had not the first idea of how to respond to such a statement. She occupied herself with looking out the window instead.

"You are right not to answer," Sir John said. "I have been too rash. It is better that I speak to your father first."

Kitty felt her heart drop to her knees. Speak to her father? Surely he could not mean...she must put a stop to that idea immediately. She did not know him well enough, she had not even decided what her view of him was.

"There is no reason anybody should speak to my father at this moment," Kitty blurted out.

"The lady demurs," Sir John said. "Very prettily done."

Demurs? Kitty was certain she had not claimed some false reluctance. She had said what she meant to say. There *was* no cause for anybody to speak to Lord Penderton just now.

"Sir John, I must insist—"

Kitty was tapped on the shoulder. She spun around to find her mother standing behind her. "It is time we take our leave, Kitty."

Kitty curtsied to Sir John, never happier over her mother's strict ideas about a call.

GILES HAD WRANGLED Sir John's address from Lady Milton, under the ruse that he had some old books he wished to dispose of that Sir John might take an interest in. Lady Milton had joked that he was down to selling off his books on account of the dukes' pact. It had been an irritating exchange—it seemed that nobody was beyond joking over his father's ridiculous pact with the other dukes.

Nevertheless, he'd got the address and made his way over. He and LaRue dismounted their horses a full block from the house and his valet paid a boy to hold the reins.

The house itself was not too far from St. George's church and Giles thought if anybody were to spot him, he might claim he was on his way there for a wedding or a christening. Not the most likely story, as those things were always in the newspapers, but it was all he could think of.

He must find some clue or evidence that Sir John was at the bottom of the Royal Society's mystery. The more he pondered it, the more it seemed likely that Sir John was Veritas, or was working with Veritas, or knew the identity of Veritas. The man came from nowhere, he claimed to have received the note from Veritas, and furthermore, he was an irritating person. Unraveling the mystery was the only way he could see that he'd be able to convince Miss Dell that he was in earnest, and therefore, Dalton had made up the story about bets in clubs. And therefore, everything was Sir John's fault.

Giles knew very well that Dalton had likely only invented *part* of the story he'd told Miss Dell. While it was true that he'd had nothing to do with any bets taking place regarding his interests, it was also true that there were probably bets being made. He did not know why gentlemen could not mind their own business! The ladies were always blamed as terrible gossipers, but at least they only whispered—they did not lay money and they did not write anything down to live forevermore in the club's book.

Further, if there *were* wagers, Miss Dell should never have been told of it. There were always bets laid involving ladies—who would they accept, what sex the first child, would a wife countenance her husband's latest flirtation. Great sums had changed hands over whether Lady G would allow Lady H to sit at her table when all and sundry knew Lord G was following Lady H round the town like a lovesick puppy. Yet, nobody *told* Lady Gordon that fortunes had been laid relating to her current disposition!

In any case, he would not approve of bets laid regarding Miss Dell. Oh, it had been one thing to hear of the bets for and against Lady Sarah. That particular lady had led him on a merry chase and had been well able to look after herself. Miss Dell, though. She was different. He could not say why, exactly. She simply was and nobody should be laying wagers with her name attached.

"That is the house," LaRue said, his voice dripping with boredom and ennui. "What do we discover?"

"I will not know until we discover it," Giles said, looking critically at the rather non-descript abode. It was one of those houses that masked the finances of those who lived in it. It was not large, but it was not small. It was not rich, but it was not poor. It was the sort of middling place one might pass a thousand times and not remember a thing about. Very like Sir John himself.

It was fronted by a fenced garden with two old trees that must block any sort of sunlight attempting to make its way indoors. It seemed kept up well enough, at least from the outside. Of course, if Giles had read Sir John's temperament correctly, the inside of the house was likely to have not a pin out of place. The fellow was far too grim for anything approaching a jolly lived-in hearth.

The front door swung open and Giles pulled LaRue behind a standing carriage. "There he is," Giles whispered.

LaRue peered around the back of the carriage and then

turned back to his master. "Sérieusement? He is absurd."

"He is, rather," Giles said, though he knew LaRue's sole measure was Sir John's rather uninspired dress. He watched Sir John call down a passing hackney and get inside.

"He is gone," Giles said. "Now we must just keep a watch out for whatever servants he keeps."

"In *that* house?" LaRue said. "A cook and a parlor maid, no more."

Giles was not certain of it. He really did not see how one could survive with only a cook and a maid.

"Surely," he said, "there must be at least a butler. Who would answer the door?"

LaRue rolled his eyes to the heavens. "Who knocks on the door of the absurd man? Nobody."

"I appreciate your theory, LaRue," Giles said, "but we ought to be careful all the same. I have yet to set foot in a house that did not have a butler."

LaRue examined his carefully polished nails. "And yet, you ride through the neighborhoods of filth, pickpockets, and diseased ladies. Who is *their* butler?"

That was true, of course. But for all his disdain of Sir John, he was a titled person. A low and foreign title, but title all the same. It seemed incredible that he would not employ a butler.

LaRue, seeing his master's dubiousness over his claims, muttered, "Les riches sont tellement stupides."

"I will pretend I did not hear the word stupid just now," Giles said. "Rather than argue what servants are in the house, we will saunter over and see if we can have a look in the windows. If we can slip into the garden unnoticed, we can use those trees for cover. If someone spots us, I'll say I heard the house was empty and being sold."

LaRue did not comment on the plan, though Giles was certain his thoughts were aggrieved. His valet would be affronted to be forced into doing two things he excessively disliked—walking and being out of doors.

The street was not a busy one, and he and LaRue bided their time, strolling along the front of the house until Giles saw their opportunity. A couple had turned the far corner and a governess had just hustled her charges into their house. The street was deserted.

Giles sauntered to the gate as if he had meant to go there all along. It was unlocked and they were inside the garden in a moment.

Giles made his way to the front of the house, using the trees for cover and ignoring his valet's various mutterings. He peered through a set of wide windows to a room lined with empty shelves in dark wood. There was a desk to one side, and a chair behind it.

"Very odd," he said.

"Naturellment," LaRue said, leaning against the house.

"It is a library," Giles said. "A library with no books in it."

"Nothing to read. A dream for you, yes?"

Giles ignored this latest insult hurled from his valet and said, "Sir John runs round the town advertising himself as a scholar. What kind of scholar has an empty library?"

LaRue shrugged and Giles made his way to the other side of the house. Peering through those windows, he saw a near desolate room. The only furnishings were a chair and side table pulled up to the fireplace. The only item in the room was a small book on the table.

Behind him, he heard the whine of the garden gate swinging open. He pulled LaRue behind the trunk of the nearest tree.

A charwoman carrying a bucket hobbled past them and to the doors. She took out a key and let herself into the house.

"The butler?" LaRue whispered.

Giles did not answer, but pulled LaRue from the garden. They decamped to their original post across the street.

"It is extraordinary," Giles said. "There is nothing in that house. He surely does not receive callers, there would be no place to sit. He cannot belong to a club, nobody would have him.

Where does he meet people?"

"Does he meet people?" LaRue said.

"There is a book in there. I suspect it is his appointment book."

"That is how he meets people?"

"I do not know, but I want that book."

"Tout simplement fantastique," LaRue said. "The day becomes more and more wonderful. Now we will be housebreakers for a book. Why did I leave France?"

"We will not break in," Giles said. "You will pay that charwoman to hand it over."

"Pay with what!" LaRue cried.

"I'll sell some of my coats," Giles said. He had no idea what the going rate was for a charwoman to steal possessions, but he would soon find it out. He was certain a book of appointments would reveal something underhanded about Sir John Kullehamnd.

KITTY SAT WITH her mother and Frederick in the drawing room after breakfast. It was not the usual place to find Frederick, most days he would be on his horse already, gone off to nobody knew where. This day, however, they awaited a particular delivery.

It was the day of Lady Blakely's masque, an event taking place every year that both delighted and terrorized her guests. The lady wielded a terrific sense of wit and expressed that wit with a gift—all of her guests were expected to wear the mask that Lady Blakely had specially designed for them.

One could hardly avoid the invitation—were one to stay away, the talk would fly round about what sort of mask it might have been that the lord or lady dared not don. It would not be a day before the details were known everywhere. Lady Penderton said it was far better to brazen it out and take the laughter that might come one's way than sit home in a fit of temper.

Of course, Kitty thought her mother would say so, as she had always been treated very kindly by Lady Blakely's hands. As for this morning, carriages and footmen had set off from Lady Blakely's house in every direction and half of London sat in their drawing rooms, nervously waiting to discover what would be delivered to their doors.

What the night was comprised of had already been revealed in the initial invitation. Some years, it was only a dinner and fewer people were invited. Other years, if Lady Blakeley were feeling particularly energetic on the mask-making side of things, it would be a ball. This was to be a ball and Kitty was grateful for it. More people meant she would just be one among many, even if her mask turned out to be ghastly.

Kitty felt a little tremulous in the waiting. She and Lady Penderton had called on Lady Blakely weeks ago and she'd found the woman exceedingly kind. She'd even been encouraged to speak about her discoveries relating to Cornish eyebright, though later she wondered if she'd bored the lady.

"Oh, mama," Kitty said, breaking the silence, "what if Lady Blakely masks me as a bore? I should have tried to be more amusing when we called on her. I know everybody cannot be as interested in eyebright as I am."

"So true," Frederick said.

Lady Penderton laid down her sewing. "Kitty, Lady Blakely is a kind and intelligent woman. Had you worked to be more amusing, she would have seen there was something false in it. As you presented yourself as you are, I think you have nothing to fear."

"Good God," Frederick said, dropping his newspaper. "I was seated next to Lady Blakeley at a dinner last week and I *did* work to be amusing. I hope I am not punished for it. Jost says that if she jokes about him not being terribly talkative with ladies he will not come."

"And so forever cement himself with the reputation," Lady

Penderton said. "Though I do not happen to think Lady Blakely would be so cruel to one so young."

The trio fell into silence once more. Kitty pretended to read, but for once she could not lose herself in a book. Lady Blakeley's masque was only one thing on her mind. She could not dismiss Sir John's behavior from her thoughts.

Despite wishing to like him, despite feeling she *should* like him, she was becoming more and more convinced that, in fact, she did not like him. She had not at all liked the way he spoke to her at Mrs. Herschel's salon. Their other conversations had made her feel he viewed her as his intellectual equal. *That* conversation, though. There had been so much condescension in it. Scolding, almost. As if she had been a child and did not know her own good.

It was as if a curtain were pulled back and his real temperament revealed. He did not care to be questioned or crossed. In truth, he'd seemed surprised that she would pursue an avenue of inquiry that he had already informed her was pointless. He might have even seemed a little angry over it—as if she defied him and had no right to do it.

Is that what life would be like with a person such as Sir John? Would she be free to speculate on intellectual notions, but only if they aligned with her husband's opinions? His condescension had been palpable, and that had been in a drawing room with a lady only recently met. What stance might he take with a wife? Rather stronger, she feared. It felt a heavy yoke she did not care to wear.

As she mulled it over, Kitty began to think that she must not trade everything away for intellectual stimulation. Yes, it would be a grand thing to discuss the findings of the day over dinner. But she must remain her own independent person. She would not be treated like a child and ordered about. Her father did not treat her mother so. Kitty Dell would need respect, and she would need to like the person more than she liked Sir John.

Along with those ideas, Kitty could not quite push away the idea of Lord Grayson. Dashing, charming, and, as her mother said, fun. She doubted very much if Lord Grayson would be bothered if she held a differing opinion. He certainly had never spoken to her as father to a daughter. But he was also dangerous, or so it seemed. Danger or no, it was the lord who made her heart beat faster. Had he been a more reliable choice, she could not say where her feelings might have led her.

Where was the man in the middle of those two? An intelligent, reliable man who was just a little bit dashing and fun? She had not met that man yet. She could only hope that she might.

A loud knocking on the door pulled Kitty from her reverie. She waited with anticipation for Hidgson to answer it. She would very soon discover how she was to walk into Lady Blakeley's ballroom.

After what seemed an hour but must only be a minute, a footman opened the door and Hidgson came through with four beribboned boxes.

"Lay them on the table, Hidgson," Lady Penderton said.

Hidgson looked far more animated that was his usual countenance. Kitty was aware that the entire household waited with bated breath to discover the contents of the boxes. Lady Penderton said they were firm in their belief that the masks were a direct reflection on themselves. They would not rest until they knew their fates.

Hidgson laid down the boxes and slowly walked toward the door. Exceedingly slowly, Kitty thought. Two of the footmen were standing just outside, looking as if they hardly knew how they got there. Nobody was doing anything usual.

"Hidgson," Lady Penderton said kindly, "you'd best stay in case we need something. You may leave the drawing room door open."

Hidgson stopped in his tracks and did his best to hide his smile, as he had long advertised the opinion that a butler ought not smile more than four times a year.

Kitty was handed her box and opened it hurriedly. The entire morning had been one long wait, she would not delay longer.

The mask was sequined and the design was of two very wide purple eyes that sparkled in the sunlight pouring through the drawing room windows. The lashes were of the same color and broad, like the petals of a flower. "It is lovely," Kitty said, "but what can it mean?"

"Those eyes look as if they've seen a ghost," Frederick said.

"When you have gone to enough of Lady Blakeley's half-masques, you will be quicker in divining her meaning. I believe I know it—read the note, Kitty."

Kitty unfolded the small paper included in the box. *For the lady who studies flowers. Fondly, Lady B.*

"Flowers. Eyebright," Kitty said. "The mask is eyes made bright?"

"Just so," Lady Penderton said. The baroness turned to her son, who was tearing open his box. Kitty suppressed a smile. It was possibly the only time eyebright had been mentioned that Frederick had not teased her over it. He was far too taken up with discovering how he would be portrayed.

He pulled out the mask and said, "It is a depiction of an empty chair. Blast! She finds sitting next to me is akin to sitting next to an empty chair! I really did try to be amusing!"

"I very much doubt you are correct in that assumption," Lady Penderton said. "I find you very amusing."

Frederick scrambled to unfold the accompanying note. His shoulders relaxed and he heaved a sigh of relief. "It says: Empty chairs all round, as no lady sits out thanks to Frederick Dell."

"She has observed your good nature at more than one ball," Lady Penderton said. "She once commented to me that every hostess in London must seek out Frederick Dell, as his efforts surely must stop tears in retiring rooms and otherwise bruised feelings."

"Does it ever really come to that?" Frederick asked. "Crying because one has had to sit out?"

Kitty did not think *she* would cry over it, but then, she had not experienced it. It certainly would be uncomfortable to be so publicly left behind.

"It most certainly does come to that from time to time," Lady Penderton said. "It is not the lack of dancing that stings, it is the many pitying eyes while the lady sits that does it. Now, let me see what your father and I have got."

Kitty was just as interested as her mother. Lord Penderton did not attend very many functions, but he was a particular admirer of Lord Blakeley's liberal politics so he would rouse himself, and even don a mask, to encounter the gentleman.

"Ah yes," Lady Penderton said. "I am to be Gaia and your father is Zeus. He is the god of the sky and I am mother of the earth. She writes: Like a kite on a string, every philosophical man must be pulled down to earth for dinner eventually." The baroness clapped her hands in delight. "Oh, how very apt!"

Kitty let out a breath she did not even realize she'd been holding. They were to arrive to Lady Blakeley's masque unscathed.

CHAPTER TWELVE

Sᴀ Jᴏʜɴ Kᴜʟʟᴇʜᴀᴍɴᴅ, as he currently called himself, sat in his empty drawing room. He held the book in his hands, though he did not read it. He had memorized every page and found that just holding it gave him comfort.

When he'd first discovered the book, he'd realized it had been sent to him by God to lift him from his misery. He'd spent his life educating himself, ready to take over his father's small estate in Peterborough when that gentleman passed on. He intended to increase the family's holdings and take his place in fine society and, therefore, he must be educated, erudite, a person of standing that one wished to have at one's table.

As fate would have it, his father had not managed well. The old man might have done better had his wife still lived, as he remembered his mother as a sensible sort of person. As it was, his father had made disastrous investments and was deep in debt. No possible mortgage would cover the mountain to be paid. All of that, and the fact that the estate must be sold, was unknown to him until after his father was laid in the ground.

What was he to do if he was not to be the master of the hall?

He was a landowner with no land.

He'd taken a lease on a small property nearby, though with no money coming in, he knew that could not go on forever.

He'd ruminated for months, certain he had been badly used.

His fate could not be what it was. A mistake had been made somewhere.

His days and nights blended together as he walked the small, rented house searching for an answer. He rarely slept. Who could sleep with the world closing in upon one? His options dwindled away, one by one. He thought he might marry and regain his footing that way. But to who? The only eligible girl, Miss Agnes Rosings of Rosedale Farm, had laughed in his face and told him he was both poor and a bore. He would have slapped her had her mother not been in the next room. As it was, he'd been forced to admit to himself that he had not that charm that might make a girl blind to his financial shortcomings.

He thought he might buy some small plot of land with the money he had left, he might work his way up again with diligence, making a profit and buying more land.

That possibility had faded to nothing. He'd had too many pressing needs to fulfill—rent, food, drink, firewood, and especially, laudanum. That helpful draught was the only thing that kept him sane. He must have it. And yet, it took up so much of his resources.

One day, as he searched the little rented house, always hoping to discover some cache of coins somebody had forgot about, he'd found a book. It was small in size and tucked neatly above a rafter. Certainly, it must be of some value if someone had hidden it so well. He might sell it.

He'd sat down in front of his woefully small fire and read it from beginning to end. It was a diary, by he knew not who. It was only signed *A faithful servant to Sir John Hill.*

There, he'd read a story very like his own. This faithful servant detailed an intelligent and resourceful master who'd made many contributions and was cast aside by the very place that should have welcomed him—The Royal Society of London.

The parallels to his own life were unmistakable! Sir John Hill had been wronged, as he had been wronged! John Hill had not been allowed to take his proper place, just as he had been barred from it! In truth, he had fared even worse than John Hill—he'd been rejected by *everybody*. Nobody asked him to dine anymore, they just gave him pitying glances and avoided his eye.

It was then that it became clear to him that the whole of society was rigged. The powerful made certain that the ones with no power never got any. A duke might be foolish beyond measure and mortgage his estates, and yet he was still a duke and ate a fine dinner every night. Money and credit were thrown at those who did not need it and denied to those who did. A man like himself always teetered on the brink of disaster. One small push was all it took to send a man flying down a pit he could not climb out of.

The laudanum, as he increased the doses, helped him see how things were in the world even more clearly than he had before. He had not lost everything and been sent to this house only to die in misery. He had been sent to find the book, as the only person who could understand its significance. He had been sent to revenge John Hill and raise himself up in the process. John Hill had been wronged by Martin Folkes and Lord George Penderton. Neither of those fellows were responsible for his own losses, or even alive at this late date, but they were the keys to his rise. Like Jesus, he would be born again, and the descendants of those two criminals would pay for his restoration to life.

Once he'd realized that God had sent him on a mission, that he was meant for great things, the plans came to him fast and quick. It was not a month before he'd sold all of his furniture and rented the house hard by St. George's church.

As he read and re-read the book, he was more and more encouraged that the wrong would be righted through him. He would take his place as a rich man, given courtesy and inspiring fear. Further, he would do it in a rather elegant fashion—he would rip back his fate with the help of John Hill. Society would know the tables had been turned, certain persons would know that every crime had its price, though the bill had been a long time coming due.

It was a modern-day crusade and he was its only and most powerful knight. He was veritas and lux—truth and light.

He must just tread carefully now. Though he was well-aware that he was not particularly talented at unraveling the nuances of other people, he was certain Miss Dell had tried to put him off when he spoke to her in Mrs. Herschel's drawing room.

Why, though? She gave every appearance of being a lady who wished to discuss scientific discoveries and theories. And he *had* discussed them with her. What was there to oppose him? Certainly no other gentleman would humor her so.

And why had she been so obstinate as to suggest Grayson's theory that there was a connection between John Hill and Veritas? He'd made his opinion on the matter very clear in Lady Milton's drawing room. That avenue of inquiry was to be discounted. Why had she gone on with it?

Though he could not imagine that Lord Grayson held sway over the lady, she did not give up on his idea.

It was confounding.

Rather than spend hours trying to divine the incomprehensible, he decided he must just move forward in his plan. He did not think Miss Dell was in love with him. He guessed that she attempted to put him off because of that fact. He also knew it would be quite beyond his powers to transform himself into some dashing rake, leading women into corners to whisper frivolous compliments. As far as he could tell, women lost their reason over such fellows, had they much reason to lose.

No, a strategy such as that was doomed to fail. What might not fail, though, was family pressure. He would present himself to Lord Penderton. His credentials were convincing enough and it was likely that the lord would jump at the chance to marry off his bookish daughter. Lord Penderton would be only too aware that suitors would not be falling from the trees to secure the lady librarian. She might be comely, but what fellow would welcome being lectured to on all manner of subjects? She fancied herself an intellectual over some staring at flowers she'd done. Any man of sense would recoil from it.

The only obstacle, as far as he could see, would be if Lord Penderton had secret hopes of Grayson stepping forward. It would be delusional, everybody knew Grayson was an unrepentant flirt, but many a father had deluded themselves with high hopes.

He must just lay out the facts and appeal to Lord Penderton's commonsense.

He stood and headed toward the library to find some paper in the desk. He would write to Lord Penderton and request an interview.

GILES FELT AS if the walls around him were closing in. He'd gone along so jolly these past years, with really not a care. He knew, of course, that people talked about his flirtations, but he'd felt it was all said in good humor.

Suddenly, in the past few days, the humor had seemed to fade. First Dalton had used his history against him by telling Miss Dell there were bets laid with her name on them. Now, he was in receipt of his mask for Lady Blakely's ball.

The lady had always been rather amused by his way of going on, but it seemed her amusement had faded.

LaRue examined the mask. "You will look terrible," he said, pulling at the curls.

The mask consisted of a tricorn hat, a black half-mask emblazoned with a white V on the forehead, and a flowing white curled wig.

"I will look worse than terrible," Giles said. "Lady Blakeley writes: *To our own Valmont and his dangerous liaisons.*" He threw down the note and said, "Dalton is very lucky he escapes this year over some family thing he's forced to attend. Why cannot I have a family thing? I cannot be painted as Valmont!"

LaRue succumbed to a rare fit of laughter. "*Les Liaisons Dangereuses?*" he cried. "You? As Vicomte de Valmont? I am amused."

"Stop your amusement this instant. Do not you see? Last year I was a collector of hearts. Now, I am cast as the worst sort of seducer! I am not a *seducer!*"

"Naturallement," LaRue said, looking over Giles' person, "no lady would agree to it."

Giles ignored his valet's latest salvo. "If I stay away, I will be the talk of the evening, it is always so. The honor usually goes to Lady Montague, as Lady Blakeley always manages to send her a barb. But this year it will be me!"

"And so, you must go?"

"How can I go…wearing this?" Giles asked.

"You will not go?"

"I have to go," Giles said.

"Très bien. You go."

"But then I am sure Miss Dell will attend and for her to see me in this?"

"Not going again?"

"On the other hand, she would never have been exposed to *Dangerous Liaisons*. Nobody would have ever mentioned such a book in her presence. I doubt anybody would dare it this evening. Of course, that's the case. No person in their right mind would discuss the subject of that tale with an unmarried lady. There will be those who know, and those who do *not* know. She will not know."

"And finally, you are going."

"I might come up with a different explanation, should she ask. I might say the V is for…valor?"

LaRue snorted.

Giles paced the room. "There must be something inoffensive that will have the ring of truth. Victory, valiant, vaunted, valuable—"

"Vacant?"

"Vanishing, vanquisher—"

"Vacillator?"

"Vicarious."

"Vapid? Vain? Villain?"

Giles spun around. "That's it!" he said, nearly at a shout.

LaRue crossed his arms. "Valmont was a worthy villain. You? No."

"Not villain," Giles said. "Vain. Everybody knows I take particular care with my dress. I can go as vain. Yes, that will do nicely."

"And these fantastical white curls?"

"I don't know. Maybe I am Louis XIV. The Sun King was known to be vain. Who cares? I have my answer."

LaRue bowed. "You mean to say, you have *my* answer."

THE BEGINNING OF Lady Blakeley's half-masque was always the most interesting part of the evening. Everyone would scan the crowd to see how others had come masked. Sometimes the masks were so obvious that one need not inquire who wore it or why. Other masques were more subtle and would inspire guesses and speculation.

Frederick's mask, the empty chair, would be one that needed constant explanation and Kitty was certain he'd be at it all night. Frederick had folded Lady Blakeley's note in his pocket as proof to the doubting, as he could not bear to think someone posited that he was as boring as an empty chair.

Kitty thought her own large and colorful eyes was one which might be interpreted any number of ways, though she did not mind as she did not think any of them particularly terrible.

She nearly forgot she wore a mask at all upon entering Lady Blakeley's ballroom.

Lady Penderton had forewarned of Lady Blakeley's original decorating. She'd even told Kitty there was an Egyptian sarcophagus in the drawing room and the dining room was such a riot of color that it made one dizzy.

The ballroom was as no other Kitty had ever seen, or even imagined possible. The walls and the ceiling, which one would expect to find white or cream or a light pastel, were painted the deepest indigo. Upon that interesting background had been etched the night sky on a clear summer evening. Very tiny pieces of polished silver and cut glass had been embedded into a constellation mosaic and they winked and blinked in the candlelight. The wood floors were in direct contrast to the dark walls, as they were pale and whitewashed.

Lady Penderton leaned close to her ear and said, "We are meant to feel as if we stand on the beach at Bolberry Down at midnight. Apparently, Lady Blakeley's father used to take his children there to camp in the summer and she has fond memories of it."

"It is extraordinary," Kitty said.

"Miss Dell?"

Kitty turned and saw a tall man, broad shouldered. His mask was a somber one, showing a man standing on a hilltop and looking in the distance. She could not fathom what it meant, but she need not wonder at the gentleman's identity, as she recognized the voice well enough.

"Lord Burke," she said.

He reached for her card. "May I? For supper, perhaps?"

Kitty nodded in acquiescence.

"Very large eyes, I see," Lord Burke said. "May you reveal the meaning behind it?"

"I am afraid it will bore you," Kitty said. "I spoke to Lady Blakeley about my research into Cornish eyebright."

"Ah, I see. And there are the bright eyes."

"Just so," Kitty said.

Before she could inquire into Lord Burke's own mask, another gentleman joined their circle.

Kitty perfectly well knew who it was. If her eyes did not perceive the well-cut coat, the particular way of standing, the smile always at the ready, her heart certainly saw it. It began its thump-thump, just as it always seemed to do upon the arrival of Lord Grayson.

"Miss Dell? I am certain that is you. Large eyes? In search of knowledge, perhaps?" Lord Grayson said.

"Something like it," Kitty said.

"If you don't mind," Lord Grayson said, reaching his hand for her card.

Kitty allowed him to enter his name, though she was not certain she wished him to. No, that was not it. She wished him to, but she wished she did *not* wish him to. She knew well enough that Lord Grayson was dangerous. Both Penny and Lord Dalton had told her so and she ought to believe at least one of them. That her mind kept presenting ideas that might explain away what had been told her was confounding.

"I see Burke has knocked me out of the way for supper," Lord Grayson said.

Kitty did not answer, there was absolutely nothing to say to a comment such as that. How she felt, however, was a different matter. There was a thrill in knowing that Lord Grayson would have wished to escort her to supper. A very wrong thrill, she was convinced.

"Good Lord, Grayson," Burke said, eyeing his mask, "what is all this meant to represent?"

"Vanity," Lord Grayson said. "I am vain, you see. Just as Louis the XIV."

"Why is it marked the fifth though?" Burked asked. "There is only the V. Where are the other numbers?"

"It is not V for five, it is V for vanity. Do not trouble Miss Dell with your fanciful speculations," Lord Grayson said hurriedly. "By the by, come with me. Lord Helmer is anxious to speak to you about a horse."

Kitty could almost see Lord Burke's brows knit underneath his mask, but he did not resist and allowed Lord Grayson to lead him away.

Her thoughts were taken elsewhere as a variety of gentleman approached. Most of the gentleman she had previously met, and she examined their masks with interest to guess if they said something good or bad about their wearers. She was not surprised to see one of them masked as all notes and coin—she knew from Frederick that Mr. Waverly was a determined gambler. On Sir James, she *was* surprised to see two pistols crossed and was very afraid that young man had recently found himself in a duel. It was the height of foolishness. The baroness, for all her easygoing affection for her children, had told Frederick if he ever engaged himself in that sort of nonsense, he would find himself staying with a great aunt in York for a twelvemonth. His most exciting activity there would be tea time.

Frederick's friend, Mr. Jost, had become somewhat emboldened behind his mask and had put his name down on her card. His mask was a natural scene of rolling hills with fluffy clouds overhead. Kitty could not make heads or tails of it until Frederick reminded her that Jost was a painter and that he preferred pastoral scenes over portraits.

Lady Penderton had been right about Mr. Jost's treatment— Lady Blakeley would not be so cruel as to tease a young man about his shyness.

The musicians began to tune and Kitty's thoughts returned to Lord Grayson. He had taken the first.

She could enjoy herself if she wished it. She must only be careful. There would be plenty of wagging tongues at this ball. If what Lord Dalton told her was true, her name had been bandied about in the clubs as Lord Grayson's latest flirtation…no, worse, her name had been *wagered* upon, it would be wise not to call attention to it.

She was grateful that Lord Burke had taken supper. A dance was a small thing, and nobody could say much about it. But, had she been seen at supper with Lord Grayson again, it would only fuel whatever rumors there were.

To think! If there were gentlemen who wagered that Miss Dell was too clever to succumb to Lord Grayson's charms, then there were also bets that she *would*. It was humiliating!

It was also a shame. There was so much to like about Lord Grayson. He was not an intellectual by any means, at least, not in the way she thought of it. She supposed she could not discount how well he knew Shakespeare, though it would not be her particular interest. And then he had claimed he would join in the search for Veritas and that must be something. He was always engaging, particularly since he'd dropped his habit of launching compliments in every direction. He measured up well when one compared him to the grim Sir John. And Lord Grayson's person was, well, it was wonderful. There was no point in denying that.

If only his standards were better. As it was, his moral compass would not exceed that of a tadpole. And that made him a dangerous tadpole.

It was quite the conundrum. How did she allow herself to enjoy dancing with the gentleman, but at the same time protect herself from him? How did she ensure that her feelings remained in check?

GILES HAD PULLED Burke into a room just off the ballroom. It was blessedly empty.

"Nobody wants to talk to me about a horse, do they?" Burke said.

"Of course not," Giles said. "I had to think of something to stop your wonderment over my mask."

Burke folded his arms. "Why?"

"Well, because…it is not the sort of thing to discuss in front of an unmarried lady."

Burke peered closer at Giles' mask. "What is it, though? What does the V *really* stand for?"

Giles felt his face grow hot. He had hoped he would not be relaying the truth of the mask to anybody. Yet, Burke was taking Miss Dell into supper. He must be certain his friend did not entertain any more speculations over it in her presence.

"The V is for Valmont," he said sullenly.

"Valmont? Comte de Valmont? From the book?" Burke said.

"Yes, that one," Giles admitted. "Deuced unfair of Lady Blakeley is all I say."

Burke sat down on a broad leather chair. "*Is* that all you say?"

"What else is there to say? One moment Lady Blakeley thinks me amusing, the next she thinks me a scoundrel."

"You have always been a scoundrel, whether Lady Blakeley has ever mentioned it or not."

"I would not go so far as that…"

"I would," Burke said resolutely. "Every year it is the same thing. Grayson runs after a lady, then abruptly disappears from view. Every year some lady is left red-faced for her foolishness. You have used your position as bait to dangle in front of ambitious females."

"It was all in good fun. In any case, why should this year be any different?" Giles asked. "Lady Blakeley has always been perfectly aware of my infatuations."

"Because you toy with Miss Dell. She is a good sort of girl, I think. Not quite as…hardened as some others you have run after."

"She is not just a good sort of girl, she is the best sort of girl!" Giles said heatedly.

"Then why, for God's sake, would you wish to damage her?" Lord Burke said. "Why would you wish to drag her into your stupid little games? Why would you choose her as one of your victims?"

"Victims!" Giles nearly shouted.

Lord Burke stood up. "Yes, Grayson. Victims. You are a shallow fellow not worthy of her. You ought to leave her alone."

"I will not," Giles said stubbornly.

"Why not? What can it mean to you? Really, Grayson, think of someone other than yourself for once in your life."

Lord Burke turned on his heel and strode out the door, slamming it behind him.

Giles stood in the middle of the floor, shocked at the dressing-down he'd just received. Among his friends, Burke had always been a bit of a scruples magistrate, reminding them all when they went too far. Dalton once called him old aunt Bess after being scolded about something or other.

But never had Burke been so…insulting.

Burke was wrong though, was he not? After all, he only…what did he do exactly? Giles could not deny that this year's flirtation was different from season's past. There was no battle of witty phrases or batting eyelashes or a scheming mama dropping leaden hints. And, he could not ignore that he'd read a pile of papers from the Royal Society, sent letters all over Europe, and spied on Sir John's house. Those things were rather beyond what he'd ever done for any lady in the past. In truth, he'd never done anything for a lady beyond flattering words and unsigned posies.

He slowly sat down. Burke said Miss Dell was a good sort of girl. That was not even close to what she was. She was a marvelous sort of girl.

Burke was right on one point, though. She was a *different* sort of girl. She had not the wiles and tricks of his other flirtations. Those ladies had been as armored as himself and could handily come out of battle unscathed. Miss Dell was a different sort.

He ought to let her go.

Giles slowly sank down into the chair so recently vacated by his friend. A truth that had lingered in his mind, just below his conscious thoughts, began to make its way forward.

As the fog fell away from that truth, he felt a near overwhelming tension. It was very like the few moments before a battle began, those moments when all life teetered on the balance and nobody breathed.

The outer shell of his heart, that shell he had so relied on always, began to crack and crumble. He felt it almost collapsing into itself and despair rushed over him.

He was in love with Miss Dell.

Not the other loves he'd so fleetingly enjoyed across the years. Not the surface gayness that held no personal danger. This was a deeper more permanent thing. It felt as if it lived at the core of him. Almost as if it had always been there, waiting to be revealed. It was as Shakespeare and Byron described it. It was as Miss Austen had portrayed. An everlasting thing that could not be denied or forgotten. It was awful and wonderful.

And, in that moment, he knew just as clear that she'd never have him. He was not good enough for Katherine Dell. Not even close.

Despite all his planning and efforts, the worst had befallen him. He had put himself in a lady's power. Valmont had been defeated by his own machinations.

"What am I to do?" he whispered. As he whispered it, he knew what he must do. He must leave her alone. He must stop dancing and dining with her. He must allow her the time and opportunity to meet with some fellow more worthy than himself.

As he ruminated about fellows more worthy, Sir John came into his mind like an unwelcome houseguest. Giles was certain the fellow was a villain, just as he himself was a villain, though in a different manner. If he would protect Miss Dell from himself, he would protect her from Sir John as well. She fancied she liked Sir John, he thought. Or she admired him. He would not allow the weasel Sir John to take advantage of that fact.

At this moment, he would very much like to ride his horse out of town and closet himself at some friend's house in the country. He must stay where he was, though. He must stay until Sir John's connection to Veritas was revealed.

The best he could do for Miss Dell was protect her from *all* the villains in her orbit.

Giles heard the door swing open behind him. He turned and found Lady Blakeley poking her head in.

"Come Lord Grayson, my musicians are ready to start."

CHAPTER THIRTEEN

KITTY HAD BEEN used to Lord Grayson's banter during a dance, and now found he had none. It was a strange circumstance, as she had never observed the lord so subdued.

Despite the idea that she should have been relieved, she found herself rather disturbed by it.

What had happened? It was almost as if he did not admire her as he had done only a quarter hour before. She did not like the clenching of her heart upon considering it. She ought to be grateful, but she did not feel grateful at all.

She was very much of a mind to cheer him up. To bring him back to what he always was.

"Lord Grayson," she said, as they passed round one another, "I do not believe Lady Blakeley has named you vain. I suspect her note was of another flavor altogether."

"Perhaps it was, Miss Dell," Lord Grayson said, "but some things may be better hidden from view."

"That is mysterious," Kitty said. In truth, it was more than mysterious. What on earth must be hidden from view?

"Mayhap Sir John will look into the mystery of my mask, he seems to like that sort of thing," Lord Grayson said in a derisive tone.

Kitty was entirely flummoxed. Why were they now talking of Sir John?

"I will just say, Miss Dell," Lord Grayson said, "that some fellows are not what they seem. The clues may be in front of one and easily divined if one would only look at them."

Kitty did not answer. How could she when he spoke in such riddles? And so seriously, too. He wished to point out that some men are not what they seem and clues are there if one would only look.

She glanced up at Lord Grayson and saw him staring down at her, his curls moving with the dance and that large V on his forehead.

Like a puzzle where all the pieces seemed not to go together until they suddenly snapped in place, Kitty saw a picture emerge. The V on his forehead, the mystery, the clue one was looking at.

The V was for Veritas.

No, it could not be. Could it? Could Lord Grayson have been Veritas all along?

Why? Why would he do it?

Kitty began to get a sinking feeling. It might be a joke, some prank he and his friends had invented. She knew very well he thought the Royal Society's pursuits silly. Perhaps he and his friends laughed over sending the intellectuals running in all directions over a letter.

If he *was* Veritas, then he had certainly not written to relations on the continent to discover if there were a connection between Veritas and John Hill. How easy to say so and yet do no such thing.

Though where would he even have heard of John Hill to even inspire the jest? It was an old history, *she* had certainly never heard of it. Her father had known the story and never bothered to mention it before the letter arrived. It could not be a thing often spoken of.

Perhaps it need only be spoken of once. Perhaps Lord Grayson had overheard the story at his club? He and his friends would have laughed heartily over the botanist's revenge—the paper *Lucina sine concubitu.* That a lady might discover she was with child from the air would be just the type of low subject that would entertain.

But for all that, was Lord Grayson really so cruel? He had seen how engaged she was in solving the mystery and unmasking Veritas. Would he really have played her for such a fool?

She did not know what to think. Was he Veritas, or was he not? She might as well ask him. Regardless of whatever answer he gave, she might divine the truth from his demeanor.

"Do you say then," Kitty said, "that you are Veritas?"

"I say no such thing," Lord Grayson said, almost stuttering, "I point out that Sir John is Veritas."

"Sir John?" Kitty asked. "The notion is absurd."

"Is it?" Lord Grayson asked.

Kitty's head spun. First, the lord wears a mask with a V on it and hints that clues are right in front of her eyes. Then he says it is Sir John who is Veritas?

None of it made sense.

The dance ended, and very unsatisfactorily she thought. She must discover the truth. If Lord Grayson was Veritas, she must alert Mrs. Herschel that they had all been sent on a merry chase by a couple of scoundrels who amused themselves.

She must be certain, though.

GILES SPENT THE evening going through the motions. He worked to make conversation, though he was not in the slightest interested in the replies. He felt he must make the effort—were he to appear sullen it would be attributed to the mask he'd been assigned by Lady Blakeley. For all that, he found himself grateful to be wearing a mask, as he did not wish to be really seen.

Burke was right in his estimations. He had been a scoundrel and he must change his ways. He would never encounter another Miss Dell, of that he was certain, but he *would* marry someday.

He would marry a pleasant lady and do his best to be pleasant in return. Until that day, he must conduct himself more circumspect.

He suspected it would be all too easy. He had not the appetite for flirtations that he'd once had. Now that his heart had been exposed, his *real* heart, anything less than true was unacceptably false.

Miss Dell may have broken him, but she had also done him the favor of curing him of his worst habits. He supposed he must always be grateful for that.

As Miss Belrayton chattered on at supper, he could not help but ruminate on the nature of things. He'd always wondered why the old fellows at White's were so serious-minded. It seemed to him that they'd always been so. He now suspected that was not the case. They had just grown into men.

He felt he, himself, had crossed over that rubric. As if, somehow, he was older. He could only hope that meant he was wiser.

He would carry on with what he now knew to be right. The chasing of Miss Dell would end, he would expose Sir John, and he would retreat to the countryside to become better acquainted with this new person he was becoming. Perhaps he might ask Burke for some tips. Perhaps he might even go to stay with Burke. Certainly, he knew of no other gentleman who might guide him as well. That is, if Burke would still have him as a friend.

But first, he must expose Sir John. He had to get that appointment book out of Sir John's house.

KITTY HAD DONE her very best throughout the evening to concentrate on what she was supposed to be doing. She did not think she was entirely successful and suspected most of her partners had found her distracted.

She was far too taken up with considering how she might discover the truth about Lord Grayson. Was he Veritas? Were they all only being mocked?

Her thoughts had gone round and round and her scientific mind knew she did not have enough facts to form a rational hypothesis. She needed more information and Lord Burke just might have it.

She did not think Lord Burke, as one of Lord Grayson's friends, would give up the information so easily. Kitty decided the only way to confirm what she suspected was to pretend she already knew it as fact. She would have ample time to come to a conclusion over supper.

"Lord Burke," she said, after they'd gone through the usual pleasantries, "I know very well that Lord Grayson is not painted vain or as Louis XIV. I know very well the V is not for vanity, *vain* though he might be. I know what the V really stands for."

Lord Burke appeared thoughtful and stared at his fork as if it were a fascinating thing.

After a long pause, he said, "I wish you had not been made aware. A shocking bit of business, I am sorry you should know it."

"I think everybody ought to know it," Kitty said. "It will not be right to fail to expose who Lord Grayson really is."

Lord Burke looked alarmed and Kitty supposed he did not wish to be a part of exposing Lord Grayson as Veritas. She did not know why he should mind it, it was only his friend being exposed as a ridiculous prankster and had nothing to do with him, she was sure.

"Miss Dell," he said seriously, "this is an unsavory subject for a young lady and I dearly hope you stay well clear of it."

Lord Burke made the pronouncement with particular gravity. Kitty wondered why it was so, until it occurred to her that at some moment in time, the ruse would be exposed. All those intellectuals who had fallen for it would be mocked, perhaps even in the newspapers.

The lord did not wish her to be among those who were ridiculed.

Neither did she, for that matter. However, the truth must come out. They could not all go on searching for a villain who did not exist. They may have fallen for the hoax, but the longer they went on with it, the more foolish they would seem.

She must find a way to put a stop to it.

GILES HAD RISEN early, determined to carry out his duty. As the only thing he had in mind was to get hold of Sir John's appointment book, he had thoroughly briefed LaRue on the plan.

LaRue, upon hearing he was to have dealings with a charwoman, was just as offended as Giles had thought he would be.

"C'est en dessous de LaRue!"

Giles might have wondered at the meaning, if LaRue was not always complaining that something was below him or otherwise offending his dignity. He had the career of a valet and the pride of a king.

"What do you think you sold my coats for?" Giles said. "You understood the plan from the beginning so there's no use complaining about it. In any case, I pay you to serve me and so you should not complain at all. I'm sure other valets do not carry on as you do."

LaRue had straightened himself to his full height, which was not much of a height at all. "You *pay* me? Mon Dieu, I suffer amnesia! When did this happen?"

Of course, he had not paid LaRue in quite some time. "All right, you've made your point. I *will* pay you, at some later date. In any case, *I* cannot approach a charwoman and suggest she steal from the house. It has to be you."

"Of course," LaRue said. "And you, my wonderful employer, will wave to me as I swing from the gallows."

"I will not let you down, if it comes to that."

LaRue had continued to complain all the way to Sir John's neighborhood. They had arrived just as the sun was coming over the rooftops. It was Giles' plan that they watch the house for their opportunity. They must see Sir John leave *and then* spot the charwoman. If that good lady arrived while her employer remained in doors, they would have to take their chance another day.

They found a bench on the sidewalk, alongside a bricked garden wall, almost a block from the house. If they leaned forward, they could see the comings and goings of the house. Giles pretended to be taking in the day at his leisure, while occasionally craning his neck to see if there could be any movement spotted.

Sir John finally exited his abode three hours after they'd arrived. Giles had been on the verge of giving up, and LaRue claimed he would faint in one more minute of fresh air. Now, the fellow strode down the street in the opposite direction as if he had some important matter to attend to. Giles assumed he was on his way to some library or other to collect more dusty facts for Miss Dell. Well, he would not get away with whatever he was trying to do.

All they had to do now was wait for the charwoman.

KITTY HAD ONCE again received an unexpected summons from her father. As she hurried to his study, she prayed it was not another book arriving. On the other hand, it might be even worse. What if it had come to her father's attention that her name had been the subject of a wager in a gentlemen's club? Or perhaps he had heard that Lord Grayson had been unmasked as Veritas and he wondered how she'd been fooled with all the rest?

The facts pointed to Lord Grayson, though something in

Kitty's mind had set up a small rebellion, arguing against it.

While she had told nobody of her ideas, that did not mean that someone else had not exposed Veritas using other clues. Sir John might even have done it. It was clear enough that there was enmity between the two gentlemen—if Lord Grayson accused Sir John of being Veritas as some sort of red herring, might not Sir John also be suspicious of Lord Grayson? There would be much talk after Lady Blakeley's masque—might some of that talk include noting that there had been a certain gentleman wearing a very large V? Might some of that talk reach Sir John's ears and he leap to a conclusion upon hearing it?

Lord Penderton was behind his desk with a sheet of paper in his hand. "Ah, Kitty, do sit down."

Kitty did as she was bid and waited for her father to speak.

"I have received a note from Sir John Kullehamnd," he said. "The gentleman wishes to call on me."

Kitty was taken aback. He had proposed doing so and she had clearly told him not to do it. Certainly, he did not suggest an interview on her account.

The idea that he would not dare so much began to crumble. She got the awful feeling that Sir John might have decided to do what he liked, regardless of her opinion.

"Of course," Lord Penderton continued, "there might be any number of reasons for his call, but as he does not name them I am convinced it is in regards to you."

"I am afraid it might be so, papa," Kitty said, "though I told him there was no need for anybody to call on my father at this moment."

"I see," her father said. "You were as clear as that, and yet he insists?"

"That is what I think, though as you said, there might be some other reason for it."

"If there is not, if our surmises are correct," Lord Penderton said, "why would the fellow ignore your wishes?"

"I believe," Kitty said slowly, "that it may be because he does not put much stock in a female's opinion. I only discovered it recently, he is…highhanded, is what I would call it."

"I would call it forceful, and I do not like it," Lord Penderton said. "He does not even really request an interview, he writes as if it is a foregone conclusion that I will see him." He looked over the letter and laid it down. "May I assume you do not like him?"

"Yes, you may," Kitty said. "I tried to like him, but I do not."

"I am glad, my dear," her father said. "When a woman marries, she puts herself in a man's power. Of all the unhappy marriages I have seen, the cause is usually that the lady has married a man who exerts *too* much power."

Though Kitty would not have expected her father to be so astute on this particular subject, he had summed up all of her misgivings about Sir John. She would have been in his power and as far as she could tell, he did not mind wielding that power.

"Can you imagine how the baroness and I would have got on if I attempted to exert control over her? If I dictated and directed?"

A giggle escaped Kitty as she really could not imagine such a circumstance.

"You may indeed laugh," Lord Penderton said, smiling. "The notion is absurd. Your mother and I get on well because we allow each other to get on how we like. I would no more inform her of what her opinions are than I would howl at the moon. You are well to be clear of Sir John."

"How should I be clear of him, though?" Kitty asked. "I told him not to approach you and he has anyway. What will you say to him?"

"I shall not say anything at all. I will write that I am not currently arranging any interviews and that should be sufficient. He will get the hint unless he is an absolute block of wood."

Kitty was certain her father would know best how to handle the situation. It would be awkward to encounter Sir John afterward, but she fully expected he would say nothing of it and that would be the end of it.

The door opened and Hidgson stood in the doorframe appearing red in the face and entirely put out.

"I am sorry to disturb, my lord," he said. "There is a gentleman at the door who refuses to be turned away. He is insistent that he must speak to you and claims he wrote ahead of time and you are aware that he would arrive. He says his name is Sir John Kullehamnd."

Kitty felt herself go as cold as ice. It had been disturbing that Sir John had gone against her clearly stated wishes and written to her father. But now, he had come to the door?

It was frightening, as if there was nothing to be said or done to put him off. For that matter, the look on her father's face was frightening. She could not remember ever seeing him so incensed.

"We ought to just send him away, papa," Kitty said, "We can pretend you are not at home."

"Nonsense," Lord Penderton said, "I have no intention of hiding from this fellow. I will see him, and I will make short work of him. When I am done, he will not trouble you further. Go upstairs Kitty, and then Hidgson can show him in."

CHAPTER FOURTEEN

G ILES HAD RETURNED to Dalton's house, glad his friend was out somewhere. He would not have liked to explain what he had been doing out on the town with his valet. As it was, he was certain they looked as two conspirators as they raced up the stairs.

In his bedchamber, LaRue took the book from his pocket and handed it over.

It was a small book with a strange binding, probably expensive. It was not a usual leather, it was exceedingly soft with odd nubs. Giles briefly wondered if it were rabbit or something of that nature.

"She was an uncouth creature," LaRue said of the charwoman.

"Who cares?" Giles said. "She retrieved the book. How much did you pay her, by the by?"

"Thirty guineas," LaRue said with a sniff.

"Thirty! Are you mad? That was all we had from selling off six of my best coats!"

"Mrs. Smat, as she is charmingly called," LaRue said, "was able to explain to me the exorbitant price. One, Sir John would know she'd taken the book and so she must never return *there*. Two, he would go and tell the service she worked for, so she must never return *there*. And three, she thought Sir John an unpleasant kind of man who might resort to violence, so she must not return *anywhere*."

Giles thought that, considering her well-rehearsed reasoning, Mrs. Smat had engaged in this sort of borrowing before.

"As Mrs. Smat so delightfully put it, *if you want me to be a-stealin' then you best pay me enough to tiptoe out of town. I ain't swingin' for no fancy pants*." LaRue straightened a cuff and said, "Naturellement, I informed the savage that my trousers were not *fancy*, only well-made."

"Never mind," Giles said. "We've got the book and I suppose I still have enough coats."

"Mrs. Smat has no interest in your coats," LaRue said. "Only your fancy pants."

Giles opened the book, hoping he would find a documentation of Sir John's appointments—where he'd gone and who he'd met with. Instead, it was a diary of some sort.

He turned the page to the inscription and almost dropped the book. *By a faithful servant of Sir John Hill.*

"Now, why would Sir John have a diary written by one of John Hill's servants?" he said quietly.

"One never knows these things," LaRue said. "Why does Mrs. Smat smell like a brewery? We can only make guesses."

As Giles flipped through the pages, he followed the description of John Hill's troubles. According to his servant, The Royal Society's determination to keep out his master was blamed for all the ills of his life. In particular, Martin Folkes and Lord George Penderton, Miss Dell's grandfather, were blamed for all his ills. The tone of the writings slowly turned from irritation to unhappiness to despair to revenge. This servant wrote with glee of the ludicrous paper John Hill used to embarrass them all. Finally, there was a burning hatred. The hoax of a paper had accomplished its aim, it had embarrassed the society, but it had not got his master John Hill the standing he was due.

Giles ought to have condemned the tale outright, but he ended feeling sorry for the whole case. As it seemed to him, John

Hill was a man of many talents. *Too* many. It seemed the society had never taken him seriously as a botanist, only because he had engaged in so many other endeavors. Perhaps the society thought of him as a jack of all trades, master of none. Whatever he was, John Hill had employed a faithful servant indeed. Giles could hardly imagine what LaRue would write of him, if he ever bothered to write at all.

While John Hill may have been wronged, that did not change the fact that somebody was attempting to use that idea against the society now. Sir John was at the bottom of it, though why it should be so he could not fathom.

How little he would have cared about it if it were not for Miss Dell! If someone told him of the story of the society tearing its hair out to discover some fellow named Veritas, he would have laughed heartily and never thought of it again.

And yet, here he was.

"The old Lord Penderton is noted quite often in this book," Giles said. "He was the current lord's father, Miss Dell's grandfather. So, Sir John claims to receive a mysterious letter signed by Veritas, he attempts to ingratiate himself with Miss Dell, and he has possession of a diary written by John Hill's servant which rants and rails against her grandfather."

"Perhaps he bought the diary from Mrs. Smat's cousin?" LaRue asked.

Giles would ignore LaRue's endless commentary on the horrible Mrs. Smat, had he not raised a valid point. Sir John may have acquired the book during his own hunt for Veritas.

That particular theory did not suit and so he put it aside. He had skimmed through pages but now he would go back to the beginning and read through everything carefully. He would consult Crackwilder on whatever he discovered. His old lieutenant was perhaps the only person he could trust enough to reveal exactly how the book had come into his hands to begin.

LaRue left to do whatever his valet did when he was off on his own. Giles suspected mainly what he did was go down to the kitchens, stare at *the barbarians*, as he called them, and make insulting comments in French.

It mattered little what his valet did just now. He knew what *he* must do and for that he required quiet. He needed time to read and think.

SIR JOHN WAS not always able to read other people's feelings accurately, it was a defect that had followed him all his life. People's expressions, or their tone of voice, often had no meaning for him. He was only aware of this because his mother had pointed it out so often to him when he'd been younger. She'd scolded him that he must try harder. For all her scolding, that skill often eluded him. However, he did not think he was having trouble understanding another's feelings at this particular moment. Lord Penderton seemed decidedly irritated.

Why, though? All he had done was alert the gentleman that he required an interview, and then turned up for same. Perhaps he should have named a day and time. Perhaps the old fellow did not like surprises.

Sir John tamped down the smile that attempted to turn up on his lips. Lord Penderton would, one day not too far in future, be *very* surprised at how events unfolded.

"I cannot account for your visit," Lord Penderton said. "I understand that my daughter indicated she did not care for you to request an interview and I did not invite you to one."

"Miss Dell did demur on the subject," Sir John said, "but that is to be expected, is it not?"

"If you imply that my daughter says what she does not mean, I am afraid you are not very well acquainted with her," Lord Penderton said.

Sir John could see that some soothing of ruffled feathers was required. "My lord, let us be frank between us. Miss Dell is charming in her own way, to a certain sort of gentleman. I am that sort, but alas, that sort is not raining down from the skies. Most gentlemen, and I do not applaud them for this, wish to have a lady more interested in the pianoforte and sewing and things of that nature. A lady who likes the library too much cannot expect dozens throwing flowers at her feet."

Sir John thought he'd put the case straightforward. Even an indulgent father must see truth when it was laid out for him.

"I see," Lord Penderton said through gritted teeth. "So you do me a favor in taking her off my hands, do you?"

"If one wishes to categorize it so," Sir John said, "though I would be remiss if I did not point out the favor also being done *me*."

Sir John thought that was a particularly nice turn of phrase. Lord Penderton understood the real case of things, but it was gallant to claim Miss Dell's hand was an honor to her suitor.

Lord Penderton rose. "I do not know what is wrong with you, sir. You are either the most arrogant man I have ever had the misfortune to encounter, or you are dumb as a rock. My daughter does not like you. *I* do not like you. You may depart and never darken these doors again."

Sir John was momentarily frozen. He had, only a moment ago, thought he was very near success. Now the man was throwing him out.

"I did point out, my lord," he said, "that most gentlemen will not be interested in a bookish daughter. If you are so disdainful of a reputable offer, how will you get on?"

Lord Penderton's face grew an alarming shade of red. "Get out! Get out now. Hidgson, get this fool out of my house!"

GILES HAD READ the diary three times. There was not a page he had not turned over in his mind. He had gone to Crackwilder to talk it over.

After deftly getting by Mrs. Radish/Ra-deesh and one of her squalid children, he had jogged up the stairs.

Now, Crackwilder stared at the book in Giles' hand. "What do you mean, you purchased it out of Sir John's house? What does that—?"

"I paid the charwoman," Giles said.

"You stole it!"

"No, I paid the charwoman to steal it," Giles said.

"Good God, man, why?"

"Because it is the only book in Sir John's house and so I was convinced it must be of some importance."

"Wait, how could you know that? Have you called on Sir John?"

"No, not exactly."

"Then how—"

"I looked in his windows," Giles said. Even to his own ears, his recent activities were beginning to sound outrageous.

"Let me understand you," Crackwilder said. "You have been to Sir John's house, peeping through the windows. Then, you paid a charwoman to steal his property."

Giles nodded, as that *was* about the size of it. "You must keep all that under your hat, though."

"I will make the leap that these bizarre doings are all for Miss Dell," Crackwilder said. "You are determined to impress her with your investigative skills, which are zero, by the way. You have allowed your personal feelings to direct your activities. Another more astute gentleman may have looked at the facts analytically, but you are chasing Sir John simply because you *wish* Sir John to be Veritas."

"You have got the thing wrong," Giles said. "Yes, it is all for Miss Dell, but not for the reasons you think. I have given up the chase, in fact I have given up *all* chases. I only wish to protect her from Sir John. He is no good, I am sure of it. He has designs on her, I am also sure of that."

"Hold up. Did you just say you've given up all chases?" Crackwilder said quietly. "Do you mean to imply that a lady has finally—"

"That is neither here nor there," Giles said, cutting his friend off. He waved the book in front of Crackwilder's face. "This is a diary written by John Hill's servant, about John Hill. What do you think of *that?*"

Crackwilder snatched the book from his hands. "It cannot be," he said, as he opened it and began to thumb through the pages.

"It can be, and it is," Giles said. "So you see my instincts were quite right. Now, why does Sir John happen to have this diary?"

"Perhaps he uncovered it as part of his own efforts to locate Veritas?" Crackwilder asked.

That had been the first and only doubt that had sprung to Giles' mind when he'd realized what the book was. That had also been the doubt he'd just as swiftly cast aside. He was in no mood for Crackwilder to take it up.

"Nonsense," Giles said. "If he had unearthed such an important discovery, would he not have announced it to all and sundry at Mrs. Herschel's gatherings? Isn't that the point of those gatherings?"

Crackwilder appeared thoughtful. "It is true, I would have thought he'd submit it to us," he said. "It would be the first real clue anybody had uncovered. But perhaps he has only just found it."

"It is *you* who are being led by your feelings, not I," Giles said. "You do not think Sir John could possibly be Veritas, so you are looking for every reason to support your opinion."

"I am, indeed, because I really cannot imagine it. Sir John is, well he is an odd and awkward fellow, very serious and not very skilled at the social graces. He does not seem to know how to put another at ease. However, he is intelligent and, I believe, harmless."

"Try to imagine it is him, though," Giles said. "He's not

harmless, whatever else he may be. Read through the diary while I drink the brandy I have so helpfully supplied you with. On the morrow, I will have LaRue copy it all down as a record for us and send the original to Miss Dell."

Crackwilder laid the volume on his lap. "Send the book to Miss Dell? Would that be wise, considering the result of the last book you sent her? She might take it as some new jest. Or she might point out to Sir John that if his house has recently been ransacked, he might look to you."

"I'm not going to sign it," Giles said. "I am only going to write that it was found in Sir John's house. Even if I cannot yet prove his villainy, it will put her on her guard. While I do that, you must arrange to take me to Mrs. Herschel's salon. If Sir John meant to share the book, as you believe, he will mention it. He will tell all in attendance what he read and he will say it was stolen. If he hides it, if he says nothing, we may infer something from that. That something being, by the by, that I am right."

THE BUTLER HAD practically pushed him out the door and slammed it behind him.

The very worst outcome had occurred. He had been thrown out of Lord Penderton's house and told not to return.

What was wrong with the man? How did the lord not see the sense in what he'd proposed? Was the gentleman's judgment so clouded for love of a daughter?

It could be, though it seemed a bit farfetched. It had been his understanding that fathers were always trying to unload daughters, not keep them at home.

Now, he'd need a new strategy. Perhaps Miss Dell could be convinced to elope? It may have been a mistake to point out the lady's deficits to her father. Perhaps he ought to have mentioned them directly, to the lady herself. Naturally, she could not be unaware of her oddity.

She did not love him, at least he did not think so. But then, if she were to believe that he was all that stood between her and spinsterhood, that might put him in another light altogether.

Walking home at a fast clip, his thoughts bounced from one idea to another. He used his key and threw the front door open. His mind would settle when he sat himself down.

The first thing he noticed was that Mrs. Smat had not laid the fire. The second thing he noticed was that his book was gone from the table.

"Where is it?" he cried, racing to the spot. He looked under the table and overturned the cushions on the chair.

It was not there.

He tore through the house, though he knew somewhere in his soul that the search would be fruitless. He always left the book on the side table and nowhere else.

Mrs. Smat had not done her work. His book was gone. Something very terrible had gone on while he was out.

The old witch had taken it. She had somehow divined its importance, though he could not imagine how, and she would hold it for ransom. A note would arrive, and an amount would be demanded.

If he had the money, he would pay her. He would pay all the gold in the world. The book was his Nostradamus, his ledger of prophecies. All along, when he was unsure which road to take on a particular matter, he opened a page at random and a hint or clue would be there. If only he had all the gold in the world. But as it stood, he did not have much money at all.

If that charwoman had divined its value, and she must have or she would not have made off with it, might she not offer it for sale elsewhere? Might she not offer it to someone with more gold than he?

He wracked his memory. What had he ever said to the woman? Had he ever said he was going to Mrs. Herschel's salon? Had he ever mentioned any other acquaintance's name? Would she take it somewhere without even trying him first? He would be undone if she did.

No, certainly she would try him before taking it elsewhere. Perhaps he should murder her when she came to collect payment. But what if she brought associates? Mrs. Smat surely knew all sorts of low people.

Even if she did not, how would he dispose of the body? How could he be certain that her dead body would not be traced back to him? Who had she told of her extortion scheme? What would the service think had happened to her? Certainly, if they were questioned, they would point to him as being one of the places on her daily route.

He had been a fool to leave the book out as he had done. But how was he to know anybody but himself would be interested in it? Who, outside of Mrs. Herschel's small circle, would even understand the significance of it? It was only he who saw it for what it was—a crusade against the powerful. That secret, he had told nobody. God had placed the book in *his* hands, the almighty had placed the plan in *his* hands. *He* was the new faithful servant. It belonged in no other hands.

As he raced through the empty rooms above stairs, the book was not anywhere to be seen. His thoughts felt scrambled, as if he did not know what to think of first. He turned and went to his sparse bedchamber, rummaging through a drawer, and pulled out a vial of laudanum. He drank deep, knowing the liquid would settle his racing ideas and consider what must be done.

He sat at the edge of the bed, allowing the draught to ease him as it made its way through him. His terror began to recede and his rational mind resurface.

He began to think how he might talk round it if Mrs. Smat sold the book to Mrs. Herschel or any other person involved in the search for Veritas.

He could say he'd uncovered it in his own investigations and had been studying it for clues. How had he uncovered it? That, he did not yet have an answer for, but God would send him one when the time was right.

It would at least buy him some time. Would it be enough time, though? If this morning's interview with Lord Penderton had gone well and had he found himself betrothed to Miss Dell before sunset, he might have thought so. However, the meeting had gone terribly wrong and he still had not worked out how to overcome that particular obstacle.

There were steps to the plan! God and the book had given him all the steps. Everything must go in its proper order, that much he knew. He must marry Miss Dell, and *then* reveal that he was Veritas, the inheritor of John Hill's revenge. The inheritor of all the wrongs done to all the men like himself.

Miss Dell must come first. The revenge would be paltry if not for that. Once that was done, he'd have her dowry, take his proper place in the world, and thumb his nose at her father, George Penderton's son. The weak would rise up and the mighty would fall.

It might be a long and difficult climb to convince her to go against her father's opinion. He was not certain—how much did daughters really listen to their fathers these days?

But might there not be a way to skip over the long and diffi-cult climb? It would be risky and take some planning. On the other hand, it appeared he was in a risky position already.

As the laudanum coated every nerve ending and muted its activity, he began to think everything was as it was meant to be. God wished to challenge him. He was God's knight—veritas and lux, the truth and the light—and he must only prove himself.

CHAPTER FIFTEEN

KITTY HAD BEEN near terrified when she went above stairs upon Sir John's arrival to the house. She had seen his long, dark shadow lingering in the foyer and it had seemed to her something menacing. It had not been a quarter hour before she'd heard her father shout that Sir John was to get out of the house, and then Hidgson confirming that idea all the way to the front door.

Why would a gentleman comport himself in such a manner?

Perhaps she was naïve and did not understand the ways of the world. She had only witnessed her own parents' marriage and had based all her ideas on their happiness. Of course, she understood that a man was meant to be…the decider? In charge? Superior? To be obeyed?

She was not particularly clear on that point, but it had to do with the gentleman being given the courtesy of having the last word should there be a disagreement. She hadn't thought of it as actually true. She'd taken it as an idea society throws around, suggesting it was the way things *should* be, not as they really were. Frederick was always talking about a gentleman's purview, but he collapsed in a heap of ash in the face of Miss Crimpleton's opinions. Her father and mother did not have any sort of hierarchy, as her father had so recently confirmed.

As for money, she was well aware that the man theoretically

controlled it. Her dowry would one day cease to be her own. Yet, it was her mother who ran the household and consulted with the steward on occasion. Her father steered well clear of anything to do with the accounts. Kitty suspected Miss Crimpleton would do just the same with Frederick.

The outside world, though. That might be different.

Sir John was different. He was as her father had painted him—forceful. Frighteningly forceful.

She did not like it at all and she never wished to encounter Sir John again. While she *did* like Mrs. Herschel and would very much wish to attend her Tuesday gatherings, she began to think she would not. At least not right now. She would not put herself in a position where he might attempt to run over her wishes again.

But then, she did so want to attend. She wanted to hear of any discoveries relating to Veritas. She especially wanted to hear for herself if anybody else suspected Lord Grayson. And, after all, she would be with her mother. There was not anything Sir John could actually do to her and she doubted the gentleman would dare an unpleasantness in Lady Penderton's presence. In fact, she was likely to encounter Sir John somewhere at some time in future—perhaps it was best to get it over with and have her mother by her side while she did so.

There was a gentle knock on the door and Kitty knew it to be her mother's own hand. The baroness entered and said, "Ah, here you are. I am certain your father will wish to speak to you at some point, but not just now. He is so rarely in a temper that I think it has exhausted him. I have sent him in a tea tray to bring down his temperature."

"Sir John," Kitty said flatly. "I heard him being thrown from the house."

"Indeed," Lady Penderton said. "And I do not believe anybody was sorry to see him go. Hidgson was doing his very best not to smile and *I* was positively delighted."

Kitty took her mother's hand. "You did not like him from the beginning," she said. "Were you able to see something that I could not? For that matter, that Penny could not see either? She did think he would be so suited to me, and I did think maybe, at least, if I tried…"

"You should not *try* to like anybody. As for Sir John, I found him a tiresome person," Lady Penderton said. "Though, I cannot claim that I could have predicted precisely how arrogant and insistent he would turn out to be."

"I am relieved to hear that, at least," Kitty said. "I was beginning to think that perhaps his true nature was there for everyone to see, and then I did not see it until we had come to this."

"I will not say I comprehend anybody's true nature outside of my own family," the baroness said. "However, I *will* say that Sir John seems a tedious person who cares little for anything other than his own feelings and opinions. His wife, whoever that poor soul may someday be, will lose her sense of self. Her own opinions will dry up as she is forced to take on his own."

"Yes!" Kitty said. "That is what is so frightening about him. When I told him an opinion he did not wish to hear, he did not hear it. It was as if I'd said nothing at all."

The baroness played with the wisps of hair that framed her daughter's face. "And let us not discount his dullness. He is so dreary with that grim visage of his and taking everything in the world so seriously. Who would wish to live with *that* day after day?"

Kitty realized she had never really considered that aspect. "I initially thought, that is, I wondered if it would not be pleasant to be always having intellectual conversations."

The baroness looked kindly at her daughter. "Perhaps consider that it might be pleasant to marry somebody who is actually pleasant. There is no sin against fun, my dear."

Kitty nodded. She suspected her mother might be right. Her mind had been so consumed with the idea that she must find a gentleman who was interested in her thoughts and opinions on the discoveries of the day that she had not considered anything else.

"What about Lord Grayson?" Lady Penderton asked. "He is handsome, he is fun, and his prospects are excellent. I think, when you'd buried yourself too deeply in your books, he would reach in the pile and pull you out into the sunshine."

Before Kitty could answer, the baroness shook her head as if she remembered something amusing. "Oh, I know, they all say he is an unrepentant flirt and he will never be caught. It's all noise of course, every gentleman is caught eventually and I do not think him the type to carry on with that nonsense after he marries. And, I *do* think he takes more than a passing interest in you."

Kitty had no idea how to explain to her mother all that she thought of Lord Grayson. He *was* handsome, he *was* fun. She was drawn to him as she had been to no other. But she feared he would never have any real feelings for anybody. Beyond that, he might well be Veritas and playing them all for fools. At least, all signs pointed in that direction.

"Never mind," the baroness said. "Do not answer me. It is only your first season and you need not decide on anybody."

Despite Crackwilder thinking it a horrible idea to take him to Mrs. Herschel's salon, Giles had insisted upon it. He would see for himself what Sir John said of the missing diary. What a man did not say was often as illuminating as what he did say.

Though he had nearly convinced himself that observing Sir John was his sole reason for going, his more honest self knew there was another cause. He would likely see Miss Dell there too.

He had made a commitment to himself and he would keep it, he would cease his chasing of Miss Dell. Though, might he not look upon her? Or even have a civil conversation with her?

It would have been ideal if he'd been able to deliver the diary to Miss Dell ahead of time, and then she could have revealed she had received it anonymously. Everybody might question why Sir John had not immediately let the company know that he'd had it and that it had been stolen from him.

However, LaRue was taking ages to copy it out. Never was a valet so complaining! To hear LaRue tell it, his arm was nearly broken, his fingers gripped with the rheumatism, and ink stains were appearing in his dreams.

No matter, the scoundrel ought to be done with the job by the morrow. In the meantime, he would see what he could discover in the lady astronomer's drawing room.

As they entered Mrs. Herschel's drawing room, Giles could not help but note the looks of surprise on the other faces in the crowded room. Not the least of which was the look of surprise on Miss Dell's features. He supposed he could not fault her for her astonishment, it was the last place he might be expected to turn up.

She was lovely as ever, startled though she might be. She reminded him, just now, of a lovely sprite in the forest who had been amazed to be seen.

Giles had not initially spotted Sir John, though he had done a quick scan of the room. Now, he suddenly saw the fellow peer around a column and look straight at him. Though curiosity was on most of the attendees' faces, Sir John's expression was far different. It seemed some combination of fear and wrath.

The only person not in wonderment or otherwise put out by his arrival was Mrs. Herschel. Crackwilder had spoken to her prior of his wish to attend. Giles was not certain, but he believed his lieutenant had told some story of his having an interest in mysteries in general and had offered to lend his assistance. Whether or not Mrs. Herschel believed that story, or was interested in whatever help he might offer, he knew not. At least the lady appeared friendly enough.

"Lord Grayson," she said, "Mr. Crackwilder has told me of your fascination for the details of our current mystery. We are always happy to welcome more minds to the case."

Giles bowed and said, "You are too kind to invite me into your circle, Mrs. Herschel. I must confess that I do not attempt to understand all that you have contributed to our understanding of the heavens, and so you must allow me to be only a member of the admiring public on that score. In this matter, however, I am at your service."

"Charming," Mrs. Herschel said. "Very charming."

Giles thought he had indeed been sufficiently charming, though he could almost feel Crackwilder's eyes rolling to those just mentioned heavens.

"I believe you know some who are here," Mrs. Herschel said. "The baroness and Miss Dell, I think?"

As Giles bowed, Lady Penderton smiled at him and said, "How interesting to see you here, Lord Grayson."

Miss Dell, on the other hand, said nothing at all and only nodded to acknowledge the acquaintance.

"And Sir John, I believe?" Mrs. Herschel said, looking round the room.

Sir John stepped forward reluctantly. "We have met," he said dully.

Following that less than gracious greeting, Mrs. Herschel took Giles round to meet her other guests. Most were fellows he would not have been likely to meet anywhere. They were gentlemen, but not the sort who hung around a club gambling and socializing. He had of course heard of Lady Stanhope and her remarkable travels. The lady was as sunburnt as one would imagine she would be, but just as lively too. Mr. Lackington was introduced to him, and Giles made sure to mention that he had recently bought a book in the fellow's shop. He would have expected Lackington to seem more grateful over the purchase, but it seemed that shopkeepers of books viewed themselves in a higher realm from shopkeepers of everything else.

The niceties having been accomplished, Mrs. Herschel gained everyone's attention.

"I will leap straight to the heart of it, ladies and gentlemen," Mrs. Herschel said, her small person taking control of the party. "We are gathered here to share any discoveries anybody has made regarding the identity of Veritas. I am hoping there is some small string or breadcrumb mentioned today that we might follow, as I am at my wit's end. We do not understand what this villain's next move might be and I am very afraid we are running out of time. I do not think he will stay silent forevermore, some plan is likely in the works. Now, has anybody found out anything?"

The drawing room had fallen so silent that one might have heard the sound of a needle pulling thread through fabric.

While Giles noted Miss Dell staring at him out of the corner of his eye, he kept his focus intently on Sir John. The man's face remained neutral and he could not divine what the fellow was thinking. What he was *not* doing, though, was talking about a diary that had been recently stolen from his house.

Quite suddenly, Sir John stepped forward. Giles held his breath. Would he say it? Would he claim he'd had the diary?

If he did, Giles felt all of his ideas might go up in smoke. It was only by his silence that Giles could assure himself of Sir John's guilt. Saying nothing about it confirmed he was in some way connected to Veritas and did not want it discovered. That he most likely *was* Veritas. If he were to tell of it, that would portend an openness that would muddy the waters quite a bit.

"Sir John?" Mrs. Herschel asked.

"I do not claim to have come to a verified conclusion, Mrs. Herschel," Sir John intoned. "But as we are intending to share any bits of information or clues we may have stumbled across, I will note that it has been mentioned in my vicinity that Lord Grayson attended Lady Blakeley's ball wearing a large letter V on his forehead."

Giles took in a breath. What was the man saying? Where was he going with this?

"I only mention it as nobody seemed to know what it

meant," Sir John went on. "There was much speculation about it among a group of gentlemen in Hyde Park. As they mentioned the composition of the mask within my hearing, I did not move off, but rather listened to their chattering. None of it was particularly noteworthy, other than the very large V on the lord's mask and one fellow claiming there was some secret attached to it. And now, here he is, most unexpectedly among us."

The party turned and looked warily at Giles. "That is ridiculous!" he cried. "What do you even hint at?"

Sir John clasped his hands behind his back. "I hint that the V stood for Veritas. I hint that Lady Blakeley is in on your secret. I suspect it is some elaborate joke played upon a society that would never have you. I understand men of your ilk are fond of such things."

"My ilk? This is sheer nonsense," Giles said. He would very much like to say all he knew. That it was Sir John who was in receipt of a diary about John Hill. That it was Sir John who failed to mention that fact.

He could not, though. If he did, he'd be admitting he stole it from the house.

He glanced at Miss Dell, and she looked away from him. Surely, she would not believe Sir John's scurrilous claim.

"Lord Grayson," Lady Penderton said, "perhaps you might clear up the mystery and put Sir John's mind at rest. What *did* the V actually stand for?"

"Vanity," Giles said. "It was Lady Blakeley's joke on how much care I take with my clothes." He glanced derisively at Sir John. "More care than some others."

Sir John smoothed his coat reflexively and said, "Lord Grayson told all and sundry that story, at least that was part of it. The mask was also comprised of hair styled in white curls. I believe we have all seen the copies made of the portrait of John Hill and note he was styled just the same. Lord Grayson was heard to claim that he was painted as Louis XIV as some explanation of the hairpiece, though with only a V noted. It was a thin story, not believed by anybody."

"Sir John," Mrs. Herschel said, "you make a terrible accusation. Lord Grayson, how do you answer it?"

Giles knew not what to say. Of course, he'd known the story he'd told about his mask had been a flimsy one. But how was he to know the V would be taken as Veritas? It was absurd.

"Sir John hints that I must be Veritas. It is irrational. Veritas is not likely to wear a confession on his forehead." Giles stared at Sir John and said, "No, that villain will blend in and attempt not to be noticed. He will move in your circles and you will take him as one of your own."

Giles could see Miss Dell looking back and forth between himself and Sir John. She could not be in any doubt. How could she be? Surely, she esteemed him more than that? She might think him an unreliable fellow, but certainly not a villain.

"I can confirm your notion is ridiculous, Sir John," Crackwilder said. "Grayson is not Veritas."

"Then what was the V really for?" Sir John asked. "Why would its meaning be such a secret?"

Giles could see his story about the V was not going to hold up. However, he certainly could not reveal the truth, that the V was for Vicomte de Valmont. Not in Miss Dell's presence. He must only attempt to turn the tide in another direction.

"Perhaps," he said, "the gentleman doth protest too much. Perhaps one who really has something to hide attempts to throw suspicion elsewhere."

"Do you accuse *me* of something, Lord Grayson?" Sir John said, his voice dripping with outrage.

"I only think it unusual that it was *you* who received this mysterious letter. Why you? Why not Banks? If one wished to threaten the Royal Society, one would go direct to its president. Why does Veritas go to one so recently arrived? To one nobody seems to know much about? It seems convenient, were one wishing to commit a fraud of some sort."

"I would not think a gentleman such as yourself," Sir John

said coldly, "should presume to know more than the educated minds in this room. Your deductive reasoning, if that is what it can be called, is laughable. Leave the thinking to minds that think."

"To minds that think?" Giles said, feeling very close to losing his temper. "What is it, in your *thinking*, that you congratulate yourself upon? What does the society find itself so smug about? If you were interested in providing any useful information to mankind, you would ponder the nature of love, or why an innocent child is taken while a wily old man is left, or why men go to war, or what spurs us to have thoughts, or where do the heavens end and what lays beyond. Instead, you spend your time wondering how a housefly sits on a wall. You have mired yourselves in the minutia. You are absurd."

"Say no more, Grayson!" Sir John shouted.

The party turned to him in shock. Giles only smiled. "It is *Lord* Grayson, to you. And what would you propose to do to stop me? I advise avoiding any gauntlet throwing, I may appear a dandy, but this dandy is well-versed in pistols."

"Gentlemen!" Mrs. Herschel said. "I will not have such talk in my house."

"Quite right, Mrs. Herschel," Giles said, "My apologies. However, I think you will discover that Sir John knows far more about Veritas and his connection to John Hill than you imagine. And now, I will take my leave before this argument goes further and I am forced to do something about it."

After taking his leave of Mrs. Herschel, Giles bowed to the baroness and Miss Dell, though Miss Dell only studied her hands.

If Sir John had somehow turned her against him, he would pay for it. Not because he still chased Miss Dell, of course he had given that up, but because Miss Dell must not fall prey to Sir John.

SIR JOHN WATCHED Grayson depart Mrs. Hershel's drawing room, all the while working to restrain himself. If he had his way, he'd find a weapon and shoot the gentleman's head off or run him through. How dare that fop attempt to interfere with his plan. How dare he make accusations.

As his temper began to settle, an uncomfortable feeling stole over him. Those who only moments ago had stayed close and sought his opinion had moved off. He stood alone.

They could not believe the lord's claims, could they? After all, what could Lord Grayson really prove? What could he really know?

A sudden realization came over him. Lord Grayson had told Mrs. Herschel, in fact he'd told *everybody*, that they would discover that he knew more about Veritas and John Hill than he'd said.

It was Grayson. He'd stolen the diary. It must be so.

He cursed himself for his foolishness. Why in the world had he thought Mrs. Smat would have use for it? The charwoman might have read it all day long, assuming she could read, and not seen any kind of significance in it.

Grayson though, he would know the importance of its author being the faithful servant of John Hill.

But how would he have known the book existed at all?

He hadn't known. The lord had come sniffing around, determined to make him out a villain to Miss Dell. He'd interviewed the charwoman. Perhaps Mrs. Smat had even let Grayson into the house for a fee.

That must have been it. Grayson had gone in to look around and there was the book. It would have stood out, as there was very little else in the place. He opened it up, and he'd seen that it was written by the hand of John Hill's faithful servant. He'd slipped it into a pocket and made off with it.

As he listened to the whispers swirling around him, he found some comfort in hearing that the majority of them had nothing to do with him. Grayson had insulted every one of them down to their bones.

His thoughts were interrupted by Mrs. Herschel. "This seems a bad business, Sir John. I suspect there is some rivalry or discontent between you and Lord Grayson that has led to this unfortunate display."

"Perhaps you are right, Mrs. Herschel," he said. "Perhaps my own disdain for gentlemen such as Lord Grayson has led me to make surmises that may not prove true."

"And he, *you*, no doubt," Mrs. Herschel said, seeming relieved that her opinion was correct. "I suppose I am most sorry for Lord Home, as news of Grayson's opinion on his latest paper is bound to get back to him."

Sir John nodded, though he could not care less for Lord Home's or his housefly's bruised feelings. Lord Grayson would pay for stealing his book. He would pay for unsettling his plan. He would pay for it all. Though it would be best that Mrs. Herschel believe he held no grudge against the scoundrel.

He would decide what to do when he had time to think. For now, he must pursue his original goal for this visit. He must find time alone with Miss Dell.

Chapter Sixteen

"That was quite the performance," Crackwilder said, leaning back in the carriage.

"Yes," Giles said, "exactly as I predicted. He pretended the diary never existed, he did not say a word about it."

"I meant your own performance. *This dandy is well-versed in pistols*, indeed."

"I am well-versed!" Giles said. "I'm an excellent shot."

"Yes, I know it, but imagining you getting so wound up as to attend a duel is laughable. The time of day would put you off, for one. For another, you might wrinkle your coat at such a meeting, or worse, have a hole put through it."

"I will avow, duels are ludicrous," Giles said. "Mackinjay and Plester shot at each other last year over Mackinjay suggesting Plester's hair color resembled a carrot. They both missed and it was a waste of a morning for everybody involved. However, if there was ever a fellow I would meet on a green at dawn, it is Sir John."

"Do not allow your feelings to cloud your judgment," Crackwilder said.

"I do not," Giles said. "Are you not convinced I am right, though? In all that talk there was no mention of the diary. Rather, he attempted to throw the suspicion on me. On me, of all people."

"Yes, I heard, I was there. You may be right, but there is nothing conclusive to point to just yet. Not mentioning the diary does not equal guilt—he may have his reasons or some plan to get it back."

"Ha!" Giles said. "If he does think he'll get it back he's very much mistaken. I wonder who he imagines has it?"

"Probably the charwoman who stole it in the first place."

"The delightful Mrs. Smat. He'll never find her, she has tip-toed out of town."

"Further," Crackwilder went on, "it was hardly necessary to mock the publications of the society in such a manner."

"I read those papers," Giles said. "Not a one of them was less than ridiculous."

"As you see it. By the by," Crackwilder said, "what *did* the V on your mask really stand for?"

Giles cleared his throat. "A rather unsavory character named Valmont."

Crackwilder roared with laughter. "The seducer Vicomte! Of course. How stupid I did not guess it."

KITTY SAT ALONE in the drawing room. She had her sewing things spread out everywhere, as she often did when she wanted time to think. It was unlikely that anybody in the house was fooled by it, as she only very rarely produced a finished piece of work.

The gathering at Mrs. Herschel's house had been entirely unsettling. She had hoped to go there to hear of new information regarding Veritas. She supposed she had, but what information it had been!

First, Lord Grayson had come, which had been a shock. He'd looked especially handsome, surrounded as he was by rather rumpled individuals. She knew she could not fault the rumpled, those gentlemen had their minds on other matters. Her own father often appeared so after a long morning in his study. Still, their frumpiness came into sharp relief when compared to the immaculately starched Lord Grayson.

And then, what came next! Lord Grayson accused Sir John of being Veritas, and Sir John accused Lord Grayson of the same.

Her mind had circled round and round on the subject. She found she was torn in two different directions—the facts as they were known, and her less logical but just as compelling instincts.

The facts, stripped of any feeling, must point to Lord Grayson. Lord Burke had not outright said the V on his mask stood for Veritas, but he'd come close enough in his words to confirm the idea. Lord Grayson's own words, too, had felt a confirmation.

Against Sir John was only Lord Grayson's questioning of why it had been he who had received the letter from Veritas. There might be all sorts of explanations for that.

Her instincts, though, ran in the opposite direction. As the two men argued and Kitty sat apart, watching it like a play, it seemed Sir John must be Veritas.

Of the two men, it was he who seemed a villain. Lord Grayson's countenance appeared open and confident. Sir John's more wary and hiding.

She was not a fool, though. She perfectly realized that her opinions of Sir John had undergone an unfortunate transformation since he had approached her father. Must that not cloud her judgment?

And then, she well knew that Lord Grayson always displayed a rather open countenance, and he was likely skilled at acting that part.

For all that, Veritas might be *neither* of the gentlemen. There was enmity between them, they were far too different sorts of men to have a congenial acquaintance. Perhaps they accused each other out of hostility alone.

She blushed as she remembered Lord Grayson's accusation that they were all absurd. They were not, were they? Surely, the society's efforts were valuable to mankind's advancement. In any case, why should scientific men take on questions that could not be answered? Only God knew why the baby was taken and the wily old man left behind, or where the heavens ended. As for the nature of love, well, that could not be studied at all. It made perfect sense that science trained its eye on matters that *could* be explained. Like how a housefly stays on a wall…

Kitty nearly shrank in her chair as she recalled what had occurred after Lord Grayson had left Mrs. Herschel's drawing room. There were whispers everywhere, and Sir John had been left to stand alone.

Kitty had watched with trepidation as he made his way toward her. She hoped he would pass by and take his leave, just as eager to be gone as Lord Grayson had been.

He had not passed by. He had stopped in front of her and made commonplace conversation about the weather.

Comments about the likelihood of rain should not have affected her. But after he'd gone to see her father and been thrown from the house and just been accused of being Veritas, there was something deeply unsettling about it.

It seemed to her that any rational person must have either avoided her or raised one of those subjects. He acted as if nothing at all unusual had occurred. She was beginning to think that things that did not sit well with him were simply dismissed, as if they never existed at all.

And then, he seemed to take no notice of her mother's icy stare! Could he not feel her irritation?

When he'd run out of comments about the weather, he'd said, "Miss Dell, there is an interesting volume on one of Mrs. Herschel's shelves I would have you examine."

No circumstance slowed him down at all! He came on like a runaway carriage.

The baroness had risen and said, very decidedly Kitty thought, "I think not, Sir John. My daughter and I are just taking our leave. In future, there can be no cause to pull Kitty aside for a book or anything else."

Sir John had seemed on the verge of challenging Lady Penderton. She had stared at him as he stood in their way and said, "If you please?"

She'd said it in a tone Kitty had not heard from her mother. It was cold and steady and felt cloaked in animosity.

Sir John had reluctantly stepped aside and let them pass. Her mother had laughed about it in the carriage, but to Kitty it had felt a lucky escape.

Hidgson brought her mind back to where she was, safe in her own house. He'd softly knocked and now brought some letters into the drawing room. He held a package too and Kitty looked at it inquiringly.

"It is addressed to you, miss," Hidgson said. "I will present it to Lord Penderton as soon as he emerges from his study."

Kitty could well guess it was a book, and as she'd ordered several of them recently, from a variety of shops. Whenever she passed a shop window stacked with books, she could not help drifting in and inevitably found something she required. She saw no need for her father to review this particular package.

"I can take it, Hidgson," she said. "It is not from any suitor, but one of the books I have been waiting for."

Hidgson looked dubious and glanced down at the package. Kitty could see for herself that it did not have a return address.

"It will be the one from the tiny shop on James Street, I am sure of it," Kitty said, reaching out her hand.

Hidgson handed it over, albeit reluctantly.

After he had closed the door, Kitty tore off the brown paper wrapping. If it were the obscure little book on Devon flora she'd ordered, perhaps that would engage her thoughts for an hour or so.

It was not that book at all. It could not be, the shopkeeper had expressed quite clearly that the book was bound in brown leather. This was some strange sort of very pale leather. Was it even leather? It was soft, and yet bumpy.

She opened the book and a note fell out. She unfolded it and read:

Found among the possessions of Sir John Kullehamnd.

A friend.

"What on earth," Kitty whispered. She put the note aside and opened the book. There, inscribed on the first page:

An account by a faithful servant to Sir John Hill

Kitty began turning the pages. It was a diary of sorts, though an unusual one. Most diaries documented the writer's experiences, this one documented somebody else's.

That somebody else whose life unfolded on the page was John Hill.

Was it real? Had it really been found in Sir John's things? If it had, why was it not still in Sir John's things? Why had Sir John not mentioned anything of it? Who had sent it and how had they acquired it?

There were so many questions, and Kitty did not think she could begin to answer them before she had studied the book and was fully acquainted with its contents.

She stuffed her sewing things back in their basket and hurried up the stairs with the volume tucked under her arm.

GILES SAT IN Dalton's library, mulling over what he ought to do next. He'd sent Miss Dell the book and had every confidence that she would show it round, including his note, at Mrs. Herschel's next drawing room. As all those fellows congratulated themselves on being intellectuals, he hoped they could use their incisive minds to figure out the obvious. Sir John would be condemned and that would be that.

He would be off to the countryside to rehabilitate himself. At least, he would try. He had not the first notion of what would be involved, though he suspected it would be a self-reflection of sorts.

"There you are," Dalton said, coming in with a letter in his hand. "This is addressed to you and appears to have made a world circle before arriving."

Dalton handed over the worn and crumpled letter. Giles had nearly forgot he'd written to all of his unknown relatives on the continent. Now, it seemed one of them had finally written him back.

He opened it. It was from Count von Fersen, whoever he might be. Fortunately, it was written in English.

My dear relation of some kind,

I cannot claim to understand our exact connection, but as your dowager insists on writing us every year, I presume there is one. However distant.

In regard to your inquiry, I have not the slightest information about either a Sir John Kullehamnd or a Sir John Hill. As it is preposterous, I believe you have invented this for your own amusement, though I fail to see the wit.

I make the leap that this inane English jest is in the name—kulle meaning hill and hämnd meaning revenge.

Neither the countess nor I are smiling. Please do not write again.

Von Fersen

Giles dropped the paper. "That's it!" he cried. "Von Fersen styles it a joke and so it is. Sir John Kullehamnd. He's made up the name using two Swedish words to describe his aim. Hill and revenge. He revenges John Hill, who was knighted in Sweden. I knew I was right! Sir John is Veritas!"

Giles paused, an entirely new question presenting itself. Why was Sir John, whoever he really was, attempting to revenge John Hill? What connection was there? What purpose could it serve? What would be gained by it?

"Have you entirely lost your wits?" Dalton said, staring at him.

"No, not in the least. I am only going to solve Miss Dell's mystery, as I knew I would."

"Miss Dell's *mystery*?" Dalton's lips tightened and Giles could see he was getting ready to launch into a tirade about avoiding the altar again.

"Do not even trouble yourself, Dalton," he said. "I have quite given up Miss Dell. In fact, you'll be happy to know that I've given up on flirtations altogether and so there is no danger I will somehow end up married."

"And what, pray, has led to this remarkable transformation?" Dalton asked suspiciously.

"Miss Dell, of course. She is far too good for me. Burke pointed it out, you see, and I realized I must give her up."

"One can only applaud Burke, then. But what is this mystery and why should you solve it for Miss Dell, the lady you claim to have given up?"

"To save her from Sir John, obviously," Giles said, re-reading the letter.

"Nothing about this is obvious to me," Dalton said.

"Then order some wine and I'll tell you all about it," Giles said happily. "The story, as it were, is coming to an end."

As he said so, though, he wondered if he were not too optimistic. He still did not know who Sir John really was or why the man had set this whole scheme in motion. What he *did* know, though, was that Sir John had some kind of designs on Miss Dell and he was not who he said he was.

KITTY HAD CLOSETED herself in her bedchamber until the late afternoon, reading the diary and then reading it again. It documented John Hill's lofty dreams and aspirations, his new ideas, his hopes, and how they all unfolded. Some of his ambitions were realized, but his crowning ambition was not—entry into the Royal Society.

Throughout the volume, the writer's feelings on all of these happenings appeared to become more and more agitated. Kitty could not know if John Hill himself suffered greatly from his disappointments, but it was clear enough that this servant who kept record had felt them all keenly. The tone grew darker as the writings went on until they almost hinted at madness. The end most definitely hinted that the writer had gone down a very dark path and would not turn round. She read the last page again, wondering what had ever happened after it had been written.

My bones are consumed with the bitterness that has turned into a cancer and eats me alive. My master has been cheated, the world has stolen from him, and I see no way to avenge him. Pray to God somebody else finds the strength to do it for me. May some worthy soul become the truth and the light.

It was an extraordinary thing to think of, that one's servant should live their life so vicariously through the ones they served. Kitty did not think Hidgson would ever be so affected. On the other hand, whatever affected Hidgson would only be known to Hidgson, as that particular man did not share his feelings with anybody as far as she knew.

This servant lay dying, praying that someone else become the truth and the light. What did he even mean by it?

Truth. Veritas.

Whatever this poor, mad soul had meant by it, it seemed somebody had taken up the charge.

Kitty closed the book and rubbed the binding with her palm. She could not help, as she read the book, notice the odd binding that rested in her hand. It was strange, and yet familiar. It felt as if she should know what it was, though she had never seen anything like it. It was very like pig skin, and yet she did not think that was quite it.

She finally pulled out her microscope to have a closer look at it, as she was certain it was not anything usual.

Focusing the lens, a latticework of lines came into view. It looked very much like the crisscrossing of footpaths across countryside. Hair follicles were spaced apart. It was similar to the skin of a pig, but the lines were not nearly deep enough, the follicles appeared too close together.

She had seen this somewhere before.

Kitty abruptly sat up. She thought she knew where she'd seen this before. In the book of illustrations her father had given her along with the microscope. In one of van Leeuwenhoek's drawings that purported to be his own skin under a lens.

She stared at the book that now lay on her desk. It was bound in human skin.

The servant, the writer of this volume, had sounded as if he were going mad. It seemed now that he *had* gone mad. Completely mad.

What had Sir John been doing with this book? Why had he not told Mrs. Herschel of it?

Or was Sir John being somehow accused of something he had nothing to do with? Was this all part of Lord Grayson's jest?

"No, it cannot be," she said softly.

Whatever her roiling ideas of which man was guilty, she was absolutely certain that Lord Grayson would not bind a book in human skin. He would not purchase one so bound either. He would never send such a thing into her house. However little she might understand his nature, she was certain she understood that much at least.

Would Sir John do such a thing, though? Kitty was disturbed to realize that she could not be quite so certain of him.

Who had sent this book? Had it really been in Sir John's possession?

SIR JOHN KULLEHAMND, as he styled himself these days, paced his floor. It seemed a cold and empty space. The book was gone and not even a fire laid as Mrs. Smat had absconded too.

A few candles were lit, but they did not shed much light nor warm the air.

This room had once been one of comfort. It was here that he'd gleefully written the letter claiming to be from the mysterious Veritas. That letter that was to put all on notice that John Hill would be revenged. *All* of the John Hills of the world would be revenged. It was here where he'd reflected on how satisfactorily his plans were unfolding. It had seemed as if luck had been raining down upon him. He'd wondered how to further his acquaintance with Miss Dell, and then it had been the letter he wrote that drew her into his company at Mrs. Herschel's. Everything flowed smooth and easy.

Now, what had happened? His book, his very bible, was gone. Grayson had called him into question in front of his colleagues. Had the reprobate been able to raise any real doubts about him?

He sipped his laudanum, carefully managing the amount. He had not the funds to keep buying the stuff. He'd not thought he'd need funds much beyond this point, as he should be well on his way to married by now. He could have got ample credit once the banns were read and the size of Miss Dell's dowry understood.

What if Grayson spurred one of Mrs. Herschel's set to look into him more closely? He had counted on his intelligence and education to be the calling cards that would invite confidence and dispel suspicion. But what if someone asked to examine his patents? He'd had them forged and planned to use them on Lord Penderton, that fellow was unlikely to know much about Swedish documents. But what if someone like Mr. Mathews asked to see them? He did not think they would fool Matthews, expert on European patents that he was.

He'd done his best to dismiss Grayson once the fool had left Mrs. Herschel's drawing room. He'd also done his best to get

Miss Dell alone.

That confounded mother of hers! The baroness had looked upon him with what he thought might be hatred. She had refused to allow her daughter to leave her side and then just as quick, took her out to their carriage.

It felt as if his dream was slipping away.

It could not slip away! There was no other course he could take. He was practically penniless, having sold all of his worldly goods to set himself up in London. He could not start over somewhere, there was nothing to start over with.

Even if he had the means to flee, would he do it?

"Of course I would not," he said, looking up at the ceiling. "I am your knight, the veritas and the lux. I am only being tested, that is all."

He was certain God heard his words and hoped God would send an answer. If he were being tested, how would he pass the test? How would he succeed in the end?

He swigged the last of the bottle of laudanum and stood staring at the cold hearth for some minutes.

And finally, heaven-sent, came the answer. He remembered a particular line in the book, as if it had been sent to him to consider. *My master has determined that what has not been given freely must be taken.*

Of course he must take what was necessary to his success. He was a knight of truth and light, after all.

CHAPTER SEVENTEEN

KITTY WAS DETERMINED to put aside the mystery of Veritas for at least one evening. It was the night of Lady Hathaway's themed ball and she had looked forward to it for months. Penny had told her all about it—last season had been the remarkable Tudor ball in which Lily Farnsworth had been carried off by Lord Ashworth.

This year was to be Valhalla and Kitty had every expectation of encountering the God Odin and his Valkyries.

It would be a welcome diversion. The season had been meant to be one of entertainments and interesting visits to Lackington and Allen, but the cloud of the mystery of Veritas had hung over everything. Finding herself in possession of a book bound in human skin had seemed to wake her from an over-engrossing and dangerous dream.

She must put all of this aside! It was not her responsibility to unmask Veritas. Further, it was hardly a life and death matter if Mrs. Herschel's friends failed and the society was embarrassed in some way. And really, that ridiculous society did not even allow women through its doors! Why should she have all her thoughts taken up by this?

She found she could not help but be influenced by some of the things Lord Grayson had accused them all of. She *had* been a little ridiculous. If Lord Grayson was Veritas and laughed at her expense, perhaps she deserved it, if only a little bit. She could not ignore the sense of absurdity she'd felt as she'd read through the society's papers looking for clues. She knew the subjects were all worthy, nothing discovered was unworthy, and yet there was something silly in the over-formal language used to describe a fly's ability to land on a wall. It was the sort of style one might use to make a speech in Parliament.

It was as if Lord Grayson had shined a light on her doubts and brought them out for her to examine.

She blushed to herself as she thought of how often she'd spoken of her research into Cornish eyebright to people who likely had little interest in it. Frederick always teased her about it. Perhaps he was in some way right and she had been tedious.

It was not that she thought she ought to give up untangling the world's mysteries, or fail to be fascinated by others' observations, but perhaps she need not be so fixated on it. Perhaps one interest had blinded her to any other. Perhaps she might make more room for other things. She would not like to end as the faithful servant of Sir John Hill had done—obsessed with a single subject all her life.

She was young and she ought to be more carefree. She knew her mother thought it, and so far, her mother had been right about things.

Kitty had wrapped the book in layers of cloth and put it away. She did not know what else to do with it. Until she did, she would forget all about this nonsense and go to a ball.

Thinking of the ball naturally led, or so it seemed to Kitty, to thoughts of Lord Grayson. How unhappy a circumstance it was that he was not more genuine. What would it have been if he had come as a real suitor when she'd met him at Newmarket? What would it have been if all the world approved of him and were confident of his motives?

Kitty sighed. But then, she supposed, he would not be Lord Grayson at all.

"Are you ill, miss?" Martha asked, fussing with the folds of her skirt.

"Goodness, no," Kitty said, pulling her thoughts to the present. "Why do you say so?"

"It's all the sighing. I never heard so much sighing from one who wasn't pained."

Kitty smiled. She supposed she *was* pained. But if she was, it had been all her own doing. Further, what had been done could be undone. She was a young woman, fortunate enough to have been born into a family who had both the love and financial means to see to her every comfort and happiness. There was a ball this evening and, for once in her life, she would not overanalyze. She would go, she would dance and laugh, and she would analyze nothing.

LaRue brushed one of the few good coats Giles had not sold. Lady Hathaway's ball was this evening and it seemed the Viking theme was less than a closely-guarded secret. He had ordered that he would wear his dark blue coat with the silver buttons. It had a military air and was as close as he could come to an homage to a marauding Viking.

As LaRue fussed, Giles had spent quite a bit of time laying out all the facts in an attempt to unravel Sir John's motives. None of his speculations added up to much.

LaRue was not generally helpful, but this time he might have been. When Giles had finished listing everything he now knew, La Rue had said, "Mon Dieu, he is insensé. So many mad Englishman. It is in the water, no?"

Despite the insult of hinting that the English were all prone to madness, LaRue might have made a point. If something did not seem to make sense, perhaps the cause was that there was simply no sense in it.

Sir John was exceedingly odd, there was something not quite

right about him. He might very well be unhinged in some fashion. There *were* people that might pass themselves off as relatively sane when they were not. Hadn't he had an old great uncle who believed he could talk to trees? The fellow had got on well enough as he was convinced that the trees had made him promise not to tell anybody outside of a blood relation, and so he hadn't. If there was something wrong in Sir John's head, that would explain why there seemed to be no motive, no gain, in creating Veritas.

Now, his book was gone and Giles had revealed to Sir John that he knew him to be Veritas. What if Sir John were to become desperate? What might he do then?

But then, maybe the madman did have a gain in mind. It occurred to him that Sir John's real interest in Miss Dell must be her dowry. His house was empty, he clearly did not have the funds to furnish it. Wishing to make an advantageous marriage was not madness though, and it certainly would not have necessitated creating Veritas.

"My God," he said.

LaRue looked at him critically. "Your cloth is perfect, what more can you want from poor LaRue?"

"It is not my dress," Giles said. "It occurs to me that, yes, Sir John is on the hunt for a large dowry. But not any large dowry. In particular, it must be Miss Dell's dowry. He is out for money *and* revenge and only Miss Dell's dowry will do. It was *her* grandfather and Martin Folkes that stopped John Hill from becoming a fellow of the society. Folkes doesn't have a granddaughter of marriageable age. Only Penderton does. Marry Miss Dell and he ends with both—money *and* revenge. Though, I still do not comprehend why he attempts to revenge John Hill. Perhaps he is a relation of some sort and has taken it on as a family honor sort of thing."

"Miss Dell will hardly agree to marry the proprietor of funerals in the badly cut coat," LaRue said disdainfully.

"No, I think you may be right on that point, though not because of his clothes," Giles said. "At least, I would hope she has more sense. But what will he do if he is refused?"

"Carry her off like a Valkyrie?" LaRue said, clearly amused by his own wit.

"He might try something like it," Giles said. "Sir John's Valhalla being Gretna Green."

"It takes many days to reach the border."

"That is no matter," Giles said. "One night in a carriage alone and she'd be ruined. She'd have to marry him."

LaRue gave a final tug on Giles' coat to straighten an imaginary wrinkle. "As I say, the English are mad."

Perhaps they *were* mad. Perhaps he was mad. He was inventing plots in the air. It was highly unlikely Sir John had the fortitude to attempt such a thing. It would be a kidnapping. No, certainly not. The persnickety Sir John was not up to such derring-do.

On the other hand, what if Sir John *was* truly mad? If that were the case, commonsense could not dictate what he might try. Was there not madness in this whole mystery? Sir John attempted to avenge a man long dead for what cause? Only the mad worked to no end.

It could not hurt to be careful. Miss Dell must be put on her guard. Much more on her guard than she had been. He must tell her he sent her the book, and what he had discovered about the name Kullehamnd. She should not go to Mrs. Herschel's salon until Sir John had been dealt with. It was the one place he knew to find her.

SIR JOHN HAD kept a careful watch on Lady Hathaway's house. It had continually amazed him how easy it generally was to discern where a person would be in this town. That was, where a person from any kind of consequential family would be.

The newspapers outlined what parties would be held, where and when—most likely with the assistance of the hostess. For small affairs, one might see reference to particular guests. *Mrs. Jamison and Lord Reager are both expected to attend,* or some such phrasing. For larger scale events, particularly balls, no list of guests was provided, but usually a number to indicate the size of the gathering. In this case, *Lady Hathaway will host upward of two hundred.* Along with the size of the ball, it was noted that this was an annual ball and would have a theme. The newspaper claimed that the theme was always a closely guarded secret that was delightfully revealed to her guests upon their arrival.

It was not so secret as far as he could tell. As he watched the first comings and goings, it was clear enough to be a Norse theme. The front doors had just been topped with a papier mâché bow of a ship, a statue he thought might be Odin had been carried to the back of the house not a half hour ago, an enormous mural depicting Valkyries swooping a battlefield followed. Carts full of gold-painted shields had arrived. What he also noticed was the looseness of the preparations.

On a usual day, it would be impossible to penetrate the walls of such a great house. The front doors would be manned by footmen and a butler, the servant's entrance would lead into the kitchens and a territorial cook. On this day, the back garden was being transformed for the ball, and various workmen came and went as they pleased.

He occasionally saw a man in a stiff black coat walk among the chaos, his hands clasped behind his back as if he surveyed his kingdom. The butler, no doubt. But what that man never seemed to do was question anybody about their right to be there.

He could not initially see how any of this was to his advantage. He was certain Miss Dell would attend the evening, and he was certain that he must act quickly. He must do something before too many questions or suspicions were raised. He must whisk Miss Dell away. But how was he to do it? He had not even a carriage to carry her off in or a pistol to inspire some coachman to lend his vehicle.

Once he had calmed himself with a draught, a part of the *how* presented itself. As the hour grew late and the sun had already disappeared behind the rooftops, God took pity on his confusion. A large cart pulled up with all manner of costume piled high in it. As far as he could tell, there were long black capes and brass breastplates and metal headgear sprouting large black feathers. The helmet had a front piece of hammered metal with two slits punched out to go over the eyes. He very much suspected it was a costume meant to suggest Valkyries.

Sir John casually edged closer to the cart and overheard the driver's conversation with a servant who'd come jogging to it.

The footman peered into the cart and said, "Ah, yes, this will be for the footmen to wear as they lead the guests over the water to Valhalla."

The driver had snorted and said, "The *ton* do got their notions, don't they?"

The footman had appeared entirely affronted and said, "I suppose you've been paid well for the *notion*, as you call it."

"Aye, don't get your back up over it," the driver said.

The footmen nodded and said, "Never mind, carry them to the back entrance and somebody will take them from you."

The footman strode off to manage the thousand other things that must be attended to. The driver began to haul the contents of the cart to the back of the house. The old man could not carry it all at once, though.

His first idea was to take a costume for himself and bring it home. But it was too bulky! He would be noticed carrying it!

No, he must get a costume off the cart and hide it somewhere. A place deep in a stand of bushes where he could retrieve it when needed.

He hurried across the street and grabbed a breastplate, cape, and headdress. He casually walked to the back garden as if he were only one of the hundred workers swarming the site.

He must only take this first step of finding a way into the ball.

The next step would be revealed to him at the right time. He must trust that everything he needed would be provided.

KITTY'S ENTRANCE INTO Valhalla had been everything she imagined. No, that was not sufficient, it had been *more* than she could have imagined.

Lady Hathaway's back garden had been transformed into an eerie place, suitable for the dead to be led into the company of Odin. The trees were hung with wisps of black gauze that were like so many phantoms waving their arms in the breeze. The pathway was lighted by candles in dark-waxed shades, giving the way forward a ghostly amber glow.

It might have been amusing to see footmen dressed as lady-Valkyries, had the costumes not been so menacing. A black cape covered their uniforms, black plumes rose from helmets of dark metal that descended over the nose with only slits for eyes. They appeared expressionless and it gave her a shiver.

One of those footmen silently led them onto a replica of a Viking ship, with an opening in the back to step in. The outside hull of the ship had long narrow brass poles running along the bottom on either side that were fitted into a metal track leading into the darkness. The boat's tall and pointed bow seemed to reach yards ahead of them.

The footman-Valkyrie turned and pointed dramatically to the wooden benches that lined the middle of the boat. The party quickly seated themselves, hardly knowing what was to come next.

To Kitty's delight, four Valkyrie-footmen boarded and pretended to row with the oars. The boat slid forward on the track, and Kitty assumed it was being pulled by ropes from the front. As she craned her neck, she saw they headed into some sort of dark tunnel. It appeared an arbor covered in heavy black cloth.

Kitty gripped her mother's hand on one side and Frederick's hand on the other.

Frederick squeezed back. Though he was forever teasing her, he would not tease when she felt the need for his hand.

She knew she was being ridiculous, but this trip into the darkness felt almost ominous. She found herself glad to be so surrounded by her family.

They sailed into the black abyss. The party fell silent. The only sound that reached their ears was the quiet shush of metal along a greased track each time they slid forward.

It seemed as if they would be in darkness forever, Kitty could see nothing but black ahead. She almost began to feel claustrophobic and squeezed Frederick's hand harder.

Suddenly, the darkness gave way. A black blanket hung over the end of the tunnel had been flung off to reveal gay lights ahead.

"Well," Lady Penderton said laughing, "Lady Hathaway has quite the imagination."

"I have never experienced anything so marvelous," Kitty said. "It was as if we really journeyed to Valhalla. I cannot imagine what awaits us inside."

"Nor can I," the baroness said, "though I expect we will have roasted boar at supper. Lady Hathaway always gets all the details right."

"It will be a nice change from last year's conger eel," Frederick said, laughing.

They were helped off the boat and it began its backward journey into the tunnel to ferry more guests into Lady Hathaway's house.

The corridor they were led down had been turned gold with painted shields in place of wallpaper. Lady Hathaway stood at the end of it, wearing a headdress even more elaborate than the footmen and clothed in a flowing gauze gown, belted and accented with bits of brass to give the illusion of armor.

She greeted Lady Penderton warmly, and Frederick too. She

was delighted with Kitty, mostly because Kitty was so delighted with her garden Valhalla.

It was the ballroom, though, that took Kitty's breath away. It had been transformed into Odin's golden palace. The floor and the walls had been painted gold with flecks of the real article reflecting the candlelight. The ceiling, just as in Valhalla, was armored with gold breastplates. A boar's head was mounted over the doors, and a large mural of Valkyries swooping down onto a battlefield to choose their men hung over the musicians. At the far end of the ballroom stood a statue of Odin, placed where he might view all of the recent arrivals to his Valhalla.

"There's Jost," Frederick said, making his way off.

"Miss Dell," Lord Grayson said, suddenly beside her from she knew not where.

Kitty felt the usual flutter. In fact, even more so, as he had come upon her so suddenly.

He held out his hand for her card and she allowed him to put his name down. Kitty saw that he had taken supper. She felt a hesitation over it, but only for a moment. This night was to be too glorious to fret over whether Lord Grayson was Veritas or concern herself with wondering if she did not like him a bit too much for her own good. He looked smashing, as was his habit, the fit of his coat was perfection. She would dance and dine with him. Whatever the morrow might bring, she found she could not care less what had been said about her in the gentlemen's clubs. She could not care less what would be said when it was noted that they dined together.

She really felt quite reckless. Perhaps it was crossing over to the afterlife and finding herself in this magnificent ballroom. Perhaps it was because she had decided not to involve herself so much in the mystery of Veritas.

For all her carefree feelings, she could not help but notice that Lord Grayson seemed more serious than his usual self. Perhaps he ruminated over his encounter with Sir John at Mrs. Herschel's salon. He ought not to, this evening was not meant for ruminations.

After politely inquiring after her and Lady Penderton's health, he had moved off and crossed the ballroom to his friend Lord Dalton. Kitty's mother said, "Lord Grayson looks well, does he not?"

Kitty smiled. "He always looks well, mama. It is the one thing we can always count on him for."

"Oh, I think you can count on him for a bit more than that."

Before Kitty could question her mother's meaning, or scold her because she very well knew her meaning, a stern-looking older gentleman stepped forward. He was a rather frightening visage and looked as if he were on the edge of a fury. He was accompanied by Miss Danworth.

"Lord Childress," Lady Penderton said, her voice strangely devoid of its usual friendliness.

The lord bowed.

"This is my daughter, Miss Dell," the baroness said to him.

Lord Childress looked at Kitty in what felt like a critical manner. She had already gleaned hints that he was not the most pleasant person in the world. She thought she could see now how he'd earned the reputation.

She curtsied and it seemed as if he barely acknowledged it.

"I suppose I might leave my daughter in your care?" he said to the baroness. It did not exactly sound like a question and he did not wait for an answer. "I have another engagement and will return later."

"Of course," Lady Penderton said, though she could not entirely keep out a note of surprise.

"I imagine I'll have to fight my way through that ridiculous display I just came in on," he said. With that, he turned on his heel and strode off.

There was an awkward silence in his wake.

Finally, Miss Danworth broke it. "I apologize for my father, Lady Penderton, and you are not to fret over it. Nobody need look after me, I am quite accustomed to looking after myself."

Lady Penderton smiled kindly at Miss Danworth. "No doubt you are, but nonetheless you are to come to me for anything you need. One never knows when one may rip a hem or have a pin disappear from one's hair."

"Very kind," Miss Danworth said.

Kitty, herself, hardly knew what to say. Her own father would never have acted so. The man had talked of his daughter as if she were a grocer's box and he only looked for a counter to put her on.

Lady Penderton's attention was turned to an acquaintance and Miss Danworth leaned close to Kitty and said quietly, "Now that you have encountered my dreaded father, not even the Palaskar collection shall be enough to tempt you to my house."

"Not at all!" Kitty said. Though, really, Miss Danworth might be right. She would not relish encountering Lord Childress in his own house if he could barely be civil at a ball.

"But perhaps you might visit me at my house?" Kitty said. "I have not yet seen you there. I cannot claim to have anything as interesting as the Palaskar collection, but our cook does make a divine savarin if that would tempt you."

"You are very kind, Miss Dell," Miss Danworth said. "Though my father does not allow me many calls. Particularly he would not approve it if there is a single gentleman in the house who does not come into at least an earldom."

Kitty almost recoiled. What was said was in a different tone, almost as if the cool demeanor that had been so recently dropped had been put back on again. And what was actually said! Lord Childress would not think Frederick elevated enough? Lord Childress was only a viscount, after all, not so very high over a baron.

She supposed the lord had grand plans for his daughter. Kitty was grateful her own father did not dictate to her in such a manner.

"And here comes Lord Dalton," Miss Danworth said, in an even cooler tone. "He will thrill us both with his amusing personality and jolly wit."

Though Kitty did not know Lord Dalton so very well, she certainly understood that comment to be mocking of his general seriousness.

"Miss Danworth. Miss Dell," Lord Dalton said, in the tone lacking all jollity that Kitty had been accustomed to. "May I?"

Miss Danworth handed over her card and said, "I was just telling Miss Dell how amusing you can be. Your lightheartedness is striking."

"My lightheartedness is only equal to your own," Lord Dalton said, seeming not at all offended by the slight.

"Perhaps I am only not lighthearted in your presence," Miss Danworth said.

"Perhaps I jest all the day long, until I encounter you. Though neither circumstance seems likely."

Kitty hardly knew where to look. Perhaps she was not sophisticated enough, but she failed to understand the way they spoke to one another. Were they joking? Were they not?

As it happened, there was little time to debate the matter. Lady Hathaway's Viking ship was bringing guests in with alacrity and Kitty's card began to fill.

Sir John had lingered out of doors, watching the carriages arrive one after another. His stolen costume was safely hidden in the bushes in the back of Lady Hathaway's garden.

He had originally thought he must capture Miss Dell either going in or out of the ball. But how would that be possible? He needed to encounter her alone, not surrounded by her family.

This was further confirmed when he saw her arrive. He might have tried such a gambit had Miss Dell only been escorted by her mother. But the brother was there, too. He did not think he'd find success attempting to subdue the brother.

Further, if anybody was to see him make off with Miss Dell, the alarm would be raised. He would need time to get out of the city. He had mapped out an obscure route that would take longer, but would avoid having anybody on his heels. The coachman of the last carriage lining the road was already under the weather, thanks to his kind offer of ale laced with laudanum. All he need do was catch Miss Dell alone, pretend to have a pistol, and tie her up in the coach. He would drive the vehicle himself. God had given him the steps and all he need do was follow them.

He had the note in his pocket and felt confident he could count on Miss Dell's determination to uncover Veritas.

GILES HAD ARRIVED to Lady Hathaway's house shockingly early. Though it had never happened before, this night he'd been the very first to come to the doors. Or sail to the doors on a Viking ship, as the case may be. To say that Lady Hathaway was surprised to see him so soon was an understatement. The butler had gone to fetch her as she was not even yet lined up to receive her guests. Then she had peered at him as if to be certain her eyes did not deceive her.

He'd made some mumbled excuse of having to make a stop first and then that person not being at home and hurried into the ballroom.

It had been a strange feeling, being in there alone. Every other ballroom he'd ever come into was well to being filled. He'd felt foolish, standing there under the gaze of a footman who hardly knew what to do with him.

It had been necessary, though. Far too many times, he'd approached Miss Dell, only to find her supper already claimed. It could not be so this evening. He had much to tell her and it could not wait. He was certain she was in danger, and she must be convinced of it.

He'd thought of going straight to Lord Penderton with the information, until he considered how bizarre it would all sound. It was likely Lord Penderton knew Sir John, and just as likely he admired the fellow. After all, they were both of that intellectual ilk and probably had a lot to talk about. He, himself, did not know Penderton well. The gentleman was so rarely out on the town.

He had set his course and he would stay the course. He had secured Miss Dell's supper and now he moved through the motions of attempting to entertain other females as he danced with one after another.

As he did so, he began to wonder if it would really be necessary to retreat to the countryside to cure himself of his flirtations. It was beginning to seem as if he had been wholly cured already. He had not the least desire to compose a compliment and no amount of frothy gowns or gentle shining curls seemed to inspire it in him.

His eyes no longer drifted in search of beauty, except in the direction of Miss Dell. It was as if she were a magnet pulling him toward her. Just like a magnet, he would have to pull hard in the opposite direction to come loose.

Would he ever, though? No matter how hard he pulled, would he ever be free of her? Shakespeare would tell him a resounding no—he described love as *an ever-fixed mark that looks on tempests and is never shaken.*

Wherever their lives took them, he was certain to see her over the seasons. My God, would he be forced to see her escorted as a married lady? Must he smile when it was mentioned that she'd borne another's child?

He knew very well that he was not good enough for Miss Dell. But then, who was?

Burke, perhaps. Though, if Burke had been interested, Giles would have noticed it by now. He was friendly with Miss Dell, he'd known her for quite some time on account of Burke's friendship with Miss Darlington and Lord Mendbridge. For all Burke's defense of Miss Dell, and the dressing down of himself,

Giles did not think it would be Burke.

Who then? And was that lucky fellow really any better than himself? Especially if he were to improve? Was he not doing that already? Who knew how much he might improve if he set his mind to it?

Giles stopped his thoughts running in that direction. It was becoming a habit and it was self-indulgent. Only a child laments the sun ought to be out at midnight. He could not allow himself to be so nonsensical.

Why was she kindly smiling at Jost this moment? It could not be Jost—the man could not gather up two words together in front of a lady.

He would put his foot down at Jost.

Giles forced himself to keep his attention on the matter at hand. Miss Dell must be protected from Sir John. She must gain an understanding of what he really was. She must come to understand *who* he really was. What happened after that would be none of his affair.

The next dance would be with Miss Dell. This current dance, with Miss he-could-not-remember-her-name, would end. Lady Hathaway would send round champagne as she always did at this point in the festivities, and then he would escort Miss Dell. He would have all the time he needed to be certain she understood the danger.

KITTY HAD BEEN gay all evening, she had not once allowed her thoughts to settle on anything serious. Not so long ago, she would have chided herself for being too lighthearted. Or, if not chided, had a vague sense of failing to attend to important matters.

It was rather a relief to throw off the responsibility. The more she tried it, the more she liked it. She did not suppose she would ever give up her studies, or her reaching for answers, or her delight in considering another's hypothesis. However, she had come to develop her own hypothesis—a varied life was a well-lived life.

She was not to be so full of conceit as to think that the world's problems and mysteries could not be grappled with without her constant gaze. There must always be made time for dancing and laughter. She further suspected that these diversions gave her mind time to work quietly, without her conscious interference. Allowing time away from her studies might just *help* her studies.

Whether that theory was right, she would discover eventually. For now, she would only look forward to the next dance. And then supper. She knew that perhaps she should not look quite so forward to encountering Lord Grayson, but she did all the same.

She had been handed a glass of champagne and that had made her mood even lighter than what it had been.

Miss Danworth stood next to her and Kitty said, "I do not know if it is all the bubbles, but I find champagne does lift my spirits."

Miss Danworth had smiled but had not answered. Kitty began to conceive a different idea of Miss Danworth. She was cool, mostly. Though occasionally the coolness warmed. Her father was frightening and seemed to have a plan for her future that he would dictate. Her mother was long-dead. Her companion, Mrs. Jellops, seemed kind, though perhaps an ineffectual sort of creature.

Miss Danworth could not live in a very happy home. Perhaps she wore her coolness like the armor of the Valkyries.

Before she could think of a way to put Miss Danworth at her ease and coax back the warmness, a footman hurried toward her. "Miss Dell?"

Kitty nodded and wondered if her mother wished her to come to the card room.

The footman handed her a note, bowed, and walked off.

"From my mother, no doubt," Kitty said unfolding it. "I hope she does not say she is tired and we leave early, I am very much enjoying Lady Hathaway's hospitality.

Though Kitty had fully expected some missive from her mother, the writing was in a distinctly masculine hand. She nearly dropped it after reading it.

"Are you well, Miss Dell?" Miss Danworth asked.

"Well enough, I suppose," she said, handing the note to Miss Danworth. "I only should have kept my guard up about a certain gentleman's schemes."

Miss Danworth read the note: *Meet me in the garden, I have proof of the true identity of Veritas. Grayson.* She folded it again and said, "What on earth?"

Kitty smiled bitterly, her amusement and levity flown from her. "Lord Grayson pretends he will solve a mystery for me which I believe I have already solved. He will reveal himself as Veritas, a gentleman who has caused no end of trouble and embarrassment to some of my friends. He will wish to laugh at my expense."

"But you will not meet him alone," Miss Danworth said. "It would be talked of, I'm sure you know."

"I certainly will not. Though it appears that Lord Grayson does not mind putting me in a compromising position. I had not believed *that* of him."

As Kitty looked across the ballroom, she caught Lord Grayson's eye. He smiled at her, as if the assignation was arranged. How naïve he must think her! She would not meet him, she would not dance with him and she would not dine with him. She had allowed her feelings to run on ahead of her, incautious and unseeing of the danger.

Now that he had been fully revealed to her—his utter carelessness of her reputation and prospects—she felt almost leaden. It was as if a black fog settled round her shoulders.

Kitty realized a very horrible truth. She was wounded by this. Not just offended, or her sensibilities shocked. She was wounded.

Deeply wounded.

She had allowed her feelings to go too far. Much, much too far. She might just have allowed herself to love him. Now those feelings had turned back around to her and shot through her like an arrow.

It was terrible! He was terrible! She must stop at once. Why should she have any sort of feelings at all for such a person? Why should she care for one who cared so little for her?

A lady alone in a garden with a gentleman was tantamount to claiming an engagement, and if no engagement was forthcoming, the lady's reputation was ruined. Lord Grayson knew it perfectly well.

"Something is not right here," Miss Danworth said.

"Nothing is right, I am afraid," Kitty said, willing her eyes not to water.

"Not quite what I meant," Miss Danworth said briskly. "I have known Lord Grayson these past two seasons. He is a rascal of a flirt and I am quite sure he's been wrong in some of it. But he has never compromised a lady. I must discover more of this. If he goes so far, we must all condemn him."

"Do as you please, condemn or not," Kitty said, swiping at her uncooperative eyes. "I will retreat to the lady's retiring room. I do not yet know what to do about supper, but I will rid myself of Lord Grayson."

Kitty turned on her heel and hurried from the ballroom.

CHAPTER EIGHTEEN

G ILES WAS NOT at all certain what was happening at this moment. Miss Dell had left the ballroom and Miss Danworth was coming toward him. He might have guessed that Miss Dell had ripped a hem or some other feminine emergency, had not Miss Danworth's expression told him otherwise. She looked like murder.

She waved a paper in front of his face and said, "Do you really go so far?"

He had not the slightest idea what she talked about.

"You cannot be so obtuse," Miss Danworth went on. "Not even *you* can toy with a lady's reputation in such a manner."

"What are you implying, Miss Danworth?" Giles asked. "Really, I will need more clues. I am not toying with anybody's reputation."

Miss Danworth handed him the note. Or, shoved it at him would be a better description. He unfolded it and read it, taking in a sharp breath. He instantly understood the scheme, though he would not have credited Sir John with such cunning.

"She is not such a fool as to meet you, I hope you understand. I am only surprised by this, Lord Grayson. I did not think you an absolute reprobate."

"Before you continue with your condemnations, this is not my hand," Giles said. "I did not write this. My God, where has

Miss Dell gone?"

"Out of your reach," Miss Danworth said, though her confidence in her recent accusations seemed to falter.

"This was not written by me," Giles said. "It was written by Sir John Kullehamnd. He is the real Veritas."

"Sir John? The scholarly gentleman who came to see the Palaskar collection?"

"The very one," Giles said. "Miss Dell is in danger. She does not know the facts—I know Sir John was in possession of John Hill's diary because I took it and Kullehamnd is Swedish for hill and revenge."

"Sir John?" Miss Danworth said, appearing mystified. "John Hill? Revenge?"

"I suspect he plans a kidnapping. Go to her and make sure she stays well away from the garden. Alert her mother and brother. I will answer this note and deal with Sir John myself."

It seemed Miss Danworth had finally comprehended the real case of the situation. She nodded and hurried away. Giles set off toward the garden.

KITTY HEARD THE door to the retiring room swing open. She dabbed at her eyes and turned her head away. She had closeted herself in the very last alcove of the cavernous room. She'd already told the maid who attempted to attend her that she suffered allergies as a cause of her dripping eyes, the most ridiculous story in the world. She did not wish for anybody else to see her cry.

"Miss Dell! Where are you?"

It was Miss Danworth come to comfort her. It was kind of the lady, but Kitty did not think she could be comforted at this moment. She had done the stupidest thing in the world. She had fallen in love with a man who did not love her. Worse than that, the gentleman did not have even the *slightest* regard for her. She'd been the mouse who played with a cat and could not understand why it was dying. It had always been in the cat's nature to toy with its prey.

"There you are," Miss Danworth said, coming round the corner. She sat next to Kitty on the peach velvet sofa and said, "Thank goodness you are safe."

"Of course I am," Kitty sniffled. "I told you I would not meet Lord Grayson in the garden."

"The note was not from Lord Grayson, I am convinced of his veracity. He says it was written by Sir John to lure you out there and you are in very much danger. Something about a diary and John Hill and Kullehamnd meaning hill and revenge in Swedish."

"Kullehamnd? Is that what it means?" Kitty said, horror creeping into her voice.

"I wished to make sure you were safe in here before I go to find your mother and brother. Lord Grayson even went so far as to speculate that Sir John may have kidnapping on his mind." Miss Danworth paused, then said softly, "Though Sir John? Kidnapping?"

"It was Sir John all along!" Kitty cried. "It really was. No wonder he was so forceful with me and came to my father for my hand. My grandfather and Martin Folkes kept John Hill from the society. Therefore, my dowry would have been John Hill's revenge!" Kitty paused, her thoughts racing. "But who is he really? Why does he seek revenge? Perhaps he is a grandson of John Hill?"

Miss Danworth patted Kitty's hand. "I cannot claim to make heads nor tails of it, I am only glad you are safe."

"But do not you see? Sir John must be mad! He had a diary bound in human skin!"

Miss Danworth recoiled at the idea. "I am almost afraid to hear further of this bizarre circumstance," she said. "Stay here and I will fetch your mama. She will know what to do next."

Miss Danworth hurried from the retiring room.

Kitty sat for a moment, the facts all falling into place as if the bits and pieces flew from various directions to finally come together in a cohesive whole.

She leapt to her feet. Lord Grayson was in very grave danger. Whether or not Sir John was some relation to John Hill, he was most certainly mad. A madman never stopped to consider the outcomes of his actions. Rationality fled and wild ideas reigned. Anyone stepping in the way of a madman's plot would be dispatched.

Of course, that was precisely who Sir John was. How did she not see it? The man did not entertain anything that did not suit him. He just plowed on.

She must go out and attempt to stop whatever was about to happen.

She fled past the maid, who would by now be convinced that it was Kitty herself who was mad.

Mad or no, she felt filled with courage. Lord Grayson had not attempted to lure her alone into the garden. Whatever he was, he was not that. Whatever his intentions, if he ever had any intentions, he had not sought to compromise her.

GILES STEPPED INTO the back garden. It was eerily quiet. Lady Hathaway's guests had long ago been ferried in, the footmen had decamped inside, and all that was left was the Viking ship standing alone under the sputtering candles along the walkway.

Giles moved forward cautiously, cursing his luck. He'd been in battle enough times, but rarely had he sought it out. He'd certainly never sought it out without even a weapon in his hand.

He must assume Sir John to be armed. How else could that weaselly person hope to carry off a kidnapping? He might be able to overpower Miss Dell, but without a weapon to threaten her with, it was unlikely he could stop her from raising the alarm with her screams.

Giles paused, listening for any sound. There was nothing, beyond the sound of leaves rustling in the breeze.

Perhaps Sir John had lost his nerve, or perhaps he'd seen that it was Giles who arrived and not Miss Dell and decided to make a hasty retreat.

He slipped along the path that ran next to the Viking ship, its grass beaten down by the footmen who had toiled at pulling the ship back and forth with ropes.

Giles reached the stern of the ship and paused, listening.

A sudden crack exploded in his head and he fell to the ground.

SIR JOHN CLUTCHED his metal helmet. It was all going wrong!

The last of the laudanum had worn off and he felt as if his muscles twitched of their own accord. It was like trying to wake from a bad dream, but he could not wake up!

Where was Miss Dell? How dare Grayson turn up in her place.

He had taken care of Grayson. The popinjay just now lay on the ground, having had a brick to the head.

But where was Miss Dell? Would he have to go in after her? He had not planned for that. He did not know how to do that. Why was God forsaking him when he was so close to victory?

He was just as close to defeat, he knew. There was no other option but to go forward. There was no other plan. He could not retreat and regroup.

Just as despair was settling over him like a shroud, he saw a peek of light ahead. The doors had opened and Miss Dell's figure silently slipped into the garden.

Grayson moaned. He put his boot on the lord's head to stop him. God had sent him a reprieve and he must act!

He took his foot off Grayson's head and stepped forward. He would approach Miss Dell swiftly and be off.

Before he got another step, Grayson grabbed hold of his leg and pulled him down.

⟫⟫⟩⟨⟨⟨

KITTY STEPPED INTO the darkness and paused. For a moment she did not hear a sound. Perhaps she was too late? Was Lord Grayson injured or dead and Sir John had run away? Or worse, was Lord Grayson lying somewhere and Sir John still lurking in the darkness?

She ought to go back in and get help.

The silence was suddenly broken. She heard a crashing sound and curses from somewhere near the stern of the ship. She swept up one of the last candles still burning along the path and ran toward the sound.

The two men rolled on the ground. Lord Grayson yelled, "Go back inside, Miss Dell!"

Though Kitty ought to have done as she was told, she felt rooted to the spot. "Oh dear, oh dear, oh dear," she repeated to herself. She looked round her, searching for something she could use as a weapon.

Spotting one of the oars the footmen had used to pretend at rowing, she picked it up. As Sir John rolled to the top of the melee, she swung it down as hard as she could.

It made a sickening crack, and Sir John collapsed lifeless. Lord Grayson rolled him off just as shouts were heard behind them.

Frederick, leading a cadre of footmen, came running to the scene. He was just as quickly followed by the baroness and Miss Danworth.

Kitty's brother stopped, attempting to take in the scene. Lord Grayson got to his knees and said, "Dell, be so good as to grab a rope from that confounded ship and tie the villain up. He breathes despite Miss Dell's valiant effort."

Frederick sprang into action; the baroness rushed to Kitty's side. "Are you all right," she said. "Are you unharmed?"

"I am perfectly fine," Kitty said, though she was not certain that was true. She had dropped the oar and her empty hands now shook. "You are alive," she said in wonder, staring at Lord Grayson.

"Very," he said, rising and rubbing his head. "Thanks to you."

"But your head," Kitty said, watching the lord rub it.

"Sir John complimented my head with a brick," Lord Grayson said. "Though he did not realize how hardheaded I actually am."

"I am afraid I've been hardheaded myself," Kitty said. "I did at first think, when I got the note…"

"That I had written it," Lord Grayson finished.

"Yes."

"But I would never…"

"No, I know," Kitty said.

Frederick had tied up the still-unconscious Sir John. He directed the footmen to haul him into a room well away from the guests and send for the magistrate. All the while, Kitty and Lord Grayson gazed at each other.

The baroness, now assured that her daughter was unhurt, looked interestedly back and forth between her daughter and the lord. "It seems you have defeated the villain together," she said. "Two people of different strengths combine to victory."

"I cannot say what strengths I brought to the case," Lord Grayson said, "other than a foolhardy idea to come out here alone."

"It was very brave, though," Kitty said.

"Was it?"

"Oh, I think so."

"But then, you were so brave with that oar!"

"Well, perhaps."

"I wonder, Miss Dell, if one were to improve. If a particular gentleman who was perhaps not quite up to snuff were to…apply himself. Well, what I say is there is no reason in the world I could not read every book in Lackington & Allen. If I had reason to."

"Or," Kitty said softly, "I might say that a certain lady might not study absolutely all of the time. That lady might make room for other things like poetry and plays. Perhaps science is not to be one's constant companion."

"Is it not?" Lord Grayson asked.

The baroness smiled and had the good sense to move away from the couple. Frederick returned from disposing of Sir John, but Lady Penderton caught him halfway there and halted his progress.

Lord Grayson grabbed Kitty's hands in his own. "I know I am not worthy, but if you'll have me, I will improve! I'll force Crackwilder to tutor me all the day long."

Kitty squeezed his hands back and said, "You'd better not harass poor Mr. Crackwilder in such a manner. Further, I do not see where any particular improvement is necessary."

"But you would not mind that I so rarely know what you're talking about," Lord Grayson said, coming closer to her.

She could feel his warm breath on her cheek. Kitty looked up and whispered, "Perhaps I should not talk so much then."

Lord Grayson's lips touched hers to stop her talk. After a gentle kiss he said, "There is no one in the world I love so much as you."

"Shakespeare?" Kitty said.

"Yes. Much ado about nothing."

"And so it has been, I fear."

"We are a ridiculous pair," Lord Grayson said. "But what care we? And this, our life, exempt from public haunt, finds tongues in trees, books in the running brooks, sermons in stones—"

"And good in everything."

"As you like it, Kitty Dell."

Sir John, whose name was finally revealed as John Clover of Cloverhill Hall was committed to Bethlem. His story, which he told authorities willingly in the hopes that they would provide him a supply of laudanum, was published in the newspapers in horrid detail. It captured the peoples' imagination, as it was frightening to think that a once ordinary person who had fallen on hard times had set in motion a devilish plot on account of a found diary. Readers of the tale whispered among themselves that there might be more Sir Johns lurking about.

The Royal Society was both relieved that Veritas had been unmasked, and relieved that so little attention to their own participation in the scheme was paid. The Royal Society's involvement was entirely crowded out by the fairytale of romance. Miss Dell was said to be a delicate, trusting, and innocent creature. Lord Grayson was styled a veritable warrior coming to the rescue. In particular, he was quoted as having said, "We have been to Valhalla and returned unscathed," which sent the ladies near swooning. No mention was made of the real case of the thing, that they were of equal intelligence but wildly different interests, and neither of them saw a reason to correct the facts.

Lord Grayson's application to Lord Penderton for the hand of his daughter went remarkably smooth. It might not have, had Lady Penderton not explained the matter thoroughly to her husband.

"But I hardly understand what you say, my dear," poor Lord Penderton said after having been woken up upon his wife's return from Lady Hathaway's ball.

"He has asked Kitty for her hand and she has accepted, is that not wonderful?"

Lord Penderton rubbed his chin. "So you say, there was a struggle in the garden, Sir John was there, planning to make off with Kitty, then the dandy Grayson proposes marriage?"

"Just so."

"It cannot be right, though," Lord Penderton said. "He is too stupid for Kitty. Remember? The book?"

"He is not stupid at all," the baroness said. "He is different from Kitty. He has the soul of a poet and he reminds me of Frederick, without all the rule-making about what women should and should not know."

"You mean, his feelings are easily hurt? God, I've tried to explain to Frederick backwards and forwards he must not take things so personally! Miss Crimpleton made one comment on his brown coat and he hasn't worn it since."

"What I mean, my dear husband, is Lord Grayson lives in his feelings as Frederick does. They are both romantics, they breathe poetry, and this will do for Kitty very well. When she has buried her nose in a book of dry facts too long, he will take her hand and pull her into the sunshine and fresh air."

"Ah," Lord Penderton said, considering. "Just as you pull me to the dining table."

"Precisely."

KITTY SPENT THE weeks before her marriage assuring all and sundry that she was indeed betrothed to Lord Grayson. It seemed nobody could quite believe he had engaged himself.

Poor Penny was particularly turned upside down about it. It was she who had introduced Kitty to Sir John and she who had warned Kitty against Lord Grayson.

She wrote—*How could I have been so wrong? Though, my dear Kitty, as I write that line it occurs to me that I should have known all along that I was wrong. I made such a muck-up of my own circumstance that I should have presumed myself the absolute worst matchmaker in the world. Now, I will have to like Lord Grayson, though I have been so used to condemning him. Though I suppose he has finally redeemed himself and so I must credit him with that. All I can say, my dear friend, is that if you are happy, then so am I.*

Penny may have credited Lord Grayson with redeeming

himself, but Lord Dalton certainly did not. Dalton was so enraged at the news that Lord Grayson thought it wise to decamp to Crackwilder's apartment lest his friend do a violence to him. Mrs. Radish-Radeesh was convinced to give over a room and Grayson and LaRue spent an uncomfortable week together in it before the duke, his father, was convinced to release him some funds.

Much to society's surprise, Miss Dell and Lord Grayson were indeed wed. They took a wedding trip to Sweden, and there Lord Grayson called upon some of his vague connections. One of those was Baron von Fersen, who was charmed by Kitty, though he remained annoyed with Grayson. He was somewhat mollified after hearing the story of Veritas. But not entirely.

In the end, they came home after a month, glad to leave all thought of Veritas behind. They settled in their new London house, their bedchamber a clear depiction of them both. Velvet and cushions and a tall bookshelf for Kitty. An enormous looking glass and one of the bookshelves given over to poetry and plays for Grayson. Even Miss Austen was given her own space on the shelf and Kitty secretly became enamored of *Pride and Prejudice*.

Kitty spent her mornings in bed, surrounded by her preferred books. As the day grew late, Lord Grayson would make his entrance as sharply composed as ever. He would pick out her dress, as Kitty herself could not be bothered with such things, and he would even direct poor Martha as she did her mistress' hair.

Lady Grayson became something of a leader of fashion, though she did not spare much thought over it. Whatever her lord thought would suit she was happy to wear. Many a young girl recently come to town would daringly approach Lady Grayson for advice on this bonnet or that silk, only to find themselves floundering in a conversation about hemi-parasitic plants.

Lady Grayson pursued her endless thirst for knowledge, though the Royal Society never did admit women in her lifetime. Mr. Crackwilder was a great help in her pursuits, as he was promptly hired as Lady Grayson's librarian. Mr. Lackington and

Mrs. Herschel remained constant in their exchange of letters.

Though her exclusion from the society was an irritation for a time, Kitty finally hit upon an idea. She created her own society of learned women who met weekly during the season and wrote to each other in the summer. As Mrs. Herschel was an esteemed member, it was not too long before members of the Royal Society began petitioning to attend the various presentations put on by the ladies. That led to the "great trading of papers" in which gentlemen and ladies could communicate freely on their discoveries and conclusions. Mankind's knowledge of how flies walked on walls was all the better for it.

Lord Grayson, to his credit, never lost his enthusiasm for listening to his wife as she explained some obscure fact, or pondered a new conclusion, or recapped the latest meeting of the Society of Women Intellectuals. He understood her perfectly well, though how long he retained any of this information might be a question for debate.

It mattered not, as it was not every day that their conversation centered on astronomy or botany or history or geology. There were many other days when Lord and Lady Grayson lounged before a cozy fire as the lord read to her from Shakespeare, Wordsworth, and Byron.

It was, in the end, *as they liked it*.

When children came, Kitty found herself perplexed over why they wept over some minor disappointment. She looked to her husband and he was always able to explain why a broken doll, or a marzipan dropped in the street, or a bedtime come too soon, was akin to the world ending.

Whenever the childhood drama reached a fever pitch, Lord Grayson would order that all the usual activities of the house were to stop instantly so that they might grieve the devastation properly. It might entail holding a somber funeral for a dead parakeet, or awarding a broken toy soldier a medal for bravery, or composing a poem that precisely captured the anguish over lost marbles, or a passionate speech condemning the sun for setting too soon.

That these impromptu events caused no end of late dinners and missed appointments mattered little, as Lord Grayson was late to everything anyway. LaRue went on just as temperamental as ever, and even more temperamental when the lord came back upstairs, having just ruined the folds of his cloth during a romp with his children. The children, themselves, were vastly entertained by the valet's loud condemnations in French and often competed on who might playact the closest imitation. When they were not making fun of the lord's valet, they entertained themselves with their parents' interests. Should an eyelash fall, it would be carefully collected and examined under the microscope. Should the rain come down in buckets, a play might be put on to glory in the moods of Mother Nature.

Lord and Lady Grayson were, in the end, of equal intelligence and different interests. Lady Grayson might contemplate the architecture of the house, but it was Lord Grayson who was the beating heart of it.

That he made his wife's heart beat faster was all the better.

The End.

About the Author

By the time I was eleven, my Irish Nana and I had formed a book club of sorts. On a timetable only known to herself, Nana would grab her blackthorn walking stick and steam down to the local Woolworth's. There, she would buy the latest Barbara Cartland romance, hurry home to read it accompanied by viciously strong wine, (Wild Irish Rose, if you're wondering) and then pass the book on to me. Though I was not particularly interested in real boys yet, I was *very* interested in the gentlemen in those stories—daring, bold, and often enraging and unaccountable. After my Barbara Cartland phase, I went on to Georgette Heyer, Jane Austen and so many other gifted authors blessed with the ability to bring the Georgian and Regency eras to life.

I would like nothing more than to time travel back to the Regency (and time travel back to my twenties as long as we're going somewhere) to take my chances at a ball. Who would take the first? Who would escort me into supper? What sort of meaningful looks would be exchanged? I would hope, having made the trip, to encounter a gentleman who would give me a very hard time. He ought to be vexatious in the extreme, and *worth* every vexation, to make the journey worthwhile.

I most likely won't be able to work out the time travel gambit, so I will content myself with writing stories of adventure and romance in my beloved time period. There are lives to be created, marvelous gowns to wear, jewels to don, instant attractions that inevitably come with a difficulty, and hearts to break before putting them back together again. In traditional Regency fashion, my stories are clean—the action happens in a drawing room, rather than a bedroom.

As I muse over what will happen next to my H and h, and wish I were there with them, I will occasionally remind myself that it's also nice to have a microwave, Netflix, cheese popcorn, and steaming hot showers.

Come see me on Facebook! @KateArcherAuthor

www.ingramcontent.com/pod-product-compliance
Lightning Source LLC
Chambersburg PA
CBHW070926190726
48292CB00004B/1120